MW01097373

EAT
SLAY
LOVE

Also by Julie Mae Cohen

Bad Men: A Novel

EAT
SLAY
LOVE

JULIE MAE COHEN

THE OVERLOOK PRESS, NEW YORK

To Ange, Kate, and Rowan, my ride-or-dies.

This edition first published in hardcover in 2025 by
The Overlook Press, an imprint of ABRAMS

Abrams books are available at special discounts when purchased in quantity
for premiums and promotions as well as fundraising or educational use.
Special editions can also be created to specification. For details,
contact specialsales@abramsbooks.com or the address above.

Originally published in the UK in 2024 by Zaffre, an imprint of Bonnier Books UK

Library of Congress Control Number: 2024943636

Printed and bound in the United States

1 3 5 7 9 10 8 6 4 2

ISBN: 978-1-4197-7235-1
eISBN: 979-8-88707-225-8

ABRAMS The Art of Books
195 Broadway, New York, NY 10007
abramsbooks.com

Ruin is a gift. Ruin is the road to transformation.

—Elizabeth Gilbert

1

THURSDAY

Opal

CELLAR STEPS: CROOKED, NARROW, BARELY wide enough for her foot. The only light came from a bare bulb hanging from the ceiling, the space below a jumble of shadows.

A strong scent of vinegar filled the air. And something underneath, something musty and unidentifiable.

Opal, accustomed to assessing every situation for the worst possible outcome, considered for the first time whether this could be a trap. Lord knew she'd given this woman a reason to hate her. Both of these women—and she'd given them reason to hate each other, too.

Maybe it wasn't the best idea to go down into a hole in the ground with them.

She paused and glanced over her shoulder. Lilah, behind her, looked terrified; but Lilah always looked terrified so that didn't mean anything. Marina's face was less readable. She was anxious, but there was another emotion, or emotions, that Opal couldn't quite suss out.

And Opal could usually suss everyone out, within a few minutes of meeting them.

For the first time she noticed that Marina was wearing a silk dress and lipstick . . . was this what normal mothers wore for a quiet evening in with the kids, here in the depths of Richmond, one of the most affluent boroughs of London?

"Be really careful going down the stairs," Marina said. "They're rickety. Hang on to the banister, okay?"

If worst came to worst, Opal decided, she'd be able to take the two of them in a fight. She doubted either of these women had ever thrown a punch in their lives.

"I'm dying to know what's so important down here," she said, truthfully, and started down the stairs.

The scent of vinegar got stronger as she descended. The floor was concrete, and the space, lined by shelves, was lit by another single dangling bulb.

In the center of the room lay the body of a man.

"Holy shit," Opal murmured.

Behind her, the other two reached the bottom of the stairs, but Opal's attention was on the man on the floor. He lay on his side, facing her. She recognized him right away, of course. It had been years, and his hair was a different color, his clothes were unfamiliar, he had cultivated a careful almost-beard.

But it was him. She would know him anywhere, even without seeing his face: she would know him by the lurch in her gut, the sensation poised somewhere between fear and fury.

Over the years, she'd thought she'd glimpsed him many times, here in London and everywhere else she went, too. All those times she'd looked twice, she'd followed him, rehearsing what she'd say, until he turned and revealed a stranger. But she'd never felt the lurch before.

Until this moment, she hadn't known that he still had that precise power over her.

Closer, she saw that his ankles had been bound together with silver tape and his hands were tied behind his back. He had dried blood on his forehead. How long had he been lying here? *Why* was he lying here?

A gasp behind her, and the sound of another body falling. Lilah lay crumpled on the cement floor.

Marina cried out and stooped over Lilah, touching her face. "Oh my God, is she okay?"

Opal leaned over the prone woman. "She's fainted, I think."

"I'll get a cold cloth." Marina ran back up the rickety stairs. Opal quickly checked Lilah over for damage. Her pulse was quick, but otherwise she seemed fine. Opal took off her Sweaty Betty hoodie and folded it under Lilah's head.

Her gaze traveled back to the man on the floor. There were two small blue Band-Aids on his forehead below his hairline. Opal squinted. The Band-Aids had pink shapes on them, like . . .

Was that Peppa Pig?

Marina's footsteps came back down, and she knelt beside Lilah and pressed a flannel to her forehead. "I didn't know she was going to faint," she said.

"This isn't the first body she's found," Opal told her. "She's probably traumatized."

"Oh no. I didn't know. I'm so sorry!"

Lilah's eyelids fluttered. She moaned and opened her eyes, which immediately widened in horror.

"He's not dead," said Marina quickly. "That was the first thing I checked after he fell down the stairs. Before I tied him up."

Lilah sat up. Her face was dead pale and her hair had escaped its clip and hung loose. "You tied him up?"

"Yes, I had to. For my own safely. *Our* safety. I've got three children asleep upstairs. I'm sorry, I didn't mean to scare you."

"Why does he smell like pickles?"

"He was carrying a jar," said Marina. "It broke. I've cleaned up the glass, don't worry."

To her own surprise, Opal laughed.

"I'm sorry," said Opal. "I know it's not funny. But it's so typical, isn't it. A woman has an unconscious man tied up in her cellar and her first instinct is to clean up a mess."

"I've got three chi—"

"I know, I know. I think I might also be in a bit of shock. I haven't seen him in three years." Opal approached the man's body, squatted next to him, and touched his neck, checking him over as she had Lilah. "His pulse is strong, and he seems to be breathing all right. Unconscious, though, obviously."

"He hit his head on the way down," said Marina. "But he only bled a little bit. I disinfected it."

"How long has he been out?"

"I don't know. About . . . an hour?"

Opal stood. "The real question isn't about pickles or cleaning. The real question is: why did you message me instead of calling an ambulance?"

"Right," said Marina. "Right. Well, exactly. Good question."

"He could have a concussion. Or a broken neck. Or a brain bleed."

"He could," said Marina. "Though his color's pretty good. I put him in the recovery position."

"Should I google the symptoms?" Lilah asked.

"No," said Opal. "Don't google anything. We need to know where we stand first. Which means that Marina needs to answer my question. Why didn't you call an ambulance when he fell?"

Marina fidgeted.

"Look, I'll tell you," she said. "But . . . I think we all need a drink first." She made for the stairs.

Opal made a quick decision. "Just a second. Where's the duct tape that you used on his wrists and ankles?"

Marina pointed at a shelf, and Opal tore a strip of tape off the roll and pasted it over the unconscious man's mouth.

"Don't do that!" said Lilah. "Why are you doing that?"

"Just while we're talking," said Opal. "If he wakes up, he might scream, and that would wake Marina's children, and we'd have a lot of explaining to do."

"Plus it would create childhood trauma," added Marina.

Lilah bit her lip, uncertain. "But what if he's sick? He could choke."

"We'll watch him."

"I'll . . . I'll go get us something to drink," said Marina, and she ran up the stairs.

Opal couldn't stop looking at the man on the floor. He'd used to have black hair, and now it was silver-gray and white. Had he dyed it? Or had they both aged so much in the past three years?

No, it was dye. She knew how he worked. Black hadn't been his real hair color, either.

But none of this was part of his plan: the basement, and the duct tape, and the Peppa Pig Band-Aids, and the three women together.

She wondered: would a normal person, a better person, feel pity for him?

Lilah sidled up to Opal. "I think Marina pushed him down the stairs," she whispered, her words trembling. "On purpose."

2

EIGHT WEEKS BEFORE THAT THURSDAY

Lilah

LILAH STOOD BEHIND THE ISSUE desk of the library, unaware that soon, she would have the single most horrific experience of her life.

She surveyed the five stacks of books that she had spent her afternoon compiling. One for fiction, one for plays, one for crime, a short one for poetry, and a counterintuitively tall one for children. The book sets for every single library reading group. Not a single copy missing, and every set containing something from the top five priority list.

There were going to be a lot of very happy readers this month. Which partly made up for the conversation she'd overheard in the break room this morning. Well, it wasn't exactly a conversation: Jimiyu had thanked Lilah for closing up for him tonight, and Alice had muttered to herself, which was supposed to be under her breath, but had clearly been loud enough for everyone to hear, especially as there were only three of them in the break room.

"Why is *she* still working here when some of us need the money? Did she win the lottery or not?"

This wasn't the first time that Alice had said something like that about Lilah. She was always dropping little passive-aggressive barbs that were supposed to be jokes, like "Going home to your yacht?" or "Don't forget your Chanel bag!" Lilah didn't have a yacht and wouldn't know what to do with a Chanel bag, unless it was a Chanel fanny pack, but why would you spend that much on a fanny pack when one from Primark held everything you could need?

When Alice said things like that, Lilah would laugh nervously. But privately she had started calling her "Evil Alice." Only in her own head, of course.

The question this morning couldn't even remotely be interpreted as a joke. Lilah had ducked out of the break room, her heart hammering. But she'd been rehearsing answers to that question for the rest of the afternoon, even though she'd never have the courage to say them aloud.

Making up the book group stacks was one of the reasons why she still chose to work here, even though she had won the lottery and technically, she didn't need to work at all.

Plus, Lilah loved her job. Ever since she was a little girl, sitting on her dad's knee listening to him read stories, she'd wanted to work around books. Initially she'd wanted to be a writer, but what had happened at university had ruined that for her. Being a librarian was just as good, though. Every single book contained an entire world. If you put them together, you got the sum of human knowledge. Reading books, finding them, recommending them, putting them in order, sharing them, taking care of them . . . what more could you ask out of life?

Lilah Nightingale knew she would never achieve anything great—she would never cure cancer, or stop climate change, or write a bestselling novel, or pen a single line of poetry that moved someone's heart—but whenever she touched a book, she touched greatness.

She'd never give that up.

"I'm going now," said Jimiyu, emerging from the back with his coat and bag. "Thanks for closing up for me."

"It's my pleasure," said Lilah, smiling. "I hope your daughter's concert goes well. I'll see you Tuesday."

The library was closed on Mondays now. Funding issues. They always used to have Rhyme Time in the Children's section on a Monday morning, and even though it was moved to Wednesdays, she thought that Mondays had been better attended.

In her opinion, it was a crying shame not to have the library open seven days a week. Knowledge should be free to everyone. It wasn't just books, either. People used the computers for all sorts—research, paying their bills, applying for jobs or benefits or asylum. Some people came in purely for the warmth and light and shelter. Or not to be alone. You could never be lonely in a library.

Zachary loved the library almost as much as she did. They'd met here, after all—and in a reading group, no less. The inaugural meeting of the play-reading group, when they were reading *An Inspector Calls*, which Lilah had chosen because it was always good to attract people with a classic. There weren't enough people for all the parts, so Lilah had had to step in. She read Sheila. The Inspector was read by the soft-spoken gentleman in the gold-rimmed glasses, who looked like a professor, with his tweed jacket and well-scuffed brogues. He had a surprisingly powerful and eloquent voice, and once, while they were reading together—the scene where Sheila finds out about Gerald's secret—Lilah looked up from her playbook at the exact same time that the gentleman playing the Inspector looked up from his.

Their eyes met, and she felt a jolt of electricity all the way down her body, like the time she'd plugged the kettle into an outlet that wasn't properly grounded.

And then the rest was history. She twisted her engagement ring around her finger. It still felt strange there, and much bigger than she would have chosen herself. Evil Alice stared at it every time they were in the same room together.

She patted the play-reading group book stack affectionately, then picked up Jimiyu's keys, ready to do a final sweep of the library to make sure everything was in order and ready for closing. An elderly gentleman was still on the computers; Lilah said a quiet word to him reminding about closing time, and then she went to check the children's section, which got left in a bit of a mess sometimes. She was approaching the picture book bins when she saw Evil Alice coming her way, wearing a sour expression.

Lilah ducked behind a shelf of Young Adult literature. She pretended to be looking for a book, but thank goodness, Evil Alice didn't notice her and carried on past towards the break room, presumably to collect her coat and bag to go home.

This wasn't the first time she'd hidden from Evil Alice. She did it all the time. And she knew it was cowardly, like it was mean for her to call her Evil Alice, even to herself. Evil Alice probably had a lot of sadness in her life to act that way. Or maybe she had a lot of outstanding bills. Though Evil Alice didn't tell anyone about it so they could help her, or offer to loan her money; she just aggressively shushed everyone and ate all the biscuits.

Lilah heard the front door shut and scurried over to look through the glass: Alice had left. She was alone. She locked the door and drew a sigh of relief.

Lilah finished up her rounds, tidying shelves and straightening papers, shutting down computers. She loved this too: having the library all to herself. All those quiet shelves and dark screens, all the safe and comforting shadows. When she was finished, she turned off the final light, then unlocked the front door, let herself out, and locked it behind her. She put Jimiyu's keys carefully in her bag and patted them, as if to tell them to stay safe. Then, before she walked to her bus stop, she took a moment to gaze at the library where she'd spent so many happy hours as a child and young woman. Its brick walls, its dark windows. Its book-return slot by the front door. The posters on the glass doors advertising community coffee mornings, book clubs, citizens' advice clinics, and of course, Rhyme Time.

Lilah did good work here, in a place she loved. And now, after a satisfying day, she would go home to Dad, who would greet her with his usual hug. He'd been gardening today, and he'd smell of fresh soil and woodchips. They'd watch *Midsomer Murders* together on the couch. He'd have his supper on a tray, and she'd keep him company even though she wasn't eating, because she loved spending time with her dad, and she worried that he got lonely when she was out at work all day, even though now that he'd retired he kept busy with his hobbies.

And then she'd have a quick bath and put on a dress, because Zachary was taking her out for a romantic dinner later. It wasn't a special occasion; Zachary said it was nice sometimes to do special things even on Sunday evenings.

She was the luckiest person in the world.

* * *

Her commute from work to home took quite a bit longer these days than it had when she and her father had lived in the bungalow, but she couldn't complain. It gave her time to listen to audiobooks, and besides, it was always a thrill to get off the bus and walk to their brand-new house, with its picture windows and its glossy door with a brass knocker and its huge garden for Dad.

Dad even wanted to try his hand at topiary. "What do you think of a fox and a hare?" he'd asked the other night, and Lilah agreed that it would be wonderful to have a fox and a hare made of bushes in their front garden, like two characters from an Aesop fable about to come to life. Though Dad thought maybe he'd start with something smaller, like a chicken.

If someone had told her when she was a little girl that one day she would live in a house like this—an actual mansion—and that her dad would be able to retire a year early from his post office job, which was a job he loved though it hadn't been easy these last few years with his bad knees, or that she herself would have her dream job and her dream boyfriend and one day soon, maybe a cat . . . well, she wouldn't have believed them.

It was enough to make her believe in destiny.

She went up to her front door, started to put the key in the lock, and realized that it was slightly ajar.

Dad was usually quite cautious—he'd seen too many packages stolen from front steps in their old neighborhood—but he also was a little forgetful sometimes. She figured it was because they were in a new place, after he'd lived most of his life in the bungalow. The neighborhood here in Chislehurst, on a private road near the golf course, was quieter than their old place in Sidcup. It took some adjusting. And he did do his word puzzles and Sudoku every day, and she made sure they included plenty of oily fish in their diet, but nevertheless she was frowning when she walked into the hallway and called out, "Dad? You left the door open."

Her voice echoed slightly against the marble tiles. Dad didn't answer.

He might be in the back garden, or in the kitchen, or upstairs. It was difficult to hear people in this house because it was so big. Last week she'd had to resort to calling Dad's cellphone when she couldn't find him. He was in the bath, but not in his own bathroom. He'd just wanted to try out one of the other ones.

She closed the door, left her keys in the little bowl, and went through the house to the open-plan kitchen, which was all marble and granite and stainless steel, with an enormous new Aga stove that she hadn't quite figured out how to use yet. The room was empty and the back doors to the patio were open. Glass crunched underfoot.

One of the panes of the patio doors had been broken from the outside.

"Dad?" she called again.

She looked around the garden. He'd been working out here—his edge cutter and spade were leaning neatly against a low wall, and one of the beds had been mulched—but he wasn't anywhere to be seen, and not in the shed or greenhouse either.

When she went back into the kitchen, she noticed that several of the drawers were open. Frowning, she shut them. It wasn't like Dad to be untidy.

She glanced into the room that the estate agent had called the "family room." It adjoined the kitchen so you could chat with whoever was sitting there while you cooked dinner. She stifled a scream.

It was a mess. Lamps overturned, sofa cushions thrown to the floor. The television, mounted on the wall, was half off its brackets and hung at a precarious angle.

Something terrible had happened. She could feel it like hands around her neck.

"Dad!" she shouted.

She ran upstairs, terror pounding in her ears. She ran past bedrooms with open doors, barely noticing that each one of those rooms had also been ransacked. Clothes on the carpets, blankets trailing, electronics ripped from the walls. The door to her father's study was open too: a large room at the back of the house, south facing for the natural light.

A great deal of the room was taken up by his model train setup. It was magical, that land he'd built on large sheets of plywood, propped up on tables, with little people, shops, trees, several intricately painted steam locomotives, even cows in the fields and dogs running in the park. As a child she'd watched it for hours, and played with it, though only under his supervision. She still helped him with it sometimes.

It had been upended. The trains lay in a jumble on the floor. People, shops, animals, all of them to scale. The tracks clung to the fake grass, perfect and empty. A bottle of model paint had smashed, filling the air with a chemical scent.

Her father was lying facedown on the floor beside the ruins of his trains.

He was still wearing the clothes she'd seen him in this morning before she'd gone to work: dun-colored corduroys, a white shirt with a subtle check, the sleeves rolled up. It was all stained with blood. Bright red on the collar of his shirt. He lay in a puddle of it, a flood of it. It mixed with the green of the enamel paint.

"Dad!" She fell to her knees beside him. The blood was still warm. The skin of his neck was lukewarm when she touched it. The back of his head, where the hair was thinning (she always told him it wasn't) was covered in blood, so much of it that it looked black.

His head was the wrong shape.

"Dad," she sobbed.

She shook him gently. She tried to wake him. She took his limp hand and wound her fingers around his. She kissed his knuckles.

She kept saying his name, even though she knew it wouldn't do any good.

3

SIX WEEKS BEFORE THAT THURSDAY

Marina

MARINA'S FIRST JOB INTERVIEW IN nearly seven years was not going well.

"I can give you six nights a week," Henri, the restaurant owner, was saying as they sat in his cramped office behind the kitchen. "Dinner service, it's our busiest time."

"I'm not sure I can do that. I've got three kids. I was hoping you'd have availability for lunchtime. Or part time? Sundays?"

"I need six nights a week."

Marina thought of all the bedtimes she would miss. The bath times. The story times. How much childcare would cost.

"What's your pay scale?" she asked.

"For prep cook—minimum wage."

"Prep cook?" Marina looked at the papers lying on Henri's desk. "Maybe you've misread my CV. My last position was chef de cuisine."

"That was a long time ago."

"I . . . took a break. To have children."

"And who hires a part-time head chef? This is not a nursery school. I need my kitchen to be a well-oiled machine. The job is prep cook, six nights a week, minimum wage. Take it or leave it." He looked at his watch.

On her way back through the kitchen she paused momentarily, absorbing the heat, the scents, the bustle of white-clad employees preparing for the dinner service—commis, chefs de partie, sous chef, each with their own roles and expertise, the chef de cuisine at the head of them all. This had been her world: the place where she felt most at home.

Beside her, the deep fat fryer was heating up in readiness for the evening's frites. Marina, clutching her useless CV, had a sudden vision of herself grabbing a block of ice from the freezer, running across the kitchen, and tossing it into the hot oil.

She imagined how the surface of the oil would ripple, and then erupt, the ice turning instantly to steam and sending plumes of lethal oil into the air. The resulting fireball explosion, the screams, the chaos, the burns.

A well-oiled machine, indeed.

She blinked. Shook her head. Where had that come from? A prep cook, slicing potatoes, was staring at her.

"Sorry," she said, and left in a hurry.

* * *

"One hundred and eighty-six pounds," her mother was saying, as Marina helped her unpack her Waitrose bags. "And fifty-two pence. I said to the cashier, I have brought up two children, and I never. The price on everything has gone up."

"I know, Mum."

"And seventy-four pounds yesterday in Mark's! I don't know how anyone raises a family."

Well, thought Marina. *I usually make everything myself, or failing that, I go to Aldi.*

But she knew better than to suggest that. She put away a packet of microwave pilaf rice.

"The fruit alone. Blueberries," her mother added, significantly.

"The kids are fine with cut-up apples and carrots."

"Don't be silly. They need their antioxidants."

"I'll transfer over some money," she said, doing the calculations and trying to work out where she'd get it from. Jake was supposed to send child support payments, but he hadn't managed a full one yet, and she dreaded having to get in touch with him to demand more. His new girlfriend kept on answering his phone.

"I know it's expensive with all of us living here," Marina added. "I'm sorry that the job interview didn't work out."

"Nonsense. Your father wouldn't hear of you handing over a penny."

"I appreciate it, Mum. I really do."

"It's fine." Her mother put away a six-pack of premade smoothies. "Children do waste an awful lot of food these days, though."

"I'm sorry."

"I bought two liters of milk and I had to pour half of it down the drain."

"I did say that Lucy Rose doesn't like it plain."

"Children need their milk." Mum shut the fridge decisively. "Anyway, it's not for much longer."

Marina paused while folding up a reusable shopping bag. "What . . . do you mean by that, Mum?"

"I just mean that you've made your point."

"What point is that?"

"That you're upset with him. For his mistakes. I was saying it to your father last night. 'Andrew,' I said, 'any day now she's going to decide that she's punished Jake enough, and she'll see sense and go back to him.'"

"Mum." She clutched the bag. "We had to sell the house. Someone else is living in it now. Where am I supposed to go back to?"

"That was a mistake, selling the house. Your father said so when it happened."

"At the time," Marina said, trying to stay calm, "I explained that it was the only way we could raise the money to pay our creditors."

Jake's creditors.

"With property prices as they are, you'll never find a place with four bedrooms. Still, as your brother pointed out, Ewan doesn't need his own room yet and when he's a bit older, he and Archie can share."

Her parents' North London semi had three bedrooms, but Marina was sharing her old room with all of the children because her mother liked to keep her brother Neil's old room free in case the twins stayed over.

"I'm sorry," she said. "I can't afford to buy any house, certainly not at the moment. I don't quite understand what you think I'm planning to do. If you need me to leave, then I understand. Maybe I can stay with Neil and Sally for a little bit. Or find a place to rent," she added doubtfully. "I'll keep looking for jobs."

"You said you were going to sort things out with Jake."

"I—no, Mum, I don't think I said that?"

"You certainly did. I was sitting right there when you said it. And I haven't rushed you, because like I said to your father, 'Andrew, she needs time to lick her wounds. Her pride has been hurt, and that's important to a woman.' And of course you're always welcome in our home, darling, for as long as you want to be here. But the children need their father, and you need to get back to your life."

What life was that?

"I have sorted it out," said Marina. "I've got divorced."

A cataclysmic silence fell across the kitchen.

"Divorce" was a dirty word in the house she'd grown up in. It was spoken in a whisper, like "cancer" or "voted for the Green Party." Her parents had been married for forty years and Marina had never heard them raise their voices with each other. Her father's parents were married for over sixty years and had died within weeks of each other. You could use a photo of Marina's older brother Neil and his wife Sally as an illustration for a Wikipedia entry on "marital bliss." Or at least "comfortable tedium."

Marina's mother had never quite lived down the humiliation of her own mother having married three times, but at least Nana Sylvia had had the sense to wait until each husband had died before starting over.

Mum's face went white, then red.

"What do you mean," she said.

"It's final. I got the email last week."

"This is nonsense," her mother said. "You don't buy a divorce online, like it's from Amazon."

"I have a lawyer. She filed the petition for me and dealt with the settlement. It's just the decree absolute that's come by email."

"Why don't I know anything of this?"

"You didn't want to talk about it."

"Because it's—" Her mother caught herself, and shook her head. "What does Jake think of this? Surely he doesn't stand for it?"

"Jake's living with his pregnant girlfriend in Neasden."

Mum's lips thinned. "First my mother dies, and I have to handle all the legal brouhaha, and then you put this on me? On the same day when we are meeting to hear my mother's will?"

"I'm upset about Nana Sylvia too."

"I'll have to talk to your father about this," said Mum, leaving Marina to unload the dishwasher.

In movies, women who got divorced behaved in predictable ways. They went on yearlong spiritual journeys to find themselves, or they held wild and sassy celebrations with all their girlfriends, or else they lay alone on a sofa and wept and ate chocolate ice cream out of the container. Marina couldn't do any of these things. Even if she didn't have responsibilities, she certainly couldn't afford a year doing nothing but trying exotic cuisine and living in ashrams. A party here in London would have been nice, but she didn't have any girlfriends anymore, let alone sassy ones. Her work friends had moved on, and all the PTA moms who she used to spend time with had dropped her as soon as she got divorced. And what mother of three was able to spare the time to lie on a sofa and weep?

She did feel like eating chocolate ice cream, but her mother only believed in vanilla.

No: since the divorce came through, the only thing Marina really wanted to do was to talk to her grandmother.

She adored Nana Sylvia. Always had, since she was a little girl and used to dress up in Nana's fancy clothes and have tea parties with her antique porcelain. She was a sympathetic ear, a wicked laugh, a subversive comment. She hated hypocrisy, she was extroverted and charming (when she wanted to be), she didn't suffer fools. She wore bright colors and ridiculous hats, talked loudly in public about sex, and only did housework when she felt like it. She was everything that Marina knew she could never be, but secretly wanted.

And she was Marina's biggest supporter. She went to every school play, every piano recital, every sporting event. Most importantly, she had taught Marina about fine food and wine. When Marina wanted to study cooking in Paris, Nana Sylvia had paid her tuition and her travel. When Marina got her first job in a trendy London bistro, Nana

Sylvia ate there every chance she got and always sent her compliments to the chef.

The only thing that Marina had ever done that Nana Sylvia didn't approve of was getting engaged to Jake Faulkner. Nana Sylvia admired the ring then took her aside and said, "He's not good enough for you, dear. No one is. But he'll do for a first, and he'll make beautiful children. You can wear my dress."

And now . . . she was gone. Massive fatal stroke while on a Caribbean cruise. They'd had to fly her body from St. Lucia.

"And," Marina's mother had said, "to add insult to injury, the company won't even refund the price of the unused portion of the cruise."

Marina's phone rang and she snatched it up, hoping it was Henri with a better job offer, or Jake offering money, or Nana Sylvia saying she wasn't really dead and it was all an elaborate prank.

But it wasn't. It was Lucy Rose's nursery ringing to say she had to pick her daughter up because she'd bitten one of the other children again.

* * *

My assets are to be liquidated, my house in Richmond to be sold, and the estate to be split evenly into quarters: one quarter to my daughter Alexandra; one quarter to her son Neil; one quarter to my granddaughter Marina; and one quarter to my surviving niece Gabriella, or to her heirs if one of her lethal illnesses actually turns out to exist.

However, if (and only if) my granddaughter Marina has divorced, the preceding clause is null and void. If Marina has divorced and is unmarried at the time of my death, my house, all it contains, and all my assets are bequeathed entirely to her. I only apologize, my darling, that you will have to deal with the Andersons who are endlessly building that monstrosity next door.

"You get the whole thing? All of it?"

"That house has to be worth at least seven million in today's market."

"Seven and a half, easy. I have twins to send to school. How am I supposed to afford their fees now?"

"You go from a quarter share to all of it, just for getting divorced?"

"You're being rewarded for failing."

"Is this why you wouldn't even try marriage counseling?"

"You've been sucking up to Sylvia for years."

Marina finally snapped. "I love Nana Sylvia! I don't want her house, or her money. I want her to be alive!"

"If you don't want it, then you can sell it and split it, like she said."

"That's the fair thing to do. None of *us* have broken up our families."

"I'd be cautious about what you say, Marina," warned the lawyer.

"Did you know she was going to do this?"

"Of course not," said Marina. "We never talked about her dying. She was always too full of living."

"You must have known something. The two of you were always chattering."

"My own mother. I can't believe it. This is just like her."

"My favorite aunt! She knew I need private medical care. And what did she mean, 'actually turns out to exist'?"

"What about everything that's in the house? There are some valuable pieces in there. The piano? The art? The dueling pistols alone are worth a hundred grand."

"It just doesn't seem fair that your children get everything and mine get nothing. Surely she didn't mean that?"

"Would it be against the will if Marina sold the house and split the money anyway?"

Marina hadn't meant to sit on the side, apart from the rest of the family, but now she looked at the row of accusing faces and wondered how they could think about money at a time like this.

"Marina can do what she likes with it," said the lawyer. "It's hers."

"See, Marina? I know a great estate agent."

"I want to live in the house," said Marina.

Everyone stared at her.

"I'm sorry," she said. "But the children and I don't have a house to live in. And I love Nana Sylvia's house. It reminds me of her. It's full of her things. I could never sell it."

"You could buy a huge house in the suburbs with a quarter of what that house is worth!"

"You could buy a new build. It wouldn't need so much upkeep. For a single woman on her own, these things are important."

"I never asked her for a penny. Never once. This is how she repays me?"

"I'm keeping the house," said Marina. "I'm sorry."

4

TWO WEEKS BEFORE THAT THURSDAY

Opal

"IT'S NO GOOD, MY FUCKING face is melting off again."

Opal dropped her arms, mid pigeon-pose, and glared. Faiza peeped over the tripod at her.

"It's fine," Faiza said. "You look great."

"It is not fine. My eyebrows feel like they're on my cheeks." Opal stormed off the yoga mat and across the studio to the illuminated mirror. She examined her face. "They *are* on my cheeks. Which is almost unbelievable because my lipstick is also on my nose. How the ever-loving fuck does makeup melt in two directions at once?"

"You were upside down for quite a long time," Faiza volunteered. "Which looked great, by the way."

Opal turned to the young girl cringing beside the mirror. She looked like all the other young girls who had crossed Opal's path in an endless stream since she had started this business. Every single person involved in social media marketing was about fifteen years old with tits that defied gravity and they spent all of their time wearing crop tops, pouting into phone cameras, and speaking every sentence with a questioning lilt at the end like they'd never been certain of anything in their lives. Even Faiza, her social media manager/photographer/producer/video editor/PA, who was more resilient than most—well, at least she'd stuck around for more than five minutes and seemed to know what she was doing—was barely out of college.

"What is your name?" Opal demanded of the young girl.

"Taylor?"

"Are you sure? You don't sound it."

The girl nodded, biting her lip.

"Taylor, I wonder if you can tell me something."

". . . Okay?"

"Are you a professional makeup artist or are you some brainless cow whose entire resume consists of makeup tutorials that you do from your bedroom on TikTok?"

"She's a professional," said Faiza in a carefully controlled voice. "She's done London Fashion Week."

"Then why do I look like a badger who has been put into a microwave?"

"I'm sorry," said Taylor. "I can try a bit of powder?"

"A bit of powder? What a great idea! A bit of powder can solve anything. Global warming, arms proliferation, cancer. Just slap a bit of powder on there! Problem gone!"

"It's . . . the makeup melts a little when you sweat?"

"No shit, Sherlock. GlowUpp makeup melts when you sweat. GlowUpp makeup melts when the sun comes out. GlowUpp makeup melts when you look at it funny. The stuff is utterly useless, especially for a fitness expert who is trying to wear GlowUpp makeup while recording a fitness video."

"Maybe if we—"

"The thing is, Taylor," Opal interrupted, "and I will say this slowly: even though GlowUpp makeup is terrible, even though it is awful slop that's fit only to be tossed straight into the bin as soon as you buy it, I have signed a binding contract to be an exclusive brand ambassador for GlowUpp. Faiza, you're the one with the alleged marketing degree. What does that mean, *exclusive brand ambassador?*"

"It means that you are legally obligated to use GlowUpp products in all of your public-facing appearances as a fitness influencer and talk about how GlowUpp products are your beauty product of choice when you're following a healthy lifestyle."

"Did you hear that, Taylor?"

". . . Yes?"

"And what that means for *you*, Taylor, is that it is *your job* to make GlowUpp's terrible makeup look good on me. This is why we hire a so-called makeup artist, instead of me slapping the stuff on by myself with a trowel and hoping for the best. Do you understand?"

". . . Yes?"

"Good. So tell me, Taylor, why, after a little light yoga, do I currently look like a dog's breakfast?"

Taylor was tearing up now. "Maybe . . . maybe powder?"

Faiza stepped in between them before Opal could get properly angry. "Taylor, why don't you take a little break? And we can get back to work in a little bit, with a fresh approach?"

Taylor fled.

Opal swore.

Faiza sighed. "This is the fifth makeup artist you've made cry. Can we maybe rethink our philosophy for dealing with freelancers?"

Opal grabbed a wipe and started trying to rub off her makeup. It was incredible how something that slid off her face so easily when she was exercising was so resistant to actual makeup remover.

"My philosophy isn't the problem. It's this sponsorship that's the problem. And the main problem is that it's the only one I've got and it is currently funding both my mortgage and your salary."

"My meager salary," added Faiza.

"My massive mortgage, because I am the talent, and your meager salary, because you are straight out of college, and I am giving you a chance."

Faiza shook her head and looked down at her phone.

"Feel free to look for a job elsewhere," said Opal.

"There are no jobs. It's all unpaid internships."

"In that case, hustle your ass and help find us another sponsorship or brand ambassadordom or whatever it is, and then we can consider a raise." Opal gave it up as doomed and chucked the wipe into a trash.

"What did Sweaty Betty tell you?" Faiza asked.

"Recession."

"I was talking with Si and they said they'd pulled out because you were too difficult to work with."

"They can't handle strong women," said Opal.

"That might be true, but also, you are a bitch."

"What is it with your generation? Has feminism entirely bypassed you? Have you given it up in exchange for collagen and avocado toast?"

"I *think* the point of feminism is to support your fellow women."

Opal snorted.

"The thing is," continued Faiza, "you can yell at me all you want, and you probably will, but if this carries on, GlowUpp is going to drop you as well. And then what happens?"

"I'll fire my staff, meaning you, and go it alone. I don't need anybody."

"I'll go try to persuade Taylor to come back."

Faiza went off, leaving Opal by herself. She grabbed another wipe and scrubbed some more.

She did indeed have a massive mortgage on her flat in Canary Wharf. And quite aside from the crapness of their product, her contact at GlowUpp had been making noises that smacked loudly of dissatisfaction. The fact was, she'd scraped this sponsorship by the skin of her teeth. She was strong, she was ambitious, she was knowledgeable, she could be extremely charming when she wanted to, and she was in the best shape of her life, but she was past the age of fifty and that meant, as far as social media influencing went, that she was the bottom of the heap. Invisible. Washed up.

And once this source of income was gone, she was all out of options. She only had herself to rely on, and bankruptcy loomed.

Again.

You're worthless and you'll always be a failure without me.

There it was. His voice again in her head, on top of her mother's voice and her father's voice and her teachers' voices. These days, his was the loudest.

And at night, in her dreams, she saw Cora. As she'd been before she died.

Opal began running in place. There was a reason they called it outrunning your demons. Except every time she thought she'd outrun hers, they came back and told her she was a pile of crap, that all of the trolls on her Instagram account telling her she was unfuckable were right, that it didn't matter that she had perfect triceps and triglyceride levels, she was washed up, and worse than that, she was a terrible excuse for a human being and she had blood on her hands.

"Argh," she said, and collapsed into the makeup chair, and reached for her phone. Faiza wasn't going to be back for a while—if at all—and so she might as well follow up some leads.

But first . . . she'd do the reverse image search. She hadn't done it yet today.

It was second nature by now; what had started out of desperation one sleepless evening had become a habit, like doing her morning workout. Select, copy, drag, drop, search. Nothing.

That is: usually it was nothing.

Today . . . it was something.

Opal leaned forward in her chair, eyes wide, hardly able to believe what she was seeing. This . . . was *really* something.

If she played her cards right, this was something that could change everything.

5

THE DAY BEFORE THAT THURSDAY

Lilah

GRIEF WAS SO STRANGE. LILAH had been very young when her mother died, and she didn't really remember how she'd felt then. Since losing Dad, she went through cycles of feeling almost normal, and then being hijacked by sadness so overwhelming that she felt as if she were being erased from the world. And she was so tired, as if nothing had any point anymore.

But, as Zachary quite rightly said, she couldn't spend all day lying in bed crying.

She was living in a suite in the Dorchester next to Hyde Park. This wasn't something she would have chosen for herself—she would have been satisfied with the Premier Inn in Chislehurst, or if she wanted to be extravagant, a Marriott—but Zachary insisted on a five-star hotel. "You need to get away," he had said, "be surrounded by life and people. And it's so much easier to have you in town, especially if I need to work late." He was working as a consultant in cyber security for a bank in the city, and often worked late. But he made sure he ate dinner with her as often as he could and checked up with her on the phone multiple times every day, because he missed her.

They had room service sent up to the suite. She didn't feel like eating most of the time, but it did her good to sit at a table with Zachary and force down at least a few mouthfuls.

Tonight, she was having the soup again. Zachary was having steak and a salad. It was nice he took the time to have a meal with her. He always turned off his phone when he was with her, left his laptop at the office, so he could give her his full attention.

"Have a bite of this," he said, holding out his fork to her. There was a piece of steak on it. Rare.

"No thanks."

"You're wasting away, darling. You need some protein and some iron."

"I'll take a multivitamin."

"That won't give you protein. Here. Just a bite. Do it for me?"

The steak was still bloody. She closed her eyes and opened her mouth. The meat tasted metallic, animal. It was too chewy and at the same time too soft. Little fibers lodged themselves between her teeth.

She swallowed as quickly as she could, feeling it go down her throat in a lump. She opened her eyes and gulped water.

"That wasn't too bad, was it? Don't you feel stronger already?"

Lilah nodded doubtfully. She worried a bit of meat caught between two molars with her tongue.

"Tomorrow you should try ordering something other than soup," Zachary said.

Her mouth still tasted of blood. "I'll try some pasta," she said.

"Carbs are terrible for you."

"I'm not sure I can manage anything else."

"At least try it with meat sauce, darling." He cut another piece off his steak. He had a point: he was older than her but so healthy. Practically glowing with it.

"Anyway," she said. "I've been thinking that I'd like to go back home."

"Hmm," said Zachary, chewing. "Is that a good idea?"

"I don't know. But it's my home. I can't avoid it forever. I have to come to terms with what happened, I think. And I can't do that sitting in this hotel, reading books."

"I thought sitting in a luxury hotel reading books was your idea of heaven."

"Well, yes. But I also miss Dad. I want to be in a place that reminds me of him. This suite is like . . . a Wedgwood prison. And I think it would be a good idea for me to go back to work."

Zachary put down his fork and knife. He took a sip of water, and he smoothed his napkin on his lap. It was all cloth napkins here and Zachary was so meticulous. It was one of the things she loved about him.

"Actually, darling. There's something I've been wanting to bring up with you, but I wasn't sure how to do it."

"What's that?"

"I don't know," he said. "Maybe I've spoken too soon. Maybe I should wait until you're a little stronger."

"Wait for what?" Lilah asked, feeling uneasy.

"I just . . . maybe I'm being overprotective. But I've waited all my life to find you, Lilah. I couldn't bear it if anything were to happen to you."

"Happen to me?"

He sighed. "Have you ever wondered . . . if maybe what happened to your father wasn't just a robbery gone wrong?"

Lilah shook her head. "No one would ever want to hurt Dad on purpose. I don't believe that. That's what I told the police."

"No, not that someone wanted to hurt your father. I agree that your dad couldn't make an enemy if he tried. Maybe it's because I love you so much, but I can't help wondering if the real target wasn't your father . . . but you."

She nearly dropped her spoon. "Me? Why?"

"You were working late that day. If you'd been following your regular schedule, you would've been home that afternoon when the break-in happened."

She'd thought of this herself, mostly in the small hours of the morning when she couldn't sleep. If she hadn't volunteered to lock up for Jimiyu, if she hadn't lingered over closing the library . . . she could have been at home. She could have done something.

Her dad might still be alive.

"The robbery theory just doesn't make sense to me," Zachary was continuing. "Why would someone break in at random in the middle of the day? They hardly walked away with anything, either. A couple of laptops and a TV. If they'd done even the most cursory of research beforehand, they would have known that you didn't have lots of cash and electronics in the house."

Lilah didn't like talking like this, as if her dad's death was part of a murder mystery in a book, and not something that had really happened and was the most painful thing in her life. But Zachary was talking about it because he was concerned for her, so she went along with it.

"Maybe they didn't do any research," she said. "Maybe it was opportunistic. That's what the police said."

"The murderer did enough research to know that you didn't have any cameras or an alarm system. And opportunistic thieves are people like junkies, who need money fast. Whereas you're on a private road, in an exclusive neighborhood."

"Well that seems like all the more reason to rob it."

"No, whoever broke in was organized. They'd planned it. Watched the house."

"Oh God this is horrible." Lilah pushed away her bowl of soup.

"Terrible," agreed Zachary, reaching over to take her hand. "But that's the way my brain works. I like to look at things logically, step by step. But you're in shock, so you're not able to think logically, my poor darling."

"So why do you think it happened?"

"As I said. I think we have to look at the possibility that whoever did this awful thing was actually trying to hurt you instead of your father. You were supposed to be home at that time, after all. I think it's possible that they broke in and were looking for you. And that when you weren't there, they attacked your father."

"But why? Why would someone be looking for me?"

"Well. You're so wonderfully modest that sometimes you forget that you are a very wealthy woman. And some people, they see a wealthy woman, and they think, *I want a piece of that.* They could have been breaking into your house to try to get access to your bank accounts, for example. To force you to give them your passwords and access codes, or transfer money to them. Or to kidnap you, for ransom. Or, God forbid, to punish you for being lucky."

"People don't do things like that," said Lilah, though there were shelves upon shelves of books in her library that said that they did.

"You have millions and millions in the bank." Zachary lowered his voice. "And what did you do to earn them? You chose a few numbers. People are envious. Especially when they think that someone has something that they don't deserve."

"But that's how the lottery *works.* It's not for whoever deserves it most, it's literally by chance. And I don't even *want* most of this money. Dad and I had been making plans to give the lion's share of it to charity, we just have to deal with setting up trusts and all the taxes and things."

"Of course. Of course, you're a good person. And you do deserve that money. Every penny, my love, even though some people might say you don't." He squeezed her hand. "But there are bad people out there. And I'm worried that some of them may have it in for you. That's one of the reasons why I wasn't keen on you talking to lots of people at the funeral."

He had been very protective of her during the funeral. He'd never left her side. And he'd stuck right with her every single time she'd spoken to the police, holding her hand, keeping her strong.

She chewed on her lip. "Dad and I did our best to keep the lottery win out of the media."

"Well . . . you did after I met you, and I explained how important privacy is. And then that photo got out anyway to the press, after your father died."

Zachary had been so angry about that photo being published, raging about violations of privacy. It had been a nice photo, though, of her and Zachary and her dad on holiday. She was glad the media had got hold of that one, at least.

"But that would mean that if someone did have it in for me, it would be someone I knew. I can't believe that's true."

"Everyone who really knows you can't help loving you," agreed Zachary. That was a little overenthusiastic—Lilah generally felt that people, other than her dad, found her inoffensive rather than inspiring of love. And Evil Alice seemed positively to hate her. But he was her fiancé, after all, and he might be biased.

He added, "But we can't discount the possibility that someone is following your movements. And that you're in danger."

"Do you think we should tell the police?"

He smiled. "I love that you have such faith in institutions. It's utterly charming."

"Shouldn't I? I work for a public institution."

"And is it always managed properly, for the benefit of the public?"

She thought about the Monday closures. The slashed budgets. "Well. No."

"I won't feel good about you being back in your home until we've installed a full security system."

"Yes, that's a good idea. If I'd had cameras and an alarm installed before all of this happened . . ."

The idea made her feel sick. She could have prevented her father's death, if she'd been a bit savvier.

"It would have been wise," agreed Zachary.

"Yes," she said, with more conviction. "I'll start doing some research and get some quotes."

"Better late than never." He squeezed her hand and beamed at her, and Lilah managed a smile back. "But you don't have to make the calls. I have contacts in the security industry."

"I thought you worked in cyber security."

"Yes, well, it's all connected obviously."

"Oh."

"I can sort it all out for you. A full security system for your home, so you can be the safest you can possibly be. State of the art. I'll get in touch tonight, and they can start tomorrow first thing."

"Are you sure, Zachary? You're so busy with your own work."

"You've got enough to think about right now. Leave it to me, I'll arrange everything. It's the least I can do for the woman I love."

"You're so good to me," she said. "I don't know what I've done to deserve it."

"I'm just like any man. I want to protect you. Nobody's going to hurt you on my watch. Meanwhile, promise me that you'll be careful, okay? Be aware of your surroundings. I know you're a little daydreamer, always with your head in the clouds. In fact, I got you this. I want you to carry it from now on."

He pushed a small cylinder across the table. She picked it up.

"Careful!" he said, and she held it at arm's length.

"What is it?"

"It's pepper spray. For self-defense. You should carry it at all times when you leave the hotel. Don't show it to anyone, though; it's illegal in the UK."

She put it down quickly. "I don't want to do anything illegal."

"It's okay, darling. It's mostly for my peace of mind. I'm sure you'll never even have to get it out of your bag. In any case, there's no need for you to go out—you can get anything you need sent to the room."

She glanced around. This place was all soft upholstery and glossy surfaces. When she ventured out into the public areas of the hotel, the staff were polite and unobtrusive, and no one else seemed to pay any attention to her. But, if Zachary was right, she'd been oblivious to threats all along.

And because of that, her father was dead.

* * *

Zachary took the keys to Lilah's house, telling her that he'd set up a meeting with the security team. "Don't worry about anything," he told her before he left. "Before you know it, we'll have your house as safe as the Bank of England."

She picked at her room service breakfast while she finished the book she was reading, a history of the bloody history of Koh-i-Noor diamond. Thinking about it rationally, this was probably not the best book for her to have chosen. It was fascinating, but she didn't need any reminders of the violence, tragedy, greed, and human suffering that was attracted by great wealth.

She needed something more cheerful.

Lilah looked through the stacks that she'd had delivered to the hotel. They took up most of the glossy desk in the seating area of the suite. She'd never been one for ebooks—she liked the feel and smell of a book, she liked its heft in her hand, and the satisfying action of turning the pages. But none of the books in her to-be-read pile quite hit the spot. She wanted something comforting and predictable and warm, that reassured her about the goodness of human nature.

All at once she knew the exact book she wanted. *Anne of Green Gables*. She hadn't read it since she was a little girl, when she read it obsessively. She still owned her childhood copy of it, a worn hardback whose paper cover was tatty around the edges. It was sitting in her house right now, in her own library, on a shelf on the left-hand side as you walked in the door. She could picture its location exactly, in with the other *M*s, for Montgomery.

She could get an Uber and pick it up. She'd be in and out within seconds. But . . . Zachary had her keys. And he'd said it wasn't safe yet for her to go back.

She picked up her phone to text Zachary and ask him to pick it up when he was at her house this afternoon. Hours from now. And then it would be hours until he came back for dinner. And what would she do in the meantime?

"This is silly," she said aloud to the room. "I have over sixty million pounds. I can just go to a bookshop."

So she did.

*　*　*

Lilah loved bookshops almost as much as she did libraries. In some ways, she loved them more. Although that made her feel guilty, because libraries were free for everyone, and you needed money to buy books.

No, she loved both the same.

Her father had introduced her to bookshops, just as he'd introduced her to libraries. When he'd taken her to the children's section of the library near their bungalow in Sidcup, presided over by a friendly woman called Mrs. Johnson, she was allowed to take out five books at once. When he'd taken her to the local bookshop—it was only a news-stand with a small selection of books for sale, but it was magical to Lilah nonetheless—she could only buy one book with money saved from her allowance. But she could keep that book forever and read it as many times as she liked, whenever she wanted.

She still had that first book. She had all the books she'd ever bought.

She had bought her copy of *Anne of Green Gables* in a different book-shop, a wonderful bookshop called Cuthbert & Binding in a tiny alley just off Charing Cross Road. Her father had brought her there. This bookshop, unlike the local Smith's, was in an old building and rambled over several floors, with narrow corridors lined with more books than you could read in a lifetime. Some books were new, and some were second-hand, and some were even rare first editions, kept behind glass. But the other books, you could touch and open and read. There were tall shelves and cozy reading nooks. There were potted plants and illustrations from favorite stories on the walls.

Lilah had got lost in that bookshop—not only lost in the stories in the books, but literally lost. Her father hadn't been able to find her. Worried, he'd asked the shop assistant to help, and they'd combed the shop for a short little girl with skinny legs, finally finding her curled up on the very top floor in a forgotten corner stacked with discounted and slightly out-of-date Survey maps, reading about a Canadian orphan.

Lilah took the subway to Leicester Square station and found the bookshop alley just where she remembered it, along the back of a theater. It was narrow, with wooden and gilt signs hanging from the buildings and book lovers scurrying back and forth, peering in windows, carrying their latest treasures under their arms.

Instantly, she felt herself relax. For the first time in days and days she felt the presence of her father rather than his absence. She remembered when she was a little girl and he'd taken her hand and led her down this same alley. She followed their past footsteps to the shop and opened the door, inhaling the scent of old paper and words.

Every single time she would go into a bookshop for the rest of her life, she would think of Dad. Not as she'd last seen him—lying bloody and cold on the floor—but as he really used to be, smiling and gentle, with his clever hands and his soft, precise voice.

While that was sad, it was also pretty wonderful.

"Can I help you?" said someone.

Lilah realized she'd been standing in the doorway, eyes closed. The person who'd addressed her was a bookseller standing behind the register near the door.

"Oh," she said. "I just love the smell in here." She closed the door behind her.

"Me too. Can I help you find anything?"

"I'm looking for *Anne of Green Gables*."

"Children's books are on the first floor in the front. Would you like me to show you?"

"No thank you, I remember where they are."

The stairs were rickety and comfortingly bowed in the middle from thousands of feet. She found the children's section and happily browsed all the shelves starting with A. When she got to M, she found a lovely hardback edition of *Anne of Green Gables* with watercolor illustrations and gilt lettering, so perfect that she wanted to sit down and read it right there. But of course, she couldn't do that when there were so many other books to look at.

Lilah had planned to pick up one book and then go back to the hotel, but by the time she reached the register, she had a stack of other books as well as the L.M. Montgomery. Including a book on the meaning of flowers that she would probably never read, but which her dad would have liked, and that she couldn't pass by. Maybe she'd read it. Maybe she'd plant a little plot in the garden in his memory, with plants that meant love and kindness, and she could sit there and remember him.

"Hi again," said the bookseller, scanning the books through the register. "Good choices."

"Thank you."

"*Anne of Green Gables* was my mum's favorite book. I've never read it, though."

"Oh, you should! It's full of such good people. It makes you feel like the world is going to be all right after all."

He paused and gazed at her. He had dark natural hair and brown eyes and was about her own age. "I know you, don't I?"

"Oh. No, I don't think so?"

"Have you shopped in here before?"

"Not since I was a little girl. I work in a library, so I usually get my books there."

"You look familiar," he said thoughtfully. "I wonder where I've . . ."

She saw the exact moment where realization bloomed on his face. It was the same moment that she realized it too: he'd seen her photo in the paper. The same holiday snap of her and her father and Zachary, taken in Bournemouth, that the press had somehow got hold of. They printed it next to that terrible headline:

MILLIONAIRE LOTTERY WINNER'S DAD MURDERED

The bookseller looked down quickly. "That'll be sixty-eight seventy-nine, please. Do you have a loyalty card?"

"Maybe, I—no, I don't think—" She took her debit card out of her bag, slotting it into the reader and deliberately averting her face as she waited for the charge to go through.

"Um," said the bookseller. "It hasn't gone through."

She typed in her pin again.

"Sorry," said the bookseller. "It says declined."

"Sorry," she said, "I'll try another card." But when she checked her bag, her credit card wasn't there. She remembered: she'd given it to Zachary to reserve her hotel room, and told him to keep it to pay for some of the security stuff for the house.

"Do you have payments set up on your phone?" the bookseller asked helpfully. She shook her head.

"I'm sorry," he said. "I know you're good for the money. In fact, you could buy this whole shop if you wanted to. If it were up to me, I'd let you take the books and pay us back later. But it's not my shop."

"It's okay," she said, hurriedly, stuffing her debit card back into her bag. "I don't really need them right now."

"There's a cash machine down the road. Should I hold these . . . ?"

"No no, no bother, don't worry, thank you, goodbye!" She turned and rushed out of the shop, her cheeks flushing violently, her ears filled with the sound of her hammering heart.

She glanced backwards as she hurried down the alley, to make sure that the bookseller hadn't called security or that no one else had seen what had happened. The pavement was empty, but she saw a man wearing a blue baseball cap leave the bookshop and stride quickly in her direction.

It was a coincidence. She ducked into Leicester Square station, hurried down the stairs, and tapped her card at the gate.

The display lit up: *Seek Assistance.*

Oh. Of course.

She turned around and the man in the baseball cap was directly behind her. He was much taller than her, with a thick chest and beefy arms that packed his jacket as tight as sausage.

"I'm sorry, excuse me, sorry." She bowed her head and rushed past him, back up the stairs to the street. When she glanced over her shoulder, he was also walking up the stairs.

A black cab approached with its light on. She waved frantically at it, and it had slowed down before she remembered yet again that she had no money to pay for it. So she danced an elaborate pantomime to indicate that sorry, she didn't need a cab after all, and to avoid the disapproving look of the driver she bolted across the road in front of him, dodging between cars going the other way, to join the throngs of tourists in Leicester Square.

Her phone was ringing in her bag, but she was in too much of a hurry to answer it. By the Mary Poppins statue, she looked back again. She thought she saw a blue cap by the performer dressed up as a levitating Yoda, so she walked faster. Sweat prickled under her arms and although she always wore comfortable shoes, she wished she'd chosen sneakers today instead of ballet flats.

For the first time it occurred to her that maybe this wasn't bookshop security. Maybe it wasn't a random person who happened to be going the same way as her, either. What if Zachary was right, and someone was after her?

What if she was in actual danger?

Her throat tightened. Phantom hands around her neck.

Her phone stopped ringing, then started again. Piccadilly Circus lay ahead of her, with its crowds and traffic. She walked as fast as she could, breaking into a run every few steps, dodging around pedestrians. In front of Eros, a tour group stood in a great cluster listening to their leader, who was holding an umbrella high in the air. Lilah squeezed between them, pushed through to the other side through a chorus of *tsks*, and ran across the road just before the light changed. Having safely gained the pavement on Piccadilly, she walked backwards for a few steps, searching the people behind her for a cap. What if she led him right to where she was staying? She had the pepper spray in her bag.

To her left ahead of her was Waterstones Piccadilly, with its black shiny awning. She hurried through its doors into blessed bookishness and pressed herself into the corner in front of the New Hardcovers section, watching the front window like a hawk.

Less than two minutes later, the man in the blue baseball cap walked by on the pavement outside. He was really quite large. She held her breath, but he didn't seem to see her.

Her phone rang again. She pulled it out, eyes watching the street through the window. It was Zachary.

"Where are you?" he asked as soon as she answered.

He sounded so concerned that she couldn't tell him about the man following her and worry him even more. "I'm in Waterstones Piccadilly," she said hoarsely.

"I've been calling the room and you didn't answer. And then you didn't answer your phone. I was worried about you."

"I'm alright."

"You don't sound alright. What's wrong?"

"Nothing, I'm fine."

"I know when something is wrong, darling. What is it?"

"I . . ." She cleared her throat. "I had some trouble with my bank card. The card was declined at the bookstore."

"Oh, poor darling! You probably demagnetized it. Were you trying to buy books? If you tell me the titles, I'll order them for you and have them delivered, and you won't have to worry."

"No, it's all fine. I just . . . don't have any cash."

"Well, you don't need cash at the Dorchester. Are you on your way back there now?"

"Yes."

"Call me as soon as you get there, from the hotel phone, so I know you're safe? I worry so much."

She promised and put down the phone. After five minutes more that seemed an eternity, and then she ventured outside the shop again, checking in either direction. No sign of him.

Her sense of direction was not great and she hadn't spent much time in this part of London, but she did her best to take a circuitous route back to Park Lane, taking wrong turns and doubling back on herself. Zachary texted her four times while she was doing this, but she only replied with one-word answers. By the time she reached the Dorchester her mouth was dry and her feet were blistered.

She hurried through the lobby, head down, glancing from side to side. The lobby was generally pretty busy, but no one was wearing hats. How would she be able to tell a regular hotel guest from someone who wanted to hurt her?

Was she going to be looking over her shoulder for the rest of her life?

She waited until no one was near the elevator to get into it and rode up to her floor alone. The corridor was, thankfully, empty. She let herself into her room and collapsed on the bed, trying to slow down her breathing and heart rate.

She tried to think rationally. Maybe the man in the blue baseball cap was, after all, a fellow book lover who happened to be going in the same general direction she was. Though wouldn't a book lover have stopped at Waterstones? No, maybe he'd already bought the books he wanted? But he wasn't carrying any. But he could have been browsing.

Most likely she had totally overreacted, but the important thing was that no one was hurt and she was safe now. And once Zachary sorted out her home security, everything was going to be fine.

Lilah sat up and took a long cool drink from the complimentary bottle of water that the housekeeping staff left on her bedside table every time they made up the room. (They tried to do it every day, but she thought it was ridiculous that they should be tidying up her messes, so she tried to remember to keep the DO NOT DISTURB sign on.) She reached for the hotel phone to call Zachary.

She wouldn't tell him about the man in the blue baseball cap. It was nothing, and she didn't want to worry him. And also, she had sort of lied to Zachary before when she said everything was fine, and it would be difficult to justify that.

Although . . . was it a bad thing to keep secrets from your fiancé?

Her phone pinged again with another text, probably from Zachary, and she checked it before she rang him, to make sure he wasn't going into a meeting or anything. Sometimes he got cross when she interrupted him at work.

The message, though, wasn't from Zachary. It was from an unknown number.

LILAH. YOU ARE IN DANGER.

6

SHE OPENED THE TEXT MESSAGE properly and stared at it. All she saw was her name and the word "DANGER" in big capital letters.

She wanted to run and hide. But where? The wardrobe? Under the bed? In the hotel kitchens? Back to her house where her father had been murdered?

Her second impulse was to call the police. She searched the hotel room desk for Detective Branston's card, the one he gave her when he'd interviewed her about her father. He'd said that if she thought of anything else, anything she might have noticed, that she should get in touch. But though she looked in the desk, her handbag, and all the pockets of her clothes, she couldn't find his card.

Then her phone buzzed again.

ARE YOU ALONE?

She could call 911. She could google Detective Branston's number.

But after all, she had possibly just evaded a pursuer in a chase through the streets of London. Maybe it was time she started trying to protect herself.

She texted back.

```
Who are you?
```

The person was typing. She held her breath.

```
I'M SOMEONE WHO WANTS TO HELP YOU.

Then why are you trying to frighten me?

YOU'RE IN DANGER, AND YOU NEED TO KNOW. ARE
YOU ALONE?
```

She looked around, suddenly worried that the man in the baseball cap had somehow appeared in her hotel room. She checked the ensuite and looked out the peephole in the door.

```
I'm someplace safe.

THAT'S NOT WHAT I ASKED YOU, LILAH.
```

The reply was quick and unexpectedly testy, in a way that reminded her of someone.

```
Is this Alice?

I DON'T KNOW WHO ALICE IS. I JUST WANT TO KNOW
IF YOU'RE BY YOURSELF. I DON'T WANT ANYONE TO
READ MY MESSAGES. AND YOU SHOULD DELETE THEM
AS SOON AS YOU GET THEM.
```

She snorted. As if she were going to do that. She'd need the messages as evidence.

```
IT'S SAFER IF YOU DON'T TELL ANYONE THAT WE"VE
BEEN IN TOUCH.
```

Who are you? she texted again.

I CAN'T TELL YOU UNTIL YOU PROMISE ME THAT
YOU'RE NOT SHOWING THESE MESSAGES TO ANYONE
ELSE.

This is going round in circles! Okay, okay, I'm
alone in my room. And I won't show these messages to anyone unless you turn out to be a
weirdo who's trying to hurt me, in which case,
I'm taking my phone straight to the police.

IT'S NOT THE POLICE I'M WORRIED ABOUT.

Lilah curled up in an armchair. If it weren't so strange, she would
find it sort of nice to have someone to have a text conversation with.

How did you get my number?

YOU'RE RIDICULOUSLY EASY TO FIND.

She felt oddly insulted by this. Well I'm not exactly an
international woman of mystery.

NO. YOU'RE AN INCREDIBLY RICH LIBRARIAN.

And you still haven't told me who you are. It's
becoming rude.

There was a pause, and then the three dots appeared.

YOU'VE GOT A FEISTY STREAK. THAT'S GOING TO
HELP A LOT.

Help with what?

IT'S NOT SAFE TO TELL YOU OVER THE PHONE. WE
NEED TO MEET.

"No way," said Lilah out loud, then she typed, I'm not meeting someone if I don't even know their name. You say you want to keep me safe, but I've not seen any evidence of it.

MY NAME IS OPAL. I'LL BE AT THE MCDONALD'S ON PRAED STREET TOMORROW MORNING AT 9:30. COME ALONE.

If I go, how will I recognize you?

DON'T WORRY. I'LL RECOGNIZE YOU.

* * *

Zachary didn't join her for dinner that night—he had an important meeting with a Malaysian client, which he had to do on Kuala Lumpur time—so she didn't have the chance to talk with him about everything that had happened. When she'd rung him earlier to say she was safe at the Dorchester, he'd seemed satisfied.

She was in bed but lying awake when he returned to the suite. He obviously thought she was asleep because he got ready for bed quietly and without turning the lights on, so she carried on pretending she was asleep when he climbed in beside her. It was just as well. He would most definitely object to the idea of her meeting some random stranger named Opal in a McDonald's near Paddington.

And Opal had sworn her to secrecy anyway, though Lilah wasn't sure of her moral obligations to keep a promise to someone who was sending her mysterious text messages.

It was all very tangled, and she wasn't sure if she quite understood what was going on, but one thing she did understand was that

Zachary would be very upset with her if she went, and she didn't want to make him upset.

He fell asleep quickly, his breathing becoming regular and even. She turned over in bed.

Of course, the obvious answer was not to go. It was ridiculous and foolish and reckless. Opal could be anyone. She might not be named Opal. She might be a whole gang of beefy men in blue baseball caps. She might have engineered this all of this to find out where Lilah was staying so she could try to hurt her. Or she could be trying to get Lilah's money. She could be connected to the person who murdered Lilah's father.

The sensible thing would be to go to the police station and show them the text messages.

Well, except she had deleted them, because Opal had asked her to, but surely the police could recover them.

Once again, Lilah wished she'd read more crime novels, particularly police procedurals.

So, lying on her left side, staring at Zachary's back in the dark, she made up her mind not to go. He wouldn't want her to go.

But then . . . she turned onto her right side, away from him.

The thing was, her father might have wanted her to go. He was always saying that she was young and clever, she should get out there and experience the world and have adventures. And she'd always replied that she didn't want adventures and she preferred to read about them. But this situation was exactly like something out of a novel. The mysterious stranger in the cap, the pursuit through the streets of Mayfair. The text messages that claimed to be from a concerned stranger, the clandestine meeting in a fast-food restaurant.

And those novels might be cautionary tales, tales that started and ended with dead women, but they were exciting.

All of this was much more exciting than winning sixty-seven million pounds.

Anyway, what did it matter what Zachary thought or what Dad would have said? Ever since her father had been killed, she'd been doing exactly what men had been telling her to do. First, it was Detective Branston giving her orders. Then Zachary was just trying to protect her, but if he had his choice, she'd be holed up in this hotel forever. She had to make decisions for herself.

Maybe she could learn something that would help solve her father's murder. And how dangerous could a McDonald's be?

So the next day, Thursday, after Zachary had gone off to work, she found an old metro card that still had money on it. Then she put on sunglasses and a hat and wound a scarf around her neck, and headed for Praed Street.

McDonald's was relatively busy. She scanned the tables, looking for a woman sitting on her own. Or alternatively, a bunch of armed thugs. Or a masked man with a large knife dripping blood.

It was all groups of youths eating breakfast sandwiches and tired-looking businessmen scrolling through their phones.

Unsure of what to do, she joined the line and ordered a cup of tea. At the very least she could use that as a weapon of some sort, if it went wrong. Pepper spray was illegal, but tea was definitely not. While she was paying her phone pinged.

IN THE BACK NEAR THE EMERGENCY EXITS.

Clutching her cup, Lilah threaded through the families. It was less crowded at the back. And sitting alone at a table was a woman.

"Opal?" Lilah said, approaching.

"That's me," said the woman. She stood up and held out her hand for Lilah to shake, as if this were a business meeting.

"Nice to meet you," said Lilah, for lack of any knowledge of the correct thing to say in this situation.

"I'm glad you decided to come," said Opal.

Opal was visibly older, in her forties maybe, though she was very well-groomed and moisturized. She had short hair, red lips, and beautifully white teeth. She was also, Lilah noticed as she sat across from her, very fit. She wore an orange sleeveless top, and her arms were smooth and muscular. She had a cup of black coffee, but it didn't look as if she'd drunk any of it.

"Wow," said Opal. "You look even younger in person."

"I'm twenty-six."

"Exactly."

"Why am I here?" Lilah asked. "Is this about my father?"

"I'm sorry about your father," said Opal. "That was a terrible thing that never should have happened."

Suddenly this was very serious.

"Do you know who killed him?" Lilah took off her sunglasses and scarf.

"No," said Opal. "I don't. This is about something else."

"Do you want money?"

"This isn't about that, either."

"Who are you?"

"It's easier if I show you."

She pushed a black iPhone with a bright pink case across the table and tapped open an Instagram account. @Hot_Fit_Mess was full of pictures of Opal in very tight workout gear. Here, she was sparring with a punching bag. Here, she was doing yoga on a beach. Here, she was in a video explaining a sixty-day abs challenge. In every image, she was wearing red lipstick. The captions were all in capital letters and said things like *FLEXIBILITY IS OUR GREATEST ASSET* and *GLOW GLOW GLOW!*

"You're an exercise instructor?" asked Lilah.

"I'm a wellness influencer." Opal pointed to her follower count, well into the several hundreds of thousands.

"Oh. Wow. Good for you."

"My personal brand is feeling great post-menopause. Middle-aged women get a raw deal when it comes to the medical and fitness establishments. It's all lithe young women or gym bros, and what works for them won't work for a woman over fifty."

She was over fifty? "Well, you look great."

"I work hard at it, and I work smart."

"What does this have to do with why you wanted to meet?"

"Nothing," said Opal. "I just wanted to show you my business so you know that I am who I say I am."

So it wasn't Lilah's dad, and it wasn't her money. "Is this something to do with the library?"

"No. It's about your boyfriend."

"Zachary?" she said in disbelief.

"If that's what he calls himself," said Opal. "It's not his real name."

"What?"

"How did you meet him? Was it in the library? Did he borrow a book and strike up a conversation?"

"This is none of your business."

"Oh, it very much is. Did you meet him before or after you won all the money?"

"This is really none of your business."

"Humor me. It's important."

She thought. "Well . . . after. But he's not—"

Opal pointed at the ring on Lilah's left hand. "Are you engaged to him?"

"Yes."

"Whose money did he use for the ring?"

"What? I don't know. His."

"Do you know that for certain?"

Lilah sat up straighter. "I don't like what you're implying."

"I don't like it either. But it's the truth. What did he tell you he did for a living?"

"He works in cyber security, specializing in online fraud. He has a PhD."

Opal tilted her head back and laughed silently to the ceiling. "Oh, that's rich."

"Why?"

She leaned forward, hands clasped on the table. "Have you had any problems with money lately? Credit cards suddenly at their limit? Bank balances looking smaller than they should be?"

The bookshop, yesterday. She'd been too distracted to investigate or call her bank, and Zachary had said something about a demagnetized card. "I don't have money problems."

"Do you have a banking app on your phone? Do me a favor, have a look."

"Are you saying that Zachary, my fiancé, is stealing from me?"

"Just have a look."

Lilah opened the app for the current account attached to her debit card. There was £1.56 in it.

"This must be some mistake," she said.

Opal shook her head. "It's very deliberate, I can assure you. Does he have access to all of your accounts?"

"He's got my credit card," said Lilah in a daze. "But that's because he's sorting out security for my house."

She checked the balance outstanding on the credit card. It was maxed out.

"What about your savings accounts? Your investments?"

"He asked me for the details so he could check my security, but I haven't got around to giving them to him yet."

"Are they something he could guess? Or find in your house?"

Lilah shook her head numbly. "I don't know. It was all set up by my father."

Her voice broke on the last word.

"This is your life," Opal said. "Try not to get too emotional."

"I'm don't know what you're trying to tell me."

"Have you signed a prenuptial agreement? Have you altered your will? Given him power of attorney?"

"No."

"Well. You might have had a very lucky escape."

"Are you trying to tell me that Zachary is a thief?"

"That's exactly what I'm telling you."

Lilah gaped.

"Why should I believe you? I've never met you before in my life."

"You don't have to believe me. Believe your bank accounts, darling."

She stood up. "How dare you!" she said, for the first time in her life. "You contact me out of the blue and start making all these accusations."

"Who else would have access to your accounts and steal all that money?"

"I don't know. Anyway, if he did take it, it's not stealing—I'm sure he's going to pay it back."

"Did he tell you he was taking it?"

She crossed her arms. "I trust him. I love him."

"Then you are very, very stupid."

Opal's voice dripped with pity, which put Lilah's back up even more.

"Who are you?" she demanded. "Why do you even care? This is none of your business."

"It is very much my business."

"Why? Do you even know Zachary?"

"Have you ever met his parents?" Opal asked. "Any member of his family? His friends?"

"He's an orphan. That's why he loved my dad so much."

"Does he have any friends?"

Well, *she* didn't have any friends. Lilah shrugged.

"Have you ever been to his house?"

"What does that have to do with anything?"

"Why did he say you couldn't visit him at his home?"

He'd said his house was an absolute mess of computer equipment. When she'd assured him that she didn't mind, he'd told her . . .

"He had an ant infestation."

Opal snorted.

"I don't have to put up with this," Lilah huffed. She turned, leaving her tea and sunglasses on the table. Opal grabbed her wrist. The other woman's grip was, unsurprisingly, strong.

"Why do you care?" Lilah asked again, wildly. "Why can't you just leave us alone?"

"I can't," said Opal. "The man that you know as Zachary, I know as Zander."

"Why does that matter?"

"Because I'm his wife."

7

"I DON'T BELIEVE YOU," SAID Lilah. "You're talking about my fiancé. Why are you doing this?"

Opal took her phone back, swiped and tapped, and pushed it over again. Lilah sat at the table and stared at a wedding photograph. Opal was younger and less muscular but wearing the same shade of red lipstick and a white satin dress. The man holding her hand and smiling under a shower of confetti had black hair rather than silver and didn't wear glasses, but it was unmistakably Zachary.

"You . . ." Lilah swallowed. "This was taken ages ago."

"Seven years and four months ago."

Opal swiped to show her more wedding photos. Opal and Zachary cutting a cake. Dancing at a reception. Kissing under a tree full of blossom.

The last one made her throat ache.

"So . . . he never told me about his first marriage," Lilah said. "That's not such a big deal. He's . . . he's quite a private person."

Opal seemed quite calm. She did not look like someone who Zachary would ever marry. He was shy and bookish, and Opal was glamorous and actually quite famous. She was also acting as if she were waiting for Lilah to do something or realize something.

"When did you get divorced?"

Opal didn't reply.

Lilah felt sick.

Opal continued on not replying.

"You're still married?" Lilah whispered.

"On our marriage certificate, the man you know as Zachary Dickens is known by the name of Alexander Bolt. I always called him Zander. He quite likes names beginning with Z, apparently."

"I don't believe you," said Lilah.

But she was beginning to.

"Are you living together?" she asked. "Do you . . . have children?"

"No children. And no, we're not living together anymore."

"How long have you been separated?"

"I have literally heard nothing about him for three years now. He walked out the door and disappeared. Not a sausage. I thought he'd left the country. But then he turned up here like a bad apple." Opal grimaced. "Sorry about the food metaphors. I'm hungry and I don't eat fast food."

"Why are we meeting here, then?" Lilah was aware that this was possibly least relevant question ever, but her brain could only take in so much at once.

"Zander can change his name, change his hair color, wear fake glasses, change his backstory . . . but I know him. He has not eaten carbohydrates since 2004. He'd never set foot in a McDonald's unless you tied him up and dragged him in."

This was true of Zachary, too. He believed junk food was poison. Lilah and her dad had quite liked having fish and chips on a Friday, and the one time that Zachary had joined them, he had scraped the batter off his portion of cod and hadn't even touched his chips.

Somehow this convinced her more than the wedding photos had.

"Do you want him back?" Lilah asked.

"Ha!" The bark of laughter seemed involuntary, and Opal visibly collected herself. "Oh. You asked that seriously. I didn't think anyone was that naïve anymore."

"I'm not naïve, I'm . . . concerned."

"No. I do not want him back. I haven't asked you to meet so that I could fight you for him or plead for you to let him go, or anything like that. Quite the opposite."

Lilah had unconsciously been twisting her diamond ring on her finger, but at this, she stopped.

"So your marriage was over. It *is* over," she corrected herself. "I don't know why Zachary changed his name, but the two of you separated, he built himself a new life and a new career, and he was planning to divorce you before he married me. He didn't tell me about it because he didn't want to worry me."

Opal raised a groomed eyebrow. "It's a big thing not to mention."

"Well. I've had a lot on my mind lately."

"Did you meet him in the library? Does he claim to be a big reader?"

"He particularly likes twentieth-century drama. He's a big Pinter fan."

"The Zander I knew wouldn't know a Pinter from a pointer. The only book I've seen him with is *The Seven Habits of Highly Effective People*. And I know for a fact that he never read any further than the first habit, because I had to summarize it for him so he could talk about it at parties."

"People change."

"People do change, yes. But they don't change their fundamental personalities. They might change their clothes and their hair and their name, though. Usually because they're trying to hide something."

Lilah considered herself a rational person. But this was too much.

She stood up. "I'm going to talk to Zachary about this. I need to know his side of the story."

"Don't do that, Lilah. That's absolutely the worst thing you can do."

"Why?"

"Because Zander, Zachary, whatever you want to call him, is an accomplished manipulator. He can charm the birds out of the trees. He'll feed you a story that's plausible enough and which plays to all of your insecurities—because he knows them, believe me—and you'll be taken in, because you love him, and you won't find out the truth until it's too late."

"I do love him!" said Lilah. "And I believe that he loves me, and that there is a perfectly reasonable explanation for all of this. And even if there isn't, I am the sort of person who trusts the person who they love, no matter what. And that is why I have to talk to him, instead of some stranger in a fast-food restaurant."

She turned to go.

"Wait," said Opal.

"What?" said Lilah, exasperated.

"You might not believe me, but I think you need to talk to this lady before you go."

Opal pointed at a woman who was crossing the restaurant towards them. She was older than Lilah, curvy and pretty. She wore a plain T-shirt and jeans, but she had a bright scarf in her hair and big hoop earrings. The woman held a tray with some fries and a drink.

"Marina," said Opal, standing and beckoning the woman over. "I'm Opal."

Marina had her phone on the tray. Lilah knew, somehow, that she had a text message on it, written in all-capital letters.

"Hi Opal," said Marina. "Sorry I'm late. Transport delays, and Ewan had the worst . . . well, never mind, that's a long and gross story, anyway, I'm here. *Why* am I here, by the way? And do I know you?"

"I'll explain in a minute," said Opal. "But first, I wonder if you could do something for us, Marina? This is Lilah."

"Nice to meet you," said Lilah, because her father raised her to be polite.

"Nice to meet you too," said Marina, setting down her tray and joining them. She looked happy, not as if she'd been dragged into something horrible at all. She had rosy cheeks and bright eyes and looked like the kind of person who might suggest they all go for a fun brunch out.

"Marina," said Opal, "I've been looking at your Instagram grid, and I've noticed that you've started a new romance."

"Oh. Um . . . yes. Actually, don't tell anyone, but I've mostly been posting stuff on Insta to show my ex and the PTA ladies that I'm not dead. It's been a bit of a whirlwind with Xavier, only a few weeks, but I'm not getting any younger. Oh wait, you're the fitness lady, aren't you?"

"That's right."

"Wow. My Nana used to love you! She said you made her fall in love with pilates." She dipped a fry in ketchup and ate it. "Oh, that is good. Guilty pleasure. Why did you text me?"

"I need you to do a little favor."

"Um, okay?"

"I wonder if you would mind showing Lilah here a photograph of your new boyfriend, Xavier."

Marina squinted, but she shrugged and smiled. "All right," she said. She unlocked her phone and held it out. "I don't have many pictures of the two of us together, but this is one."

It was a selfie of two people, their heads close together. One of them was Marina.

The other was Zachary.

8

THREE WEEKS BEFORE THAT THURSDAY

Marina

MARINA HAD MET XAVIER TEN days after moving into Nana Sylvia's house.

The house was wonderful, but this particular day had not begun promisingly.

They were in the back garden on a blanket spread out on the freshly mown lawn. Marina had filled one of Nana Sylvia's flowered teapots with apple juice, and she and Archie had put out plates of cookies and cut-up fruit pieces while Lucy Rose carefully arranged what seemed like every single toy they owned into a circle to join their tea party. As usual, the construction next door at the Andersons' was making a racket, but they were doing their best to have fun and ignore it.

Marina poured juice into Archie's cup and turned her attention to Lucy Rose, who was holding out a plastic ice cream tub.

"Snails don't eat cookies," said Archie disdainfully.

"Don't you think that Prince William would prefer some lettuce?" Marina asked.

Lucy Rose wrinkled up her nose. "Both," she said.

Marina passed her a plate with a cookie and a lettuce leaf. Lucy Rose shoved the whole cookie into her mouth, and then dangled the lettuce over the tub. "Yum yummy," she said, dropping crumbs from her lips.

"Well, doesn't this look like fun," said a familiar voice. Marina jumped to her feet, but not before Archie had run across the lawn to his father, who had come through the side gate.

"Daddy!" Lucy Rose put down her tub and ran to Jake too. He ruffled Archie's hair and picked up Lucy Rose for a hug.

"Haven't you grown?" he said to both of them. Marina lifted Ewan onto her hip and approached her ex-husband warily.

"Long time no see," she said.

Jake rolled his eyes as he always did when he thought that Marina was nagging him. "I'm here now. Anyway, you're doing just fine, it seems." He looked pointedly at the large detached Edwardian house. It had six bedrooms, a view of the Thames, and a turret.

"We have a place to live," she said. "Thanks to Nana Sylvia."

"Poor Nana Sylvia. Still, at least she went out in style." Jake put down Lucy Rose and held out his arms for Ewan. "How are you doing, little buddy?"

Ewan shrank back and clung to Marina's neck. She held him tighter; he was so young, Jake probably seemed like a stranger to him.

"Ah, this one is still attached by an umbilical cord," Jake said. "Mummy's boy, eh? You'll have to grow out of that." He chucked Ewan under the chin and Ewan buried his head in Marina's shoulder. "Not like my big boy Archie. He's a chip off the old block. Isn't that right, tough guy?" He tousled Archie's hair. Archie beamed under his attention. It broke Marina's heart.

"He's five," said Marina. "Ewan's one. It's a little soon to be enforcing gender stereotypes."

Jake laughed. "Someone's been feeding you woke nonsense, I see."

"Ewan still eats from Mummy's boobies," said Lucy Rose, who'd been listening.

"Not surprised, princess. Not surprised at all. So. Who wants to show me around the house?"

The two older children volunteered loudly. They each took one of his hands and led him to the back door, chattering the whole time.

Marina followed more slowly. She had to admit it: Jake could be great with the children. He was always the one who proposed rowdy games and who came up with fun ideas. Her nephews adored him, and so did his own brothers' kids, who were older.

It was one of the things that had charmed her so much when they'd met. She knew he'd make a great dad. And he *was* a great dad.

Well, he was a fun dad, at least. When he felt like being a fun dad. When he chose to be available for his children. He hadn't exactly changed many diapers, or done many bottle runs in the middle of the night, or ever taken any of the children to the dentist.

I shouldn't resent him, she told herself silently. *He's their father. Our children aren't being disloyal to me by loving him and being happy to see him.*

But she still felt jealous as she listened to Lucy Rose showing Jake her favorite toy flamingo, and Archie telling him about his new school.

Jake didn't have to deal with the tantrums and the projectile vomiting; he didn't suffer with bitten nipples and broken sleep. He got pure love from his children, even when they hadn't seen him in weeks.

Except from Ewan. She kissed his sticky cheek. "Never grow out of being a Mummy's boy," she whispered to him, even though she knew that he would. Even though she knew that her wish to keep him close would make him as weak as Jake said she was.

"Did I see cookies outside in the garden?" said Jake loudly, and Archie and Lucy Rose pulled him back outside to their picnic. "Love a cup of tea if you've got one going," he said to Marina as he passed her.

She made his tea just as he liked it. Personally, after the shock of him turning up out of the blue, with all of the associated emotions of their failed marriage and divorce, she could do with something stronger, like something from Nana Sylvia's extensive wine cellar.

But that would have to wait until the children were safely in bed.

When she brought him his tea, he was relaxing in one of the chairs on the patio while Archie and Lucy Rose ferried him cookies from their abandoned picnic. He took the mug without thanking her.

"This is quite a place," he said, nodding at the house. "Shame about the noise from next door. What are they building, the Taj Mahal?"

"You get used to it after a while," Marina lied, sitting down across from him with Ewan on her lap.

She'd gone over to the Andersons' yesterday carrying Ewan and a bowl of her chocolate mousse, and asked Mrs. Anderson politely if she could speak to her contractors about keeping the noise down. "My little one needs to take naps," she'd explained.

Mrs. Anderson had stared at her blankly. "Who are you, that woman's granddaughter?"

"Yes, and I've got three children who—"

"I told that woman, and I'll tell you too: we can do whatever we want on our own damn property." And she'd closed the door in Marina's face. Marina and Ewan had eaten the bowl of mousse by themselves. (Mostly Marina.)

Jake slurped his tea. "Imagine if Nana Sylvia had died while we were still married. Half of this place would be mine now."

"It wouldn't. The terms of her will said that—"

"I know. Isn't it convenient for you that your grandmother left you this mansion on the condition that you got divorced!"

"How did you know that?"

He tapped the side of his nose. "I have my sources," he said, which Marina knew meant, *I've talked with your mom.* "I can see why you were so quick to call a divorce lawyer."

She checked that the children were busy and out of earshot.

"I called a divorce lawyer because you wanted to leave me for your girlfriend," she said.

"Hm. Well, like I say, it's convenient." He leaned back in his chair, crossing his legs at the ankles, as if he were lord of the manor. "There's an argument to be made that actually I'm entitled to half of this place anyway."

"What do you mean?"

"Well, you didn't buy our last house. You weren't even working when we took out the mortgage. I was the one who funded everything. Bought the furniture, paid for all the redecorating. All out of my own pocket. And then when we got divorced, your lawyer said that half the house was yours. How'd that happen?"

"My name was on the deed, Jake, the same as yours."

"Because I'm a nice guy and put it there."

"No, because that was the arrangement we had. You worked and I gave up my job, which I loved, to have the kids. You brought in the money, but I took care of everything else. It was an equal arrangement."

"Doesn't seem so equal to me. Seems like you're out here having tea parties and playing dress-up while I'm working every hour God sends. And then when I got home, you were still on my back 24/7 to do things around the house. I had to go to work just for some peace and quiet!"

She didn't reply to this, because how could she? They'd had this discussion so many times already, when she tried to explain to him that raising children wasn't as easy as it looked, and how sometimes she missed her job so keenly she couldn't breathe. When she tried to plead with him to give Archie and Lucy Rose their bedtime baths so she could sit down for the first time since six a.m. Once, she'd dared to suggest that since the next day was Mother's Day, she'd love to sleep in until eight, so maybe he could come home sooner than usual from the post-soccer bar session the night before.

It never worked. It just provoked more arguments. It made him call her a nag, and it made her feel ungrateful, pathetic, needy, unreasonable. It made him explain to her that it was called Mother's Day because it was for *mothers*, that it wouldn't even *be* a special day unless she had children who *needed* her, and the soccer games were the one time a week he was allowed to go out and have some fun because the rest of the time he had to pay for the roof over their heads.

And how could she argue with that? He did work hard. She did love her children.

She just wanted a little bit of extra sleep, that's all.

Of course, the revelation that Jake had been having an affair with Freya at work did put a new spin on all of this. Along with the fact that he'd mismanaged the money he was supposed to be using to support his family.

But . . . what was the point of bringing all of this up on a sunny day when the children were so happy to see their father?

"The financial consent order that you signed when we got divorced means that you're not entitled to anything that I own now," she said, sticking to legal facts that couldn't be argued with. "Just like I'm not entitled to anything that you own. Although your children are."

He held up his hands. "Yeah, yeah, yeah, I knew you'd be nagging me as soon as I showed my face here. Times are tight for me, you know that, especially with another little one on the way. Not all of us have dead rich grandmas."

"Thanks for the sympathy."

"She never liked me."

She decided to change the subject. "The children are really happy to see you today. I appreciate you coming here to see them."

He smiled. Her tactics were working. "That's why I'm here. I've missed them. And Freya and I have moved into a bigger apartment. So they can come stay with us on a weekend."

The way he casually mentioned his girlfriend stung her. And she wasn't certain how she felt about her children spending time with the new woman in their father's life. Marina didn't know her, after all, and while she tried to resist falling into the easy stereotype of thinking of Freya as a conniving husband-stealer, the truth was that Freya *had* in fact stolen her husband.

But Archie and Lucy Rose missed their dad. And Ewan had to get to know him.

"That would be nice," she said.

"Kids!" called Jake. Archie and Lucy Rose looked up from what they were doing in the corner of the garden and scampered over. Lucy Rose was carrying her plastic ice cream tub.

"How'd you like to come for a sleepover with me in my new apartment? We can make popcorn and have a movie night."

"Yeah!" said Archie, matching his father's hearty tone.

"Big green booger movie," said Lucy Rose.

"I think she means *Shrek*," explained Marina.

"What've you got in that box?" asked Jake. Lucy Rose showed him.

"It's her pet," said Archie. "She takes him everywhere now."

"You have a snail for a pet? What, won't your mummy get you a puppy? You've got the space now."

"I love Prince William," said Lucy Rose loyally.

"Not sure Freya will take to having a snail in her house. So slimy."

"You can leave Prince William with me while you visit your father," Marina said. "I'll look after him and make sure he gets plenty of lettuce. When do you want to have the children, Jake?"

"Now. That's why I'm here, isn't it?"

Marina wondered if Freya knew about this. However, it wasn't her problem.

"Why don't you start with holding the baby?" she said, and handed a sleepy Ewan over to his father. Then she went to pack all of the children's clothes.

When she returned, Jake looked up and asked, "What will you do all weekend when I've got the rugrats?" Marina was so startled that he'd asked her an actual question about herself that she answered honestly.

"I don't know. I haven't thought about it. Maybe I'll read a book and do some gardening?"

Jake snorted.

"I don't know what happened to you, Marina. You used to be such a fun girl. So easygoing and carefree. You've changed so much. Freya reminds me of the way you used to be, actually. It was one of the things that made me notice her."

Ewan's nappy bag was heavy, full of wipes and bottles and cans of follow-on milk. If she "accidentally" swung it at Jake's crotch, she could hit him hard enough to hurt, maybe hard enough so that he couldn't fuck his new girlfriend, but not so hard that he dropped the baby.

Instead, she smiled and said, "Have a great weekend!"

*   *   *

At first, she enjoyed the relative silence. Then she found herself wandering the rooms of Nana Sylvia's house. She realized she felt lonely.

She missed her children. But also, without the distraction of her children, she had time to feel that she missed adult company.

She made herself a cup of tea and scrolled social media. On Whats-App, the concerned messages that had appeared soon after her split with Jake had melted away. She hadn't had so much as a *how u doing hun?* for weeks now. She'd had to mute or leave the group chats, which were all about arranging play dates in a neighborhood where she no longer lived. And she knew this was her own fault—she felt she was constantly being a downer, so it was better for everyone if she disappeared. Of course, she felt guilty about that, too, because it meant that Archie and Lucy Rose weren't seeing their friends anymore.

She saw that her PTA friend Nancy had posted a photo of cocktails, tagged: #OutOut #GirlsNightOut #DaddiesNightIn #BabyMummies #MummiesGroup #Cosmos #Blessed. Several of her other PTA friends were tagged on it, but not her.

She went over to WhatsApp to see if they'd posted about the night out on the group chat, if maybe she'd been invited but she didn't see it. All she could find was advice about school uniforms.

They'd all moved on without her, as if she'd never existed. Or maybe she was the one who'd moved on, out of their world where husbands could be trusted, where children were always happy, where friends were fun, where their lives were safe.

Before she could think better of it, she posted a photograph of the front of Nana Sylvia's big, imposing, beautiful, expensive house on her own Instagram. The turret, the wisteria, the mature gardens, the stained-glass window over the freshly painted front door. She gave it a bright filter and wrote:

Our new home! I have so many happy memories of this house and I'm looking forward to making many more memories here.

She did not add #blessed. But she did post it, for all of her former friends to see.

Then she put on some lip gloss, slightly less dirty sneakers, and her denim jacket that only had a little bit of baby spit on it and walked into Richmond to treat herself to a coffee.

Afterwards she explored the stores, which, like the bustling café with its oat milk matchas, clearly catered to the upmarket crowd. There was a florist, a gluten-free bakery, a thrift store stuffed to the gills with discarded designer wear and wedding hats, a glossy hairdresser's next to a glossier barber shop, and two interior design stores, one specifically for kitchens and one for, presumably, everything else.

Marina couldn't afford to buy anything in any of the stores, not even the thrift store. Shortly before she moved into Nana Sylvia's house, the lawyer had informed her that the estate contained very little cold hard cash. She could raise some money by selling her grandmother's antiques, but she was reluctant to do that.

All the customers and the people working at the registers seemed so well-groomed and well-heeled. Everyone had glossy hair, makeup so expensive that it could afford to look subtle, shoes that weren't worn down at heel. Nana Sylvia could swan around the stores here looking outlandish and not caring what anyone thought, but Marina was less confident of her own brashness, and definitely less confident of her leggings with their stretched-out knees.

She stood outside the kitchen store, ostensibly looking at a display of hand-glazed tiles but actually examining her own reflection in the window. Her hair needed a trim and her last manicure had been performed by Lucy Rose and far too much purple sparkly nail polish.

And then she remembered younger Marina, who was just eighteen when she picked up and moved to Paris to train in a professional kitchen, knowing no one and hardly speaking the language. When had she lost her courage?

So here she was in the kitchen store, looking at granite and planning out her dream home kitchen makeover. Nana Sylvia's was a little dated, and let's face it, she'd eaten most of her meals out. Marina would change the tiles, the layout, with an eye for practicality and style combined. A bigger sink, a better stovetop, a walk-in pantry, everything hanging in reach. And wouldn't it be fun to start something for herself—cooking videos on TikTok, or a home catering business? How did you even begin?

"Which one are you going for?" asked a voice. Marina jumped in surprise.

The man who had spoken to her was a few paces away next to the polished concrete worktops. He was fit, probably in his forties, with bright blue eyes and a full head of prematurely gray hair swept back from his face. He was very good looking. What people might call a "silver fox."

"Oh," replied Marina, flustered. "I'm just browsing today."

"Don't worry," said the man. "I don't work here. I'm not going to try to sell you anything. Do you like to cook?"

"Actually, I'm a chef," said Marina. This felt good to say, even though it wasn't strictly true anymore.

"So you know what you're doing." He gazed around him. "Personally, I'm lost. I didn't know that refurbishing a kitchen would involve so many choices. You're probably used to it."

"Not really. It's taking me ages to decide which granite I like best. Sparkles or no sparkles?"

"You are definitely a sparkler," said the man, and Marina realized that he was flirting with her. This was unexpected.

"Maybe on a good day," she said. "Are you planning a remodel?"

"Yes, I'm finding it overwhelming, though. This is very much the sort of thing my wife would have done." He looked sad. "I lost her two years ago."

"Oh, I'm sorry."

"Thank you. You have to carry on, don't you. Though I didn't expect to have to make decisions about color schemes. What about you? Is your husband any good at this sort of thing?"

"We're divorced. So the choices are all mine."

"Well. That must be liberating."

"I guess it is," she said. They smiled at each other.

"Listen," he said, abruptly, as if just now making a decision, "would you mind helping me out? You know what it's like trying to find a contractor—the good ones have a waiting list longer than your arm. And I can't book one until I've ordered everything. I basically have to decide everything today."

"Oh. Well, that's flattering, but wouldn't it be better to ask someone who works here?" She glanced around for a store assistant.

"You know what it's like in these places. They want to upsell you on everything. I don't mind paying for quality, but I'd rather have something I like and that's going to work."

She hesitated, looking down at his left hand, where there was no ring, then checking her watch.

"I'm sorry," he said. "I didn't mean to assume you had the time. I'm sure you've got someplace better to be."

It was that "sorry" that decided her. Any man who could say that word so easily and casually couldn't possibly be bad, could he?

She couldn't go on mistrusting all men just because Jake had let her down. And this man probably did just want advice. There would be worse ways of spending a free day than in the company of an attractive single man who respected her opinion.

"Sure," she said. "Actually, I think that would be fun."

His face broke into a bright smile. "Thank you," he said. "I'm Xavier, by the way."

JULIE MAE COHEN

"Marina." They shook hands. His touch was warm and a little exciting. "Now, Xavier, for the important question."

"What's my budget? Don't worry about that."

She grinned. "No. The important question is: are you a sparkler too?"

* * *

Four hours later, after a rather nice lunch courtesy of Xavier, Marina
walked back to her house practically on air.

It could be the two midday gin and tonics putting the spring
in her step, but mostly it was Xavier. He wasn't only attractive. He
was charming, respectful, funny, and—if the size of the order he'd
placed at the kitchen shop was anything to go by—very well-off. He
ran his own wealth management consultancy—Marina didn't pretend to know what that meant, but he'd hinted breezily at old family
money too. He didn't have any children, but he said he adored other
people's and listened attentively when she talked about her three.

And at the end of lunch, he'd asked for her number and said, "Would
it be all right if I called and invited you out to dinner with me next
week?"

"Oh," she'd said, a little flustered, "it depends on whether I can find
a babysitter."

"How long are your children staying with their father?"

"Until Sunday evening."

"Lunch again tomorrow? And a walk along the river?"

She gave him her number and her address. He'd kissed her goodbye on the cheek and said, "Thank you. I haven't met a woman I've
liked so much for a very long time."

Things were definitely looking up.

* * *

In between that lunch and their second date an enormous bouquet of flowers arrived at her house. Roses, freesias, lilies. Her unrenovated kitchen was filled with scent. The card said, plainly, "X."

That single letter made her catch her breath. Because it was his initial, but also, it meant a kiss.

She thought about kissing Xavier, and then she thought about it all day. What would it feel like to kiss a man who wasn't Jake? Did she even remember how to? What would Xavier smell like close up? What would his hands feel like on her waist? Would he be a gentleman, or would he be masterful and passionate? Maybe even both?

She was turned on. She felt like she was living in a romance novel. Here she was, a divorced mother of three, acting boy crazy.

It was wonderful.

She took a photograph of the bouquet and posted it on Instagram. #SecretAdmirer #MysteriousGentleman #FuckYouPTAMumsAndYourCosmos

(She deleted the last hashtag.)

She sent him a message: Thank you for the flowers!

You're worth it, he replied. I can't wait until tomorrow. X

Again, that initial with its double meaning. She touched it with her fingertip.

She considered playing it cool, but then she typed, Me neither.

For the first time in a long time, Marina fretted about what to wear. All her clothes were practical, plain, and more often than not, spotted with finger paint. The morning before her second date with Xavier, she tried on everything halfway decent she owned and thought wistfully about the little slip dresses she used to wear, back when she had a flat stomach and perky boobs. Now she looked terrible in everything.

Then again, she'd met Xavier when she was wearing yoga pants and an oversized sweater, and it hadn't seemed to put him off.

But she couldn't wear that again; the yoga pants had a little hole in the crotch. And she didn't even own any good underwear. She still wore the maternity bras that she'd bought for breastfeeding Archie.

Would she need good underwear?

She shivered with lust. She had it bad, after one lunch and a bunch of flowers.

She dropped the dress she was trying on and thrust her hand into her underwear. Within seconds she was leaning against the bedpost, gasping and a little dizzy with the force of her orgasm.

Well. She hadn't done *that* in a very long time. And Jake hadn't done it for her for even longer.

In the mirror, she looked flushed and happy. Her skin was glowing. She abandoned the dress (it was frumpy anyway) and pulled on her tightest pair of jeans. She found one of Nana Sylvia's patterned peasant blouses, which was made of pleasingly clingy material.

Then she thought about Xavier taking it off her and she had to take a second break to rub another one out.

* * *

He was a gentleman. He called for her at her house, waiting patiently in the hallway while she made flustered additions to her makeup, and then took her to a little bistro. "It's a risk taking you here, isn't it?" he said. "Given what you do for a living?"

"Not at all. It's a treat to be at a restaurant that doesn't have a children's menu."

He walked her to the table with his hand in the small of her back, which just about drove her insane. After that, she could hardly concentrate on the food anyway.

In the end, she was the one who initiated their first kiss while they were waiting for the dessert menu. They were at a tiny corner table with their knees close together underneath, a fact of which Marina was excitedly, almost unbearably aware. They'd been talking about their dream holidays and discovered that they both had dreamed of visiting Venice but neither had been. "I'd love to ride a gondola with you," Xavier said, and she couldn't help herself. She leaned over and planted a kiss on his lips. He was warm and tasted slightly of sea bream. She loved it.

When they finished, he looked surprised but pleased.

"I wanted to get it out of the way," she explained.

"I can see that you're a woman who likes to take charge."

This was so entirely untrue that Marina kissed him again, mostly out of lust but partly in gratitude for him seeing her as a strong person. This kiss was longer, lingering.

"I don't think I feel like going for a walk," she said, brushing her fingers through his silver hair.

"No? What would you prefer?"

"I think I want you to come home with me," she said. And kissed him again.

They skipped dessert.

* * *

Sex! Sex was wonderful! It was the most amazing thing in the world! It was something she had entirely forgotten about except as a way to make children and to celebrate Jake's birthday! She loved sex! There were so many ways to do it and they were all fabulous!

The only qualm she had was when Xavier saw her bedroom and said, "Wow, this is something else," and she realized that she was about to have sex in her grandmother's bed.

But that qualm lasted less than half a second, because Nana Sylvia was a vocal fan of sex and often went into embarrassing detail about

77

her exploits, so she would be pleased that Marina was getting some. Also, the mattress was excellent.

Marina didn't even care about her awful underwear. She stripped so quickly that Xavier never got a chance to see them.

Afterwards, he lay beside her and smiled. "You're a firecracker," he said.

And Marina, damp and languid from orgasms, actually believed him.

* * *

They saw each other every chance they got. Marina wasn't ready to introduce anyone new to her children, obviously, and Xavier understood, so they had to snatch time when the children were with Jake or her parents. Archie went to school full-time now and Lucy Rose and Ewan went to nursery three mornings a week, and sometimes Xavier arranged to work from home, which meant that they could meet for a quickie (or two).

He lived in a large new-build in Chislehurst. It wasn't really to her taste, but it was impressive and clearly very expensive, with polished marble floors, enormous windows, and leather furniture. He even had a library, stuffed with books that looked as if they had actually been read. His kitchen was fine as it was, a little cold and impersonal maybe, but all the appliances were bang up-to-date and the Aga was quite lovely. The contractors hadn't started work on the refurb yet.

Marina and Xavier had sex against the kitchen counter like they were in a movie. Then she cooked him *magret de canard au miel* and they ate it together, hot on the plate, feeding each other bites.

When they weren't together, they sent each other sexy messages. Constantly. Marina felt as if she were in heat, as if she were living a romantic dream. Xavier complimented her, gave her little gifts, seemed

in awe of her body. He said he hadn't even wanted to sleep with anyone since his wife died, and then he'd found her.

One time he even cried.

He sent her flowers every other day, so many that she had to unearth
vases from the cupboards. The bouquets didn't get a chance to wilt
before another would come to take its place. Her house smelled like
a garden.

She felt cherished, desired, sexy, wise, naughty. She caught herself skipping around the house. It seemed like the more sex she had,
the more she wanted it, even when Xavier wasn't around. When the
children napped, she masturbated. The housework wasn't getting
done, but she didn't care.

"I'd forgotten what it was like to be a woman," she told Xavier.

"Are you kidding?" he said. "You're not just a woman, you're a
superwoman."

She didn't explain any more, because she found she liked how he
thought of her. Knowing that he saw her as a superwoman made her
feel as if she could be one.

She felt as if she'd been sleepwalking for the past third of her life
and now, she was awake. More than awake. She was fizzing, high,
delirious, happy.

And then she got the text message.

9

NOW, IN THE MCDONALD'S, MARINA passed her phone over to Lilah, who was a slight young woman with bright and frightened gray eyes. She wore a plain shift dress with a cardigan, flat shoes, and a black fanny pack around her waist, but when she reached for the phone, Marina could see an enormous diamond set in platinum on the ring finger of her left hand.

And then that hand, with its diamond, flashed through the air and slapped Marina on the side of her face.

Marina reared back, hand to her cheek. "Did you just *hit me*?"

"What kind of a person are you?" Lilah cried. Her face was flushed and frantic, and from the pain in Marina's cheek, she was much stronger than she looked. "Why would you do such a thing?"

"Such a thing as what?"

"You're trying to steal my fiancé! You—you hussy!"

"I would never steal someone's fiancé. Who *is* your fiancé?"

Lilah stabbed her finger at the selfie on Marina's phone. "This man right here!"

"Xavier? You've got to be mistaken. He's a widower. His wife died two years ago."

"I'm his fiancée and I'm alive!"

"I'm his wife," said Opal, "and I'm alive too."

"No," said Lilah. "No, no, no, no. I don't believe it. I don't know what you two are up to, or why you want to take everything away from me, but stop. Just stop!"

She put her hands over her ears and then shook her head very hard. Then she ran out of the McDonald's.

Marina watched her go. "Who is that crazy bitch?"

"She's the woman who's engaged to your new boyfriend," said Opal. "That can't be."

"Do you usually get slapped by strangers without a good reason?"

Marina rubbed her cheek, trying to think it through, looking for red flags she'd been ignoring because the sex was so great. It was true that Xavier kept his phone in his pocket and never took it out when she was around. They conducted all of their phone conversations through texts, not aloud. And for such a good-looking man who was clearly proud of his body, he was uncomfortable with having his photo taken. Even the selfie on her phone that had turned Lilah from a mild-mannered person into a psycho—Xavier had turned his head to the side at the last minute, so she didn't get his entire face in the picture.

It was probably exactly the same way Jake had acted when he was cheating on her with Freya.

"What a dick," she said. It was the only possible conclusion.

"You're telling me."

"And who are you? Why did you text me?"

"Like I said. I'm his wife." Opal took a sip of her coffee.

"You're his wife? He said his wife was dead. He cried about it."

"He's very convincing when he wants to be. That's why I married him." She showed Marina the wedding photo on her phone. Then she showed Marina a screenshot of a photo of Lilah and Xavier together on a beach, holding hands and smiling at the camera. It wasn't great quality, but it was unmistakable.

Marina let this sink in.

"So he's cheating on you with both of us?"

"At least. You and Lilah are the only ones who I've found."

"Oh gosh. I'm so sorry. I honestly thought . . ."

"I know," said Opal impatiently. "And frankly I don't care who he fucks."

"I do. And clearly Lilah does as well." She hit the table with the side of her fist. "Damn. I thought I'd finally found a good one. And now, I'm the other woman?" She shuddered. "I feel so dirty."

"You're not the dirty one."

"I'm just a silly cow who he shagged into submission."

Opal didn't contradict her.

"You must hate me," Marina said.

"I'm indifferent to you. *Him*, I hate. Did you give him any money?"

"I don't have any money. Only a big house that my relatives would quite like to take off me."

"He'd find a way to make a profit," said Opal grimly. "He loves a long game. Did he buy you any presents? Because if he did, poor Lilah probably paid for them. He ran off with all my money, but I assume he got through that a long time ago."

"He's *stealing*?"

"It's more of a confidence game than outright theft, but yeah, that's the gist of it. He's emptied Lilah's bank accounts and he's maxing out her credit card even as we speak."

Marina felt as though she'd been hit by a bus.

"Should we go to the police?" she asked. "He might be doing this to some other women."

"All that will do is to alert him," said Opal. "If the police even bother to do anything about it. The money he took from me was in our joint bank account. He hasn't actually committed bigamy yet, because he and Lilah aren't married. And Lilah gave him access to her bank accounts voluntarily. So no police, and no confronting him."

"I'm confused," Marina said. "You don't care if he's sleeping around, and you don't want to go to the police or to confront him. So why did you go to the trouble to track us down?"

"Simple," said Opal. "I want revenge."

10

AS SOON AS SHE LEFT the McDonald's, her head spinning, Marina got a text from Xavier.

```
Can't stop thinking about you X
```

She stood on the pavement staring at her phone and wondering how on earth she should reply to this.

Xavier was not Xavier. He was also Zachary and also Zander and God knew how many other aliases. He was married to one woman and engaged to another. And he was a thief.

"What do you mean, revenge?" Marina had asked Opal, and Opal had shaken her head grimly.

"I don't know yet," she said. "I still have to work out the details. But the important thing is that none of us let on to Zander what we know. We need to take him by surprise."

"You think Lilah is going to keep quiet? She's very upset."

"She doesn't believe me. And you've seen her. She's a librarian. She's not built for confrontation. I don't think she'll say anything just yet."

She said it with an edge to her voice, a note of almost-contempt that made Marina think, *You say you want revenge on your husband, but it feels like it's Lilah and me who are suffering.*

But she didn't say that, of course. She, also, was not built for confrontation, even though she did imagine it quite a bit, often in gruesome detail.

So now five minutes later here was Marina, standing outside a McDonald's, not having had the chance to eat any lunch other than a few fries and due to pick up her children in fifteen minutes, staring at a text from a man who she knew was a love rat, would-be bigamist, thief, and con artist, and also with whom she'd had the best sex of her life.

Let's be honest. She'd also daydreamed about their wedding.

She texted back, truthfully:

```
I can't stop thinking about you, either.
```

* * *

The kids were in bed, though it had taken three bedtime stories before Lucy Rose would settle down. Marina brought the baby monitor into the bathroom with her as she showered.

The fact was—she thought as she caught a glimpse of herself in the steamy mirror—she looked better now than she had in many years. Her stomach was firmer, her hips had slimmed down. Her skin had a glow to it that had been lost to too many sleepless nights because of babies or anxiety. Even her stretch marks from three babies appeared lighter: like silvery tracings rather than the angry red smears that she'd smoothed coconut oil on every morning.

She didn't look like a baby machine or a worn-down and betrayed overweight single mom. She looked like a beautiful woman whose body was voluptuous and capable of both nurture and pleasure.

And that was all down to Xavier. Whatever he was in reality . . . in *her* reality, he had done all of this for her in a very short time.

Was she ready to give it up?

She put on makeup and dried her hair. She chose one of her new dresses that she'd splurged on in the thrift store in town. Richmond had *very* good thrift stores. Underneath, she wore a tiny wisp of silk in the shape of pants. No bra. Then she took the baby monitor downstairs to the kitchen, where she prepared a cheese, charcuterie, and salad board—only from Aldi, but it looked more impressive when you took the packaging off and arranged it on a platter with a quick homemade fig compote.

This afternoon after they'd parted ways, Opal had set up a WhatsApp group chat including Marina and Lilah, titled "Z."

THANK YOU FOR MEETING ME, LADIES. DON'T FORGET, WE NEED TO KEEP THIS TO OURSELVES FOR NOW.

Marina saw that, like her, Lilah hadn't replied. But neither of them had left the chat.

Now, there was a quiet knock on the door.

She took a deep breath and reminded herself of her new underwear.

When she opened the door, she was confronted with a huge bouquet of flowers. Roses, sweet-smelling freesias, her favorite tulips, and even a couple of those strange artichoke-y/cabbage-y things that seemed to be in all the expensive bouquets these days.

That's Lilah's MasterCard, she thought.

But she said, "Oh, Xavier, you shouldn't have. These are beautiful! I don't even think I have any vases left."

"We don't need a vase," said the man calling himself Xavier, as she took the bouquet. "We can scatter the petals on the bed."

She thought about Xavier lying on his back on a bed of rose petals as she straddled him and rode him hard. God help her, the image turned her on.

"Thank you for not using the doorbell," she said. "It probably won't wake the kids, but it's better to be safe."

"I can't wait to meet them. They sound charming."

"Well," said Marina honestly, "they're charming to *me*."

"Of course it's your choice as to when I meet them. I was reading an article about dating as a single parent, and it had some helpful advice. This is all so new to me." He hung up his jacket on the coat rack.

"Me too," said Marina.

"I'll send it to you. First, come here." He pulled her in for a kiss.

Marina had wondered what she would do when he kissed her, now that she knew the truth. Misleading someone was one thing when you were using words. But it was a totally different thing when you were using your body. Would she feel repulsed by being kissed by a liar who was dating two women at once in order to steal their money, while married to another woman who he'd already robbed? Would she be able to fake desire?

More troublingly: was Xavier faking *his* desire? Had he been lying to her when he whispered that she was sexy, when he told her what he wanted to do with her, when he got aroused by her and they had sex? You couldn't fake that, could you? There must be at least some part of him that found her sexy, or he wouldn't be able to perform.

But it might be different for men than for women. It was a cliché that men could get turned on by anything, even a pair of coconuts or whatever. He could have been closing his eyes this entire time, and picturing someone else. Lilah, or Opal, or one of his other women, or a porn star. This whole time he could have been laughing at her behind her back. Or literally between her legs. The poor desperate worn-out mom of three who couldn't even tell when a man was using her like a disposable sex doll.

That was at least one reason why she'd invited him over. She needed to know if he genuinely wanted her, despite lying to her. And she needed to know if she genuinely wanted him, despite being lied to.

So she kissed him back. She wound her arms around his neck, and swayed her body towards his so she was pressing against all of him. She opened her mouth and welcomed his tongue, warm and wet.

And she felt rising lust, felt herself getting warm and wet too.

Apparently she could desire someone even when she'd been shown evidence that he didn't respect her. This was a little disturbing, but not enough to turn her off.

"Do you want me?" she whispered. She let her hand trail down his chest and to his crotch. He stiffened against her hand.

"God, yes," he said. "I want to fuck you against this wall right now."

His words conjured up a mental image that was so hot that she moaned involuntarily.

What did that say about her? *Was* she, as Lilah had said, a hussy?

She pulled away. "Not here," she said. "We can't wake up the children. And besides, I've made us something to eat."

"I'd like to eat *you* up," he said.

She shook her head playfully and led him to the kitchen, where she put the flowers in the sink.

"This looks amazing," he said. "I don't know how you pulled it together at the last minute."

"All organic," she lied. "Anyway, I couldn't resist when you said you were unexpectedly free." She took two wine glasses from the cupboard. "You can have one glass, can't you?"

"I could probably stretch to two. If I did some exercise afterwards." He gave her a filthy, thrilling look.

Oh God. The line was cheesy, probably well-rehearsed, but it worked. She wanted to rip his clothes off.

How could she give this up? What if she never found it again and she lived the rest of her days as a dried-up prune undesired by anyone?

She cleared her throat. "Do you mind choosing a good bottle for us from the cellar?"

"You have a wine cellar?" His eyes gleamed. Now she could see it was with something more than oenophilia. "I'd love to."

"You'll need a flashlight—there's one on the hook next to the cellar door."

As he tested the flashlight by turning it on and off, she edged closer to him. "Should I choose a white or a red?" he asked.

"You decide. There are some impressive vintages down there. Why don't you choose something special? Wednesday's the new Friday, after all. Here, would you mind taking this down with you and putting it with the other preserves?"

She handed him a big jar of pickles. She'd scraped the Aldi label off and replaced it with a hand-written one.

"Will do." He opened the heavy cellar door. "There's a light switch here." She watched him flick it, but nothing happened.

"Yes, but it's not working. I need to get an electrician out. These old houses, you know."

She waited just behind him as he descended one of the rickety steps.

Then she rushed at him and, as hard as she could, she shoved him in the back.

With the flashlight in one hand and pickles in the other, he couldn't grab for the banister or the wall. He didn't cry out. He toppled over right away, and far more easily than she'd thought he would.

The jar smashed and she heard his body hit the stairs several times on the way down and then land, with a clunk, on the bottom.

11

MARINA HAD ALWAYS BELIEVED THAT she was a good person who wouldn't hurt anyone else. Sure, she might imagine it sometimes, but who didn't?

As an adolescent she'd been chubby and that made her a target for other students at her all-girls school. They whispered mean things about her behind her back and looked pointedly at what she chose for lunch. "Greedy Marina" they called her. She had teen acne, too, which didn't help.

Once the meanest girl, who was also the school's Head Girl, smuggled a slice of pepperoni pizza out of the cafeteria and put it on Marina's chair. Of course Marina sat down on it by mistake, ruining the skirt of her uniform and giving rise to the new nickname, "Greasy Marina."

It was that sort of school, but her parents believed that children needed to grow up resilient.

Sometimes she fantasized about punching these thin, beautiful, perfect-looking girls in the nose. She thought about knocking them to the ground and force-feeding them the squashed pizza. She doodled the scenes, badly, in her notebooks, using up red marker after red marker for blood, scribbling so hard that she tore holes in the pages. But she would never actually attack anyone. Desperately boring Sunday school lessons had taught her to do unto others as you would have them do unto you, and she kept following that rule, even though it seemed no one else ever did.

The only person she told was Nana Sylvia. "The best revenge is violence," her grandmother told her. "But that's illegal, so the second-best revenge is living well."

She taught Marina that her love of food was a superpower and encouraged her to learn to cook gourmet meals and study and practice to be a chef. And Marina found discipline, confidence, and acceptance in kitchens. In a kitchen, if you did your job well people respected you. All without the need to punch anyone.

But now she had pushed her boyfriend down the stairs. On purpose.

Her first instinct, strangely, wasn't to scream and be horrified at what she had done. It was to pause at the top of the stairs, head tilted, and listen for any noise coming from her children's bedrooms. There was nothing, which was a relief.

But also: there was nothing coming from the cellar either. No moans, no shouts.

"Shit," Marina said.

She peered down the cellar stairs. The only light was from the flashlight, which seemed to be lying on the floor. She saw Xavier's hand still beside it.

"Are you okay?" she called down. No answer.

She didn't have another flashlight, so she went to the living room, where there was a gilt candelabra on top of the piano. It took another five minutes to remember that she'd put the matches on a high shelf in the library, out of reach of little hands.

Candles lit and flickering gothically from the draft from the cellar, Marina crept down the stairs. The shadows seemed to dart and writhe around her.

"Xavier?" she said, when she was near the bottom. She held out the candelabra and squinted into the darkness. Xavier was lying on the flagstones, sprawled out on his back. His eyes were closed and there was a splash of bright red on his forehead.

"I've killed him," murmured Marina to herself. She should be terrified at this, but possibly because of the shock, she mostly felt curious. She reached the bottom of the stairs and stepped onto something squishy that popped under her foot.

Immediately she recoiled, picturing snails, snakes, Xavier's eyeball—but the scent of vinegar reached her nostrils and she realized she'd stepped on a pickle.

She picked up the flashlight, put the candelabra on the floor, and squatted beside Xavier's body. Her hand under his nose confirmed that he was still breathing. She put her fingertips on the side of the neck to check for a pulse: it was strong.

He wasn't dead.

Her breath hitched in her throat and suddenly, she was crying.

She didn't want to kill Xavier. She didn't want to kill anybody, not really. She had brought three lives into the world, and she knew how fragile life was, because every time her children left her side she was anxious that they were going to die. Lucy Rose's birth had been difficult—the baby had been transverse and Marina had labored for twenty-four hours, and when Lucy Rose came out she was blue and floppy. Marina had never felt such terror, until the nurses and doctors cleared Lucy Rose's airways and she turned a normal color and started shouting.

Xavier was someone's child. Someone loved him. He might be a con man, he might be an utter shit . . . but he did not deserve to die.

Marina wiped her eyes and her nose. She had to pull herself together. Crying wasn't doing any good. So she hadn't killed him, but now she had to deal with him.

She checked his head. The blood seemed to be coming from a cut on his forehead—when she looked more closely she saw the glint of a shard of glass in it. Gingerly, she felt around the rest of his skull under his hair, and found a large bump on the back of his head. He must have hit it on a stair on the way down? How could she tell if he had a skull fracture? If he'd broken his neck?

She should call 911. But then . . . what would Xavier tell them when he woke up?

Marina stood. The first thing was to get some light. It was too dark down here.

A little fumbling and some sotto-voce swearing later, and she'd replaced the fuse that she'd removed from the cellar box and was cleaning Xavier's head wound with the first aid kit she kept in the bathroom. The cut had bled quite a bit, but it was small and shallow—she remembered what head wounds were like, from the time that Archie had fallen off the swing set. She made sure it was clear of glass, and then cleaned and disinfected it and put on some Band-Aids.

Then she gazed around, considering her next steps.

She couldn't carry Xavier upstairs, and if she left him down here and waited for him to wake up, he would remember her pushing him. That would probably make him angry. Angry enough to hurt her? Maybe. She didn't know him that well, and he was a liar and a thief at the very least. What was certain was that she couldn't defend herself: he was much bigger than she was, and they were in a cellar. No one would be able to hear her scream . . . except maybe her children.

And then maybe he would hurt *them*.

Suddenly her next step seemed blindingly obvious. And she had better do it fast.

12

Lilah

THE MESSAGE CAME WHILE LILAH was in the enormous bath. She'd put some of the hotel's luxury bath soap in it, which helped her relax a little bit, maybe. Well, it meant that she could stop pacing around and sit in one place, submerged. But she kept her phone close by on the lip of the tub, even though this was a foolish place to put an expensive electronic item because it could fall into the water.

Zachary had messaged her earlier saying he had to work late tonight, and then he hadn't messaged again. This was unusual and she should be worried, but frankly, Lilah was a little relieved. She wasn't ready to talk with him about what she'd been told today. Even though it was probably a hoax and these women didn't even know Zachary. Even though there was a perfectly reasonable explanation for everything, like deep fakes or Photoshop. People could do anything with computers these days.

She wasn't ready to discuss it with Zachary. Not even in a bright, breezy way, like "Can you believe the crazy thing that happened today?"

Because . . . what if it was true, and she'd lost not only her money, but everything she cared about? Her father, the man she loved, her sense of what was real?

She didn't want to think about it. She didn't want to think about anything. She had not checked any of her remaining bank accounts yet. She wanted to stay in this bath forever.

But the message might be Zachary, with a perfectly reasonable explanation.

She dried her hand and picked up her phone, but the message wasn't from Zachary; it was in the WhatsApp group that Opal had set up. Marina had sent a pinned map of a location in Richmond. No message attached to it.

At the sight of Marina's name, Lilah had a twinge of conscience. She was a moral person. And she had slapped that woman. Actually slapped her!

Violence was never the answer. She could hear what her Dad would say. *Even if you were provoked, there's no excuse. You've got to apologize to Marina.*

"All right," she said out loud. "But I'm only doing it for you, Dad."

She reached for a towel.

*   *   *

She walked through the iron gate in the hedge and towards the house. In the dusk, it was difficult to see the house properly, but it was detached and tall with huge windows that glowed invitingly. It was older than hers, a grand old London house with wisteria growing over the front door. It was a very beautiful house, which sort of made Lilah wish that she'd chosen something older and more graceful for herself. But Dad had said that with a new build, you knew what you were getting, and he did have a point.

It was only after she'd rung the doorbell that she realized that this could be some sort of trap to lure her to a private place, that all of this was a ruse concocted by whoever had murdered her father.

To her relief, when the door was opened, it was only Marina. "Is Opal with you?" Marina asked, peering out.

"No, should she be?"

"What do you want?"

Lilah wanted to squirm, but she remembered what her dad said, and stood strong. "I owe you an apology."

Marina seemed to be considering. After a pause, she opened the door wider. "I suppose since you're here, you'd better come in. My children are asleep, so we have to be as quiet as we can."

The entranceway had patterned tiles on the floor and a floor-to-ceiling gilt-framed mirror on the wall. A sweeping staircase led upwards. Lilah noticed for the first time that Marina was wearing a little red dress and she had her hair piled on top of her head so that soft tendrils fell around her face.

Zachary's jacket was hanging on the coat rack. The nice one, that he wore when he took her out to a fancy restaurant. The sight was painful, so Lilah averted her eyes.

"Is he here?" Lilah asked.

"We need to talk about that," said Marina, which Lilah took as a no, and he'd just forgotten his jacket.

She brought Lilah through to the kitchen, which was huge and cluttered with things like bunches of herbs hanging from the ceiling, old copper-bottomed pots and a very large basket containing an implausible number of champagne corks. There was also an old pine farmhouse table with several chairs around it, including two high chairs.

"How many children do you have?" Lilah asked. For the first time, she was aware that this woman, whom she'd called a hussy, had a whole life outside of sleeping with Lilah's fiancé. She was a mother. Though for a mother she seemed to also drink a lot of champagne.

"Three. All five and under." She gestured at a platter of cold meats and cheeses on the table. It was beautifully arranged, with grapes and other fruit in a basket beside. "There's some food if you're hungry."

"Is that why you sent a pin to your house?" Lilah asked. "You wanted to invite us for nibbles?"

"No, but you might as well eat them." Marina chewed on a nail. "I actually only meant to send that pin to Opal."

There were only two wineglasses.

"Are the two of you planning something together?" asked Lilah. She felt left out, which was irrational. She didn't even like these women. Opal was a bully and Marina was sleeping with other people's fiancés. They were worse than Evil Alice.

"Not exactly."

A doorbell rang. Marina left the kitchen to answer it.

Lilah picked up a slice of cheese and nibbled on it. She wasn't hungry, but it was laid out so prettily, and she didn't know what else to do. She heard the door open and a bit of conversation, and Marina appeared a few minutes later with Opal. This time, Opal was wearing workout gear, which made her look even more fit.

"What's up?" Opal asked, seeing Lilah and the platter of nibbles. "We're not having a dinner party, are we? I would've brought wine."

"Your Instagram profile says you used to be a nurse," Marina said to her. "Is that true?"

"Briefly. Why?"

"It's easier if I show you. And since you're here, Lilah, I guess you need to see it too."

She went to the side of the room where there was a shut door that Lilah hadn't noticed before. It had a sliding bolt on it, which she opened.

"Be really careful going down the stairs," she said. "They're rickety. Hang on to the banister, okay?"

Opal went down first, and Lilah followed, with Marina at the rear. A bulb hung over the staircase, but it didn't throw much light and Lilah had to concentrate to make sure her feet were placed safely. Down in the cellar it was hardly any brighter; there was another single bulb dangling from the ceiling and the walls were lined with shelves and shadows.

She didn't see it at first, until Opal said, "Holy shit." And then she did.

Zachary lay on the floor. His eyes were closed and there was some blood on his face. And even though he looked nothing like her father, even though he was in a different position, all Lilah could see was her dead father as she'd discovered him on the worst day of her life.

She gasped. Her throat closed up, squeezed by phantom hands. And she felt herself falling as the room went dark.

13

Opal

"I'LL . . . I'LL GO GET US something to drink," said Marina, and she ran up the stairs. Lilah waited until she was gone, and then sidled up to Opal.

"I think she pushed him down the stairs," whispered Lilah, glancing after Marina. "On purpose."

"Of course she pushed him down the stairs on purpose," said Opal in her normal speaking voice. "That woman's got balls. I didn't expect it of her."

"You're not frightened?"

"Why should I be? She's not pushing *us* down the stairs. And if she wanted to keep us captive, too, she would've locked the door."

The door above them was open. That seemed to make Lilah feel a little better.

"We need to call the police," said Lilah.

"You want Marina to go to jail? A mother of three?"

"We don't know her. We just met her today."

"She hasn't told us her side of the story yet. We don't know what made her push him."

"You can't just go pushing people down the stairs. They could die."

"If she'd wanted to kill him, she wouldn't have asked us to come over," Opal pointed out.

"She asked you to come over, not me."

"Regardless. Be sensible. If she were attempting murder, she wouldn't want witnesses."

"I just think we should call the police and let them deal with it."

"Listen," said Opal. "I get it. You're scared. But Zander—Zachary— is the bad guy here. Not Marina, or either of us. The three of us are his victims."

"I don't know," said Lilah. "Am I a victim? I thought that he loved me."

Opal huffed impatiently. "He lied to you and stole your money."

"I have a lot of money to spare. I would have given it to him anyway, if he'd asked."

Lilah gazed at Zander with soft, foolish eyes.

"He's broken your heart," said Opal. "And isn't your heart the most important thing you own?"

"That doesn't mean that he deserves to be hurt."

Opal had a different opinion. But instead she asked something she'd been curious about, since finding out about Lilah.

"Did he ever hit you?"

"What? No! He would never!"

Opal decided to let it lie. "Like I said, I think we should hear Marina's side of the story first. There's plenty of time to call the police later."

"Did he hit *you*?"

"That's not relevant." She turned away to look at the shelves of wine. There were a lot of bottles down here. This whole house, with its antiques and its location and its gardens, had to be worth millions. No wonder Zander was worming his way in.

"Did you love him?" Lilah asked suddenly.

"Why do you care?"

"I need to know. Did you love him?"

Despite herself, Opal remembered the day she'd married Zander Bolt. She hadn't thought about it for a long time—good riddance to bad rubbish—but looking at the photographs this afternoon had actually stirred some memories.

Her bouquet had been roses and jasmine. Her dress had been silk. All her life, she had been contemptuous of vapid girls who dreamed about their wedding day, as if they had no higher ambitions than to give up their identity to some man in exchange for a veil and a princess dress. In her opinion, marriage was either a business transaction or a life sentence. Her parents' had been the latter; Zander and she had agreed that theirs would be the former. Meld their resources, present a united front, grow their enterprises together. She'd proposed to him, as a matter of practicality, and there were no fireworks or champagne.

So she'd expected to approach her own wedding day with a healthy dose of cynicism. But when she'd started down the aisle of the registry office (on the arm of no man—her father was long dead by then and she was no one's to give away), there had been a moment where she'd caught Zander's eye and he had smiled at her.

And her heart had fluttered. She remembered it as if it had been yesterday.

It had been her biggest mistake. Because of it, she would end up broke, and someone would end up dead.

"I loved him," she said. It was the only plausible explanation of why he'd got away with it.

Lilah nodded. "That's good enough. Okay. I won't call the police right away." She squatted next to Zander and wiped off the little bit of blood that was on his forehead.

"Why do my past feelings for Zander have anything to do with it?"

"Because if you ever loved him, really loved him, then you'll want to make sure he is all right. Even if you think that he victimized us. You won't want to make any choices that will hurt him in the long run. So I won't call the police until I've heard the whole story."

Opal opened her mouth, and closed it again. Maybe this wasn't the ideal time to shatter Lilah's romantic illusions.

Instead, she also squatted down next to Zander and began going through his pockets. Keys, wallet. No phone.

"His phone's not in his pocket," she said. "Where is it?"

Lilah stood. "He doesn't carry it in his pocket. He always turns his phone off when he's with me. Often he leaves it at home, or in the office. I thought it was because he didn't want to be distracted."

"More likely it was because he didn't want you to see what he was really up to."

Marina came back down the stairs and gave each of them a juice box. They had cartoon characters made up of fruit on the sides. Opal's was Bertha Blackcurrant.

"I thought you meant a *drink* drink," said Opal.

"Oh. Sorry. I've got kids—"

"You keep telling us. It's odd that you find it more acceptable to push a man down the stairs and tie him up while there are children in the house than to have an alcoholic drink."

"You're welcome to, I mean—" Marina gestured around at the extensive wine cellar. "Take your pick." She poked the attached straw into her own box.

"That food upstairs," said Lilah. "It wasn't for us. You had a date."

"I had a date with Xavier," Marina confirmed. "Zander. Zachary. Whatever his name is. I hadn't planned it; he'd said he had an unexpectedly free evening and asked if I wanted to meet."

She sat down on a large cardboard box labeled "Jars" and stared at the unconscious Zander. She looked exhausted. Opal and Lilah stayed standing.

"Why did you push him down the stairs?" Lilah asked.

Opal expected Marina to feign surprise, or to deny that she'd done it and pretend that he'd fallen naturally. But instead Marina said, "I'm not sure. I thought about it, but it was more like a fantasy than a real thing that I was going to do. Like, 'This guy needs to be taught a lesson.' In an abstract sense. But then I bought the pickles especially, so maybe I really did plan to do it."

Opal wasn't sure how the pickles fitted in, but she waited while Marina took a deep drink from her juice box and carried on.

"I was mostly going on autopilot. That's what you do sometimes, when you have small children. You can't think about everything all at once, because you'd go nuts, and also you are tired most of the time so you physically can't think of it all. So sometimes you go through your day and it's not until the kids go down for their naps that you realize that you can't remember what you've been doing. Somehow the kids got fed and the dishes got washed and the laundry got folded, but you can't remember doing any of it. And you've let their childhood slip away without even noticing."

She seemed to go into a reverie.

"But Zander?" Opal prompted gently.

"He was the thing, you know. The one thing that made me feel as if I were actually alive and living in the moment, for myself. I was never on autopilot with him. I felt like me, for the first time in years. And . . . it was all a lie."

Marina looked up at both of them.

"So yes. I wasn't sure if I was going to go through with it, but I suppose I did plan to push him. I gave him pickles to hold so he couldn't grab the banister."

"So you're mad at Zander," said Opal. "Fair enough, the bastard deserves it. But you made a date with him, even though you agreed not to see him until we'd had a chance to talk about what our plan was, going forward."

"There was a plan going forward?" asked Lilah. Opal waved at her to say they'd discuss that later.

"I'm sorry," said Marina. "I know. And you were right. It's a complicated situation and I should not have done something impulsive and stupid and illegal and then involved the two of you in it without your consent." She took a breath. "But the thing is . . . the thing is. I've followed the plan for most my life, never hurt anyone, and where's it got me? And also, when I pushed him down the stairs . . . it felt good."

A silence fell.

"It felt good?" Lilah said at last. "You hurt someone and it felt good? Are you literally crazy?"

"I'm not the one who slapped a random mother of three in a McDonald's and called her a hussy, so."

"I apologized for that!" Lilah turned to Opal. "This is all your fault. If you hadn't told us about Zachary, none of this would have happened."

"You're blaming me?" said Opal. "For telling the truth?"

"We would never have known. We would have gone on living our lives, being happy."

"He's been lying to you. How can you be happy if you're living in a fictional world?"

"I've lived in fictional worlds all my life and it's been absolutely fine!"

"Then you're an idiot," said Opal. "Although frankly this does not come as a surprise. And *you*." She pointed at Marina. "You have to stop apologizing so fucking much."

"Sorry," said Marina, and then she put her hand over her mouth.

Opal threw her juice box away. It landed on the unconscious body of her ex-husband and bounced onto the flagstone floor. "Screw this," she said, turning away.

"What are you doing?" asked Lilah and Marina, more or less at the same time.

"I'm getting a real drink."

She perused the shadowy shelves, which were stacked with wine bottles lying on their sides. She wasn't a wine drinker, as a rule; it had too much sugar and she hated the way the scent of it oozed out of her pores the next day. If she wanted a drink (if, on the very rare occasion, she wanted to get drunk, as falling-down-comatose drunk as her dad used to get), she drank vodka on ice.

But she was in a wine cellar, and when in Rome. If she was going to drink wine, she was going to have the best one she could. She figured that Marina owed her an expensive drink at the very least after pulling her into this mess.

Opal reached for the oldest-looking bottle on the shelf, one coated thickly with dust, with cobwebs spinning from the wax seal over the cork. She pulled it out, and in that moment two things happened at once.

Behind her, Zander moaned.

And in front of her, with a faint rattle and clank, the wine rack slid to one side, exposing a heavy wooden door with a hatch in it.

14

Marina

"WHAT IS THAT?" LILAH SQUEAKED.

Marina, who was crouching down to check that Xavier was still unconscious (he was, but he was beginning to stir), stood up and went over to Opal.

"A secret passageway." She couldn't help a little skip of delight. "This is *exactly* like something Nana Sylvia would have."

"Who's Nana Sylvia?" asked Lilah, joining them.

"My grandmother. She left me this house." Marina examined the newly exposed door. It was made of thick oak, with brass hinges and a bolt on the outside. There was a square hatch at about head height. It had a little latch on it. "How did you find it?"

"I took out this wine bottle," said Opal, holding up the wine bottle. Marina felt around the empty, cobwebby space and found a small lever. She pressed it, and the shelf slid over to cover the door again.

"I love secret passageways," said Lilah. "I've never seen one in real life."

"When I was a little girl, I searched all over this house for a secret passageway. I was convinced there was one, and Nana Sylvia never denied it. It just seemed like that kind of house, you know?"

"I assume you never checked down here," said Opal.

"I didn't like spiders. I still don't." Marina pressed the lever again to expose the door and tried the bolt—it was oiled and slid open easily.

Inside, it was dark, and the air was stale. Lilah fetched the flashlight. Marina didn't know what she'd expected, but not this: a small, windowless, but perfectly comfortable parlor.

There was a leather armchair, a mahogany side table, a made-up single bed with a burgundy velvet bedspread pulled over it, densely patterned wallpaper on the walls. A fringed lampshade hung from the ceiling. Lilah trained the flashlight toward a shelf, where there were rows of tinned food, some glass bottles that may once have contained water, and a few hardback books. There was also a fully stocked bar cart, complete with dusty glasses.

"Narnia," breathed Lilah.

"It's a bomb shelter," said Opal. She walked in and turned on the light, which illuminated the space dimly. "All this furniture is from the 1940s." She picked up a book and blew dust off the jacket. "Raymond Chandler. A first edition. This is wild."

Marina checked the expiration date on a can of oil-packed tuna. "August 2020. I guess Nana Sylvia stocked up fairly recently in case of another war. She'd be keeping safe in style, which is typical." She crouched to look at a box under the shelf. "SqueakyClean Portable Composting Toilet, Eliminates All Odors."

"Your aunt sounds like a regular Girl Scout."

"Except there's also the makings for a perfect gin martini, if you don't mind the lack of ice."

Behind them, Xavier moaned again. It was muffled, through the duct tape gag.

"He's waking up," said Marina. "Oh God. What do we do now?"

Opal met her gaze. The two of them looked at each other for a brief but significant moment.

"I'll need to give it a quick clean," Marina said. "Who knows how long since it's been dusted."

"What are you talking about?" asked Lilah. "Wait. You're not thinking about putting Zachary *in here*? This locked room without any windows?"

"Just until we can work out what to do next," said Marina. "It's definitely better than keeping him tied up and gagged."

"It's perfectly comfortable," said Opal. "I've seen less well-equipped hotel rooms."

"I'll go get the Dustbuster and some fresh bed sheets."

She hurried out. Behind her, she could hear Opal and Lilah arguing about the ethics of locking their communal husband/fiancé/lover in a luxury bomb shelter.

Back upstairs in the kitchen, it was as if nothing strange whatsoever was happening. She couldn't even really hear the other women talking, except for a low murmur. The bomb shelter might be soundproofed, too—presumably so that you wouldn't be distracted from your reading and your perfect martini by bombs falling outside.

But the lock was on the outside of the door, she'd noticed. Inside, there was only a simple latch.

First things first. She checked on the children, who were all sleeping soundly, thank God. Archie was sucking his thumb (another failure of her mothering, but boy it was cute) and Lucy Rose was clutching her plastic ice cream tub with her snail in it. That child was desperate for a pet.

Then she grabbed bed linens, the portable vacuum cleaner, and a couple of rags from the airing cupboard, and a mostly empty bottle of ibuprofen from the bathroom. On second thought, she also took the box with her spare baby monitor, the one she'd used for Lucy Rose. On her way back through the kitchen she picked up the three juice boxes that were left in the pack and shoved them under her arm. She took the cellar stairs carefully but quickly.

Opal and Lilah were still arguing.

"No. We're not calling the police. We are not sending a single mom of three to jail."

"But according to you, Zachary is a thief. He's a con man. He was planning to be a bigamist. He's broken all sorts of laws. So Marina was actually catching him, so he can go to jail. If all of what you say is true, this was self-defense."

"No. I'm many things, but I am not a snitch."

"I'm not a snitch either! But we will get in less trouble if we tell them now. They have to see our point of view."

"Here is a life lesson for you, Lilah. All these things that this man, whatever we call him, has done. The lying, the cheating, the con artistry, the theft, the manipulation. The police do not care. Believe me. They do not give a single shit about the women who this man has used up and thrown aside. And odds are, there are a lot more than three women he's cheated. Some of them have probably been to the police already. The police will say that we gave him the money out of our own free will. That we cared about him, that we loved him, that we married him, and so we consented to everything he did to us. The money he stole is long gone, and he could tell any amount of lies and the police will believe him instead of us, for the simple reason that he is a man and that we loved him enough to be fools."

"What makes you so certain?"

"Let's just say I've been there. When it comes to men being shitty to women, the odds are stacked against us. Heard of Wayne Couzens? Heard about the Metropolitan Police arresting innocent women protesting the murder of a woman by a cop? Heard of the dire prosecution statistics for rape and sexual assault? If you go to the police saying your car was stolen, they'll take you seriously. If you say your husband lied and cheated and stole, they'll say . . . well, boys will be boys and you should have chosen better. On the other hand: if a woman fights back? They *will* take that seriously."

Lilah looked as if she were going to protest further, but Marina gave her the sheets instead. "Here, you make up the bed. Opal and I will dust."

"I don't dust for any ma—"

It was then that Lilah started screaming.

She had the burgundy bedspread in her hand. She'd pulled it back to expose a human skeleton.

15

Lilah

LILAH STAGGERED BACKWARDS, DROPPING ALL the sheets and blankets on the floor. The skeleton grinned up at her with its wide toothy mouth. It had its head on a pillow, as if it had been sleeping, but its eye sockets were open and black and empty. Its fleshless hands lay folded on its alabaster rib cage.

There was a round hole in its forehead, more or less right between where the eyebrows would have been.

"What's wrong?" Marina came up next to her. "Oh my God."

Lilah's legs wouldn't hold her anymore. She sat down abruptly on the dusty Turkish carpet, her teeth clicking together with the impact and cutting off her scream.

And all at once she was sick of this. She had had enough. She was up to the back teeth with discovering bodies and screaming and fainting.

"I would like this to stop now, please," she said, quite calmly. "I would like people to stop dying."

Meanwhile, Marina and Opal were gazing down at the skeleton.

"He's wearing a bow tie," said Opal.

"Is it real?"

"The bow tie? I should think so." Opal lifted one of the skeleton's hands by the wrist. "He's fully articulated. See? All held together with wire and metal pins. Like the ones that used to be used in medical labs to teach anatomy."

Marina let out a shaky laugh. "A fully furnished secret room with a skeleton in it is exactly my grandmother's sense of humor."

"So it's a fake?" Lilah got up, more curious than frightened now.

"I think it's real," said Opal. "It's legal enough to own them. I'm pretty sure you can buy them on the internet."

"Is that a bullet hole between its eyes?"

In response to Lilah's question, Opal lifted the skull off the pillow enough to reveal a larger hole in the back of the skull.

"Exit wound," she said.

"So this is a *murder victim?*"

"Nana Sylvia liked target shooting," said Marina. "Usually she used clay pigeons. But I wouldn't be at all surprised if she thought it was funny to use a skeleton."

"You have a very disturbing family," said Lilah.

"She was wonderful." Marina began wrapping the skeleton up in the sheet that it was lying on. "She was the best person I knew and I miss her every day. And you're in her house, so I'd thank you not to insult her."

"You're the one who invited us here."

"Actually, I invited Opal."

The other two watched as Marina trussed up the skeleton like a mummy and removed the bundle from the bed.

"I said that the two of you should stop being scared and apologizing, but I hoped the outcome would be more interesting than petty bickering," Opal commented.

"Just make the bed before he wakes up." Marina deposited the shrouded skeleton in the armchair and began noisily Dustbusting.

Lilah began making the bed until Opal, behind her, huffed in exasperation and took over. "You would never pass nursing school," she said, briskly forming hospital corners on the sheets.

"I have a master's in library science," retorted Lilah.

"Hooray for you." Opal pulled the sheet so taut that it looked painful. "If we need to alphabetize anything, that'll come in handy."

A groan from the other part of the cellar, louder than before, definitely loud enough to be heard over the mini vacuum cleaner.

"Listen," said Lilah. "Let's stop arguing, okay? We can untie Zachary, and take him to a hospital, and—"

"No," said Opal and Marina together.

"But we are going to let him go eventually, right? We're not going to keep him here until there's another skeleton in that bed."

"Of course not. We'll just keep him here until we can get my kids out of the house, and we can work out a way to make him promise not to victimize women anymore."

"Or, we could just let him—"

"When are you going to stop letting people walk all over you?" snapped Opal. "You're an intelligent woman, obviously, and you'd be attractive with a little work. You need to find some self-esteem. You deserve better than him."

"Please," said Marina. "Please, let's carry him in here now. Please, before he wakes up and unties himself. I worry that he might be angry and try to hurt us."

She looked terrified. And that, weirdly, was what decided Lilah. Because hadn't she decided just a few minutes ago that she was done with being scared?

"Okay," said Lilah. The three of them went back to where Zachary was lying on the floor. Thankfully, his eyes were still closed. She didn't think she could pick him up and move him around like a trussed chicken if he were awake and looking at her.

The Peppa Pig Band-Aids on his forehead were in exactly the same place that the bullet hole had been in the skull.

"You two take his legs," ordered Opal. "I'll take his shoulders. Lift when I say 'go.' And use your legs to lift, not your back."

Zachary was tall, but he kept fit and slim, so Lilah didn't think he would be too heavy. But he was dead weight. Marina lifted his bound feet, Lilah held up his legs, and Opal had a good grip under his shoulders, but his rear end still scraped on the floor as she and Marina walked backwards towards the bomb shelter.

"We're going to need to turn around," said Opal. "The two of you aren't going to fit through the door side by side." She looked more or less at ease carrying a 170-pound grown man, but Lilah had already started sweating. She and Marina shuffled to the side so that Opal could aim herself at the entrance.

By the time they got into the room, even Opal was beginning to grit her teeth and breathe hard. They maneuvered him towards the bed. "Okay, we'll have to swing him on," said Opal, but it was then that his legs started thrashing. Marina shook her head and put his feet down. "I can't," she gasped.

"Me neither," said Lilah, with considerable relief. Opal shrugged and lay Zachary down on the floor. At least here, there was a carpet for him to lie on. He kicked and struggled, though his eyes were still closed.

Opal bent and pulled the ends of the duct tape around Zachary's wrists and ankles loose, but not off. Marina took a white object out of a box and put it on a shelf. Lilah took the Dustbuster. Then they all quickly retreated out of the room. Marina shut and locked the door behind them.

"He wasn't that heavy," Opal said. "I can bench press more than that."

"Hooray for you," said Lilah. "If we need to lift any more uncon-scious men, that'll come in handy." She wiped sweat off her upper lip, remembered her juice box, and retrieved it from the shelf where she'd left it.

"Did we do the right thing?" Marina whispered. In the dim light her face was dead pale, even her lips.

Again, seeing Marina's fear had the odd effect of making Lilah less distressed. She punched her straw through the juice box, making a perfectly round hole.

"No, we didn't," Lilah said. "But we're all in this together, now."

16

"NEVER GOOGLE ANYTHING."

They were upstairs in the kitchen stress-eating the charcuterie platter, and Opal was laying down some rules.

"It feels like every single time I read a true crime story that's taken place in the past twenty years, every single time, the perp is convicted after the police look at his search history and find something like 'how to build a bomb out of common household objects.' So: no googling how to keep a man captive, or how to convince him not to turn you in to the police, or even anything about Zachary Dickens or Xavier Sheppard or Zander Bolt or whatever name you know him as. And no visiting each other's social media platforms or looking each other up. We need time to get our stories straight, and meanwhile we don't want to produce any evidence that says anything different."

"How did you find Lilah and me if you didn't look online?" Marina asked.

"Burner phone. Can't be traced to me."

"Seriously?"

"I watch a lot of true crime, okay?" Opal spread her hands out on the table. Like her lips, her nails were painted blood-red. "Second rule is the one that Marina agreed to in the first place: we can't confront Zander about his scams until all of us together decide to. If he doesn't know exactly what we know about him, he can't twist the truth or try to manipulate us. He's extremely good at charming women. He'll lie through his teeth and sweet-talk you into believing him, and before you know it, you've forgiven him, and then he'll convince you that it was all your fault in the first place. He did it to me for years."

"Third rule," piped in Marina. "We can't leave him in my house by himself. At least one of us has to be here, in case he escapes."

"What good is that going to do?" asked Lilah. "If he got out, we couldn't stop him from leaving. Well, *you* might be able to," she said to Opal, who couldn't disagree.

"Hold on a second," said Marina. "I might have an idea."

She got up and left the room.

"I'm a little worried that Marina is a criminal genius," said Lilah.

"She really isn't. She is a divorced mother of three who is desperate for a man to bolster her self-esteem. That's why we have to agree on basic rules to keep from getting in trouble."

"Then maybe *you're* a criminal genius."

"What I have is common sense, and a certain amount of bitterness."

"Why did you ask me if he'd hit me?"

"Did you check your other bank accounts, by the way? Did he get all of your lottery winnings?"

Lilah folded a slice of cheese in half, and half again.

"All of it?" Opal asked.

"Not the investments."

"But all of the ready cash and credit? He got all of that?"

Lilah put down the mangled cheese. "It's brought me nothing but evil. I was going to sell everything and give the money away."

"That's very charitable of you." Opal pulled the fat off a slice of prosciutto, rolled it around some cherry tomatoes and ate it in two bites.

"Why don't you like me?" burst out Lilah. "Is it because I fell in love with your husband? Because if that's so, then it's not exactly fair that you keep on defending Marina and being mean to me."

"Marina doesn't love him, she's just been shagging him. But I don't care what either of you did with my scumbag husband. I wanted him to fail, that's all. I don't like Marina any more than I like you. But don't take it personally. I don't like many people."

"Even if you don't like someone, that's no reason to be horrible to them."

"But you make it so easy, Lilah. You're a frightened little bunny rabbit."

"I'm not—"

Marina reappeared. She was carrying a large mahogany box, which she set on the table next to the depleted charcuterie platter. The box had brass corner reinforcements and brass catches on the front. "These were in the attic," she said. As the other two women watched, she unlatched the box and opened it to reveal two antique pistols lying on a green felt interior. The guns had wooden stocks, silver detailing, elaborate silver workings. Other compartments held a variety of mysterious-looking implements.

"Manton flintlock dueling pistols," said Marina. "Handmade in 1797 and presented to the Earl of Devonshire, who quite liked a quarrel. Or so my grandmother told me. I was never allowed to open the box myself, but she showed me on my birthdays."

"Your grandmother had a set of antique dueling pistols and an articulated skeleton wearing a bow tie," said Opal.

"What can I say? She was wonderfully eccentric."

"Weird."

"Eccentric," said Marina assertively.

"So, you brought these downstairs in case Zander wants to duel."

"No. I thought we could use them as a deterrent. If he escapes, we can point one at him and make him get back into the bomb shelter."

"We might as well point a banana at him. Those things are ancient."

"They're in perfect working order. Nana Sylvia serviced them herself. I told you: she liked target practice."

Lilah said, "I've read enough Georgette Heyer to know that flintlock pistols take a long time to load. They're not something we could use spontaneously."

"I'm not going to load them," said Marina, shocked. "I have children. I just thought . . . we could scare him. If we needed to."

Opal sighed.

"It's a good idea," said Lilah, for no other reason than to annoy Opal.

"Okay," said Opal. "Fourth rule. If Zander escapes, we threaten him with an empty gun. How much are those things worth, by the way?"

"About a hundred thousand each."

"Right. So ideally, we don't want to use them as clubs." She turned to Lilah. "Now, fifth rule. Most important rule. No calling the police."

"Yes, yes," said Lilah. "I get it."

"I'll need someone to babysit him tomorrow morning."

"I will," said Opal. "I can prerecord my workout session and schedule the post."

"Having a man in the basement is like having a fourth child," said Marina.

"Don't we have to discuss what we're going to do with him?" asked Lilah. "We can't leave him down there forever."

"I need some time to think," said Marina. "He's not going to come to any harm down there. I can hear him through the baby monitor if he's sick. And I need to find someplace safe for my children before I can decide anything."

"We all need time to think," said Opal. "So let's convene here tomorrow afternoon."

"You are really quite bossy," said Lilah.

"It's my greatest strength." Opal picked up a ripe sliced fig and considered its blood-purple interior. "Rule six. While he's in that bomb shelter, let's only feed him carbs."

"Mean," said Marina. "I sort of like it."

17

THE NEXT DAY (FRIDAY)

Marina

FOR OBVIOUS REASONS, SHE HADN'T had time to bake a sourdough loaf the night before, but fortunately she had remembered to take a loaf of Aldi white bread out of the freezer. She lined up seven slices on the kitchen counter.

She was running a little late, rushing to prepare for the day before Ewan woke up for his morning feed—which she felt she should stop soon, he was fifteen months old, but she knew that once she finished with Ewan she was done forever. No more children to nurse, ever again. And after it was so difficult with Lucy Rose, nursing Ewan was a dream: his sweet little head on her chest, the way he curled in her lap, reached up and played with her ear softly, the dreamy look in his eyes.

But it had to stop soon. The parenting books and community health nurses all said you should breastfeed as long as you can, ideally until the child left home for university and your boobs reached your ankles.

But the truth was that once a child could walk, people looked at you funny.

She didn't get much sleep last night. Her thoughts wouldn't stop whizzing.

She buttered all the slices of white bread and lined them up on the kitchen counter. She made Archie's sandwich first: plain ham. She'd had great hopes for Archie, because when he was a toddler, he'd eat anything, including beetroot and radicchio, but the older he grew, the more it seemed that he'd inherited his father's taste for bland food. Sometimes she tried to slip a vegetable into his pasta sauce, with varying success, but it was a work in progress.

Lucy Rose's sandwich was leftover prosciutto, with cut-up green olives, cherry tomatoes, and arugula. She liked something she could get her teeth into, the spicier the better, even at age three. Ewan, still weaning, was also a work in progress, but she made his sandwich on one slice of bread, with cream cheese and a sprinkling of dill.

The fourth sandwich was for Xavier. After some consideration, she spread Nutella thickly on both slices of bread, and topped it with marshmallows, Gummi Bears, and chocolate chips. She had to press down hard on the bread to make it all stay together.

She cut the crusts off the sandwiches, cut them all into triangles, and wrapped them.

Once upon a time, and not that long ago, she hoped she'd be doing this morning routine one day with Xavier. He could make coffee and empty the dishwasher while she made the packed lunches. They could chat about how they slept, the dreams they had the night before, the day ahead.

Okay—so a man emptying the dishwasher might be a pipe dream, but surely coffee wasn't too much to ask?

She heard a distant noise—a muffled thump. Instinctively, she looked at the baby monitor—the new one, the one she used for

Ewan—but nothing came from that but a faint snoring. Ewan, her good sleeper. The sound hadn't come from the children. So it would have to wait for now.

Carrot sticks and red bell pepper sticks (these were the only two vegetables that Archie would eat, except for ketchup, which didn't count). Little boxes of raisins and cubes of cheese, and a homemade madeleine in each lunch bag. There were no juice boxes left, so she filled reusable bottles with water. Those were for the children. For Xavier, she added a half-eaten emergency packet of cookies, the plastic wrapper twisted shut, two packets of cheesy puffs, and a can of Coke from her own secret stash.

Her workdays used to be flavors and scents, knives and bubbling sauces, the kind of adrenaline that made you crave more work. It was hard to believe now; it felt like a fairy tale that happened to someone else. Her nineteen-year-old self never would have imagined that her life would turn out like this. Packing lunches made with white bread, and trying to ignore a hostage in the cellar.

In the distance, she heard a familiar raised voice, and a faint hammering. Apparently the bomb shelter wasn't so soundproof after all.

She turned on the old baby monitor receiver, the one that she'd left the transmitter for in the bomb shelter.

"THERE'S A GODDAMN SKELETON—"

She turned it off.

She'd deal with it. But first, she needed coffee.

One of many things that they don't tell you about motherhood in the books and Instagram feeds: from the moment your children were born, you would never be able to drink a coffee while it was still hot unless you made one before they woke up. That this would be the best-tasting cup of coffee all day, and you still probably wouldn't have time to finish it. And that you would usually drink it in the middle of a kitchen that was a chaos of cereal bowls, toast crumbs, used wipes, and discarded toys. Because one of the superpowers you developed when you were a mother—one of the *many* superpowers—was the ability to notice everything that needed to be done, and also to ignore it all for five minutes at a time so you could actually breathe.

She used Nana Sylvia's state-of-the-art espresso machine to make herself a small, strong coffee. Then she slipped out the back door onto the flagstone patio, which caught the early morning sunlight. She sat on a patio chair and drank her coffee, sip by bitter, restoring sip.

She didn't allow herself to think about anything.

She let the sunlight warm her face. She listened to a solitary black-bird serenading the morning. There were parrots here in Richmond, sometimes: descendants of pets who had escaped to freedom. They filled the trees with color and noise, chattering dreams of the tropics.

Two minutes later, the jackhammers started up next door.

Marina sighed. Time to get back to the real world.

She squared her shoulders, took a deep breath, and went back inside. If she could raise three children by herself while her husband was off spending their money and screwing another woman, she could do *anything*.

Inside the kitchen, the thudding from below had become louder and also more regular. She made another espresso, tipped it into a mug, and added enough hot water to make an Americano. Then she added three spoonfuls of sugar. Mug in hand and lunch bag under her arm, she unbolted the cellar door and flicked on the light at the top of the stairwell. She closed the door behind her, and carefully started down the stairs with the coffee and lunch bag.

She mentioned last night that she used to hate coming down here because of the spiders. But you live and learn—it was amazing what little fears you could get over, when there was something bigger to be afraid of.

Like the possibility of losing your children and being put away for assault and kidnapping.

She put the packed lunch on a shelf next to a bottle of wine, opened the secret passage, and unlatched the hatch in the door a crack. The thudding stopped.

She couldn't bear to look inside. Not yet.

"Good morning!" she called. She tried to sound light, cheerful, normal.

Silence.

Marina swallowed. A little bit of coffee sloshed over the rim of the mug.

"Sorry it took so long," she called, and then she clamped her mouth shut.

No. No apologies. Opal was right: they were a bad habit. And anyway, she wasn't sorry it took so long. She had to put her children first. And also, she deserved a quiet espresso, and she needed the caffeine. Who knows how the rest of this morning was going to go?

"I've made you a coffee," Marina said. "And I've packed you a lunch. I presume you're pretty hungry by now."

"Marina? What the fuck are you playing at?"

He shouted it in a raspy and thirsty voice. She winced and opened the hatch enough to look through—keeping a distance, in case he grabbed for her.

Xavier had untaped himself. She couldn't see much except for his face, because he was right up against the door. There was a pink mark across the bottom of his face from when he pulled the duct tape gag off. It probably felt a lot like having your eyebrows waxed, so Marina had sympathy.

He hammered on the door with his fists. Marina stepped back and waited for him to finish.

"You're in a basement," she told him. "The walls are thick, and also they've been soundproofed. So there's really no reason to shout. I'm the only one here, and I can hear you just fine."

He stopped hammering and swore.

"Have you been awake for long?" she asked.

"How am I supposed to know? You've put me in a fucking dungeon!"

"It's not a dungeon. It's a bomb shelter. Quite a nice one. Anyway, I told you there's no point shouting. If you can't discuss things like a rational human being, I'll have to shut the hatch again."

"Rational? You pushed me down the stairs, you cunt!"

She flinched at that.

"I really thought you were a nice man," she said. "I thought you were different from the other men out there. I thought I'd struck it lucky."

"I could have died!"

"But you didn't, so."

"You're a psycho!"

"Do you want your coffee?" She held the mug up to the hatch, close enough for him to be able to smell it but out of reach.

He clenched his jaw in a way that made it look quite chiseled, and finally nodded. Turned out that when men had tantrums, the best thing to do was to stay calm and treat them like toddlers.

She turned the mug around and passed it to him handle-first, stepping back quickly. Xavier took a sip and grimaced. "It's got sugar."

"Are you thirsty?"

He glared, but he drank more. Obviously he hadn't availed himself of the bar cart.

"How are you feeling?" she asked when he came up for air.

"How do you think I bloody feel?"

"I mean physically. Does your head hurt? I left you some ibuprofen and some juice. I didn't get a chance to refresh the water supply, so I wouldn't drink that."

"My head hurts a lot. Was I unconscious?"

"Oh, yes, for a while," said Marina vaguely.

"I need to go to the hospital! I might have a concussion. A skull fracture!"

"How many fingers?" She held up three.

"What?"

"Have you got double vision?"

He squinted. "No."

"Do you feel sick?"

"I don't know."

"Well, it's possible, but it's unlikely that you have any brain injury. Drink some more of your coffee."

"How do I know it's not drugged?"

"I guess you don't. But it's not, and if you want anything to eat or drink you're going to have to trust me, for the moment."

"It could be poisoned. If you're crazy enough to push me down the stairs and keep me hostage, you're capable of anything."

"Xavier, if I wanted to poison you, I would have put something in your glass of wine and wouldn't have bothered with the stairs."

He narrowed his eyes and finished his coffee.

"Do you feel a little better?" Marina asked. "You were probably quite dehydrated."

"Is this what you do? Do you find men and date them and then hold them captive? Is that what this skeleton is?"

"No, I found the skeleton in the cellar. I think it's one of those scientific ones."

"What do you want? Money?"

"I don't want your money, and also I've never done anything like this before."

"Is it a sex thing?"

"Ew, no." She held up the bag. "I made you a packed lunch."

"I don't understand," said Xavier, his voice gaining a pleading tone. "What are you doing, baby? I thought things were going so well between us."

"Oh, they were."

"Then what's all this? Why did you hurt me?"

This honeyed, wounded tone was hard to resist. If it was a little-boy act, it was a very good one. And she felt pretty terrible. All of this was her fault.

But it was one of the rules: she couldn't let on what she knew about him, or why she'd pushed him down the stairs. Xavier didn't seem to know yet that Opal and Lilah had been here, too. He must not have heard anything.

"I'm sorry if you're still in pain," she said. "The ibuprofen should be on the shelf next to the gin."

"It hurts too much," he whimpered. "I think I need to go to the hospital. And ibuprofen gives me a stomachache."

"I don't have anything else, except for Tylenol." What dosage of cherry-flavored liquid Tylenol would be sufficient for a grown man? If Archie had one small spoonful when he had a fever, and Archie weighed, oh, say, ten times less than Xavier, then . . . "I should have bought a bigger bottle."

"Please, baby? Can we go to A&E? It hurts so bad."

"Maybe later, if you don't feel better."

"C'mon, baby. You can let me go. Are you worried about getting in trouble for pushing me? I won't say anything. I'll say it was an accident. Which it was, right? You care too much about me to do anything to hurt me."

Marina didn't answer.

"You and I are good together, you know," he continued. "I've been so lucky to find you. I—I meant to tell you, I was going to tell you tonight. I haven't felt this way about a woman since Stacey."

According to Xavier, Stacey was his dead wife. When Xavier talked about this fictitious "Stacey," was he actually thinking about Opal? Or was "Stacey" another woman who he'd duped? How many of them were there?

"I think I've fallen in love with you," said Xavier, and his voice was sweet and rough and vulnerable and so, so incredibly sincere.

Opal was right: he was very good at this. He knew exactly what buttons to push. What woman didn't want to hear those words from the man she'd been dating?

Well . . . as of yesterday: Marina, for one.

"That's very nice of you," she said.

"I mean it, Marina," Xavier said. "I know we've only known each other a little while, but when it's right, it's right."

"I can't argue with that."

"I know this is all a big misunderstanding. You didn't mean to push me, or lock me in the basement. It was an accident, and then you panicked."

"It wasn't an accident."

"That's okay. I'm not angry. And Marina, I forgive you. I'll forgive you anything. Because I love you."

He said *I love you* as if the words were a magic spell that would get him anything he wanted. To be fair, for him they probably were.

"So just let me go, okay? We can put this all behind us and talk about our future."

"About thirty seconds ago you were calling me a psycho cunt."

"I was angry, okay? I think that's understandable. I was scared and in pain. But I know that you're not a bad person. I love you."

"I don't think that you do, Xavier."

"I do! I think you're an incredible, compassionate, kind, nurturing, clever, sexy, gentle, ethical person who always tries to do the right thing! You're amazing, Marina! You're such a good mother and you're a wonderful chef! Any man would be lucky to have you in his life! You're so strong, and caring, and—"

While he was saying this, Marina pushed the packed lunch through the hatch. It landed with a thud.

"—and you genuinely care about other people, you know, you're always looking out for others, which is why you deserve someone to look after you, to pamper you and make you feel good, and love—"

"I've got to go upstairs now," she interrupted. "But I'll check on you in a little while to see if you want anything else to eat."

"Wait. Wait, no! Don't go! Don't leave me alone down here! Please, Marina—"

She shut the hatch. Then she thought twice, and opened it a sliver.

"Xavier?" she said through the opening. "You were being more honest when you said that I was a psycho cunt."

18

BACK UPSTAIRS, SHE CHECKED THE clock: nearly seven-thirty. She propped her phone on the kitchen windowsill and started her good-morning Spotify playlist, which was mostly Beyoncé. She turned the volume up to full.

"Rise and shine!" she called cheerfully on her way up the stairs. She loved these stairs: grand and curving with a polished oak banister, built for a different era. Archie's room was first. Tenderly, she kissed him on the forehead and he woke up with a grimace and then, when he opened his eyes, a smile. "Time to get ready for school," she whispered and indulged herself in a tiny cuddle, only one, while he was still sleepy and warm and before he pulled away.

His school uniform, tiny and heart-achingly grown-up, was folded ready on the chair. "Do you want help getting dressed?" she asked.

"No," he said, already getting out of bed, tousle-headed and dogged, and so much like a tiny version of her own dad that sometimes it made her laugh and sometimes it made her worry.

In the next room Lucy Rose was awake already and on the floor with her toy flamingo, talking to it in a made-up language. She barely looked up when Marina came in.

"Time to get dressed." Marina selected an outfit from Lucy Rose's drawers, though she knew that Lucy Rose would reject it. But choosing the wrong clothes for Lucy Rose was the only surefire way to get Lucy Rose to stop playing with her flamingo and focus on getting dressed.

"No, I want *pink*," Lucy Rose said when Marina held out a pair of leggings.

"These are pink."

"The *other* pink."

There were no other pink leggings. "Which do you mean, Luce?"

Lucy Rose got up with an exaggerated sigh and started digging through her drawer. "*This* pink," she said, pulling out a pair of green striped leggings.

"Oh, I see. Do you want me to choose a top for you?"

"Go 'way." She waved her hands at Marina in a shooing motion. Thank God Lucy Rose insisted on getting her hair cut short last week, because that removed at least half an hour from their morning routine.

In the room across the corridor, Ewan was still half-asleep. She picked him up out of his cot and settled into the nursing chair with him, grateful for this gentle waking, this moment of connection.

One day, none of her children would need her. From the moment they were born, they started their journey away from you. But for ten minutes, she was a good mother, and everything that her youngest child needed.

Then she thought about Xavier.

She carried Ewan downstairs, shepherding the other two down before her. Lucy Rose wore a black top with the logo "Disco Queen" and a red cloak left over from Halloween. Fortunately, Archie had dressed himself beautifully in his school uniform, tucking in his shirt and arranging his collar perfectly neatly outside his sweater. He even had his shoes on the correct feet.

The next twenty minutes were taken up with toast, cereal, permission slips, homework, spilled juice, and a minor disagreement about using a tissue. Then there was the normal hunt for shoes, jackets, security blankets, wipes, and a small plastic penguin. The doorbell rang.

"That's Opal!" she said brightly.

"Who's Opal?" asked Archie.

"She's a friend of Mummy's who's going to look after the house while I take you to school and nursery."

Thereby proving that Marina was not only a violent kidnapper and a "psycho cunt," but also a person who lied to her children. None of this was on her bingo card for divorced life.

"What's that noise?" asked Lucy Rose.

"Oh, it must be the Andersons' construction next door."

It did not sound like construction. It sounded like Xavier discovering that his lunch contained a sandwich made of sweets.

She opened the door for Opal.

"How do you look so well rested?" Marina asked.

"Hot yoga and expensive skincare." Opal came in and put her Chloé tote on the tiled floor. "How's your guest?"

"Not as quiet as I'd like him to be," whispered Marina. She brought Opal through to the kitchen, where she stopped in the doorway and looked horrified.

"These are children," Opal said.

"Yes. This is Archie and Lucy Rose, and the little one in the high chair with jam on his face is Ewan. I'm about to take them to their gran's house."

"I'm dressed as Super Poo," said Lucy Rose.

"Lovely," said Opal in a tone that conveyed that she did not find the situation lovely at all.

* * *

At her mother's house, Marina folded up the pushchair with one arm and leaned it against the wall. "Everything Ewan needs should be in that nappy bag." She passed Ewan over to her mother.

"You haven't toilet trained him yet, I see."

"Mom, he's fifteen months old." She knelt down and whispered to Lucy Rose, "Remember not to bite either of your brothers, okay sweetie?"

"Only if I have to." Lucy Rose skipped off to the cupboard where her grandmother kept the coloring books.

"That child is strange," opined her mother.

"She is wonderfully unique." Marina put the packed lunches in the refrigerator. "Archie will need picking up at school at half past two."

"Well," her mother said. "Of course my grandchildren are always welcome here, and they can stay as long as *you* have more interesting things going on elsewhere. This rift in the family isn't *their* fault. Did I tell you about how much Neil's extension is going to cost? Even if he only hires Albanians?"

She would not apologize, nor would she rise to her mother's bigotry.

"Thank you for looking after them. I really appreciate it and I know they love time with their grandparents."

"What's so important that you have to leave them?"

"I told you on the phone—they've found some asbestos in the cellar, and it's not safe for them to be in the house until it's all been removed."

"Ah," said her mother. "Beware Greeks bearing gifts."

Marina was not sure what that had to do with asbestos, but her mother had seemingly believed her lie. Who knew it would be this easy?

"Mom, can I ask you something quickly? What do you remember about Nana Sylvia's last husband, Barry?"

"Why are you asking about him?"

"There are some photographs in the house, and I wonder if they're him," she lied, again. "I don't remember him very well."

"Well." Her mother settled into the breakfast nook with relish, to partake in her favorite pastime: gossiping about the rest of the family. "You were only a baby when she married him. I never liked him."

"Why not?"

"He was too young for her, for one."

"How old was he?"

"At least a dozen years younger than her. I said to her, 'Mum, what's in it for him?' But she didn't listen, of course."

"Mum, you're ten years younger than Dad."

"It's different for women."

She resisted asking "why?" because that was a rabbit hole that she didn't have time for. "What did he look like?"

"He was very good-looking. If you like that sort. He loved clothes. Which made me wonder sometimes, was he gay and Mom was his, what do you call it?"

"Beard."

"Who's got a beard?"

"Never mind. Anyway, he might have been bisexual but he definitely wasn't gay, because Nana Sylvia said he was the best in bed of any of her husbands, but in a showy way, like he felt he had an audience."

Her mother grimaced. "I do not want to know."

"Fair enough. So what happened to him?"

"He went off. Saw a better opportunity, probably. That sort usually do. Went out to play golf one day and never came back. And then it came out that he was having affairs right left and center, with every woman in west London practically. He liked teenage girls."

"Ew. That sounds more like a creep."

"Exactly. Anyway, good riddance, I thought. At least we won't have to share the inheritance with him." Her eyes narrowed. "Oh, is *that* why you're asking?"

"Like I said. I didn't remember much about him."

And that, at least, wasn't a lie. It was the truth. Marina had been too young, and she didn't remember much about Nana Sylvia's last, creepy, philandering, disappearing husband. Except for one thing.

He liked to wear a bow tie.

19

Lilah

LILAH HAD BEEN STANDING AT her parents' graves since the sun came up.

"All I ever wanted was what the two of you had," she was telling them. "I don't really remember you, Mom, but Dad told me once that he loved you from the moment you met, and that he loved you every day afterwards, even when you were gone. He said you'd loved each other so much that even though you died too young, you'd had more love than most people get in a lifetime. I thought that was what was supposed to happen. You met someone and they were The One, and after that, all you had to do was love them with all your heart."

She brushed a speck of dust off her father's perfectly clean headstone.

"I believe Marina and Opal. They've shown me concrete evidence that Zachary has been doing these things. And maybe not just to us, but to other women, too. He never cared for me at all. He just wanted my money, and he took as much of it as he could get. But I still love him. Maybe I'm foolish, like Opal says. Maybe there's no such thing as real love. Not for me, anyway. Maybe what you had was so rare that I'm never going to find it for myself."

She clenched her fists.

"Or maybe you lied to me, Dad. Maybe there isn't such a thing as pure, true love. Maybe this was a story you told to me, like a fairy tale, to help me sleep at night. Maybe if Mom had lived, the two of you would have disagreed and fought and hurt each other. Maybe you wouldn't have even stayed together."

She felt like she wanted to cry, but somehow she couldn't. It was as if there was a little unknown kernel of hardness in her that she'd never suspected before. She didn't like it.

"One of the most difficult things to get my head around is that Zachary said, over and over again, that he was going to protect me. I thought I'd found someone who really understood me and who I could trust. But he only saw me as something to exploit. He took what he wanted, like . . ."

She couldn't complete the sentence, or say the other man's name. She hadn't said it in years, because just saying it made her feel all over again that she was nothing, she was nobody, she was erased.

She took a deep breath.

"I don't blame you, Dad," she said. "It's not your fault that you were killed. It's not your fault that you were fooled by Zachary, too. You were a good man, and you trusted other people. And you were a good woman, Mom. I do believe that. But after what happened with Zachary, I don't know if I believe in love anymore."

She took off her engagement ring. It felt too heavy and looked too flashy. It always had, but only two days ago, she'd thought that her ring's excess was to show the bigness of Zachary's love for her. A love hard as diamond, as precious as gold.

It was all a bunch of clichés. And both the love and the money to pay for it had been stolen from her.

She looked around. The cemetery was empty of living humans, but she whispered anyway.

"I don't know if I can trust Marina and Opal. After all, I'm keeping a secret from them too." She touched her fanny pack, which held the secret. "And I don't know what we're going to do with Zachary. I hope we can make him apologize and give back all the money he stole. If he really did steal it. But what if he won't? What if he says that he's going to tell the police what we did? I don't—" She took a deep breath and said what she'd been afraid to even think, since leaving Marina's house. "I don't know what the other two will want to do. They're both so angry, and Marina has a lot to lose if she gets found out. I'm afraid . . . I'm afraid that they might hurt him. I'm afraid that they might think they have to kill him."

The last two words made her shudder.

"But Opal's right. I'm too scared to do anything about it. I'm too scared to do anything at all. I've been scared for most of my life, like a helpless rabbit. But I think the thing I've been most scared of, for all my life, is being alone. And now I am."

Lilah knelt on her parent's grave. She lay her ring on the grass between the two stones. Maybe it be trodden into the dirt. Maybe it would be found by someone. This was a waste, she knew: she could sell the ring and give the proceeds to charity. But she didn't want to poison a charity with her own disillusion and disappointment. It was better if the ring and all her hope that went with it, stayed here in the cemetery among the dead.

She kissed her fingers and pressed them first to her mother's grave, then her father's. The gesture made her feel a little better. But she was still confused and scared. She realized that she didn't know what was real and what wasn't. She hadn't since her father had been murdered, and maybe for a while before that.

So she stood up, brushed off her knees, and went to the only place that she knew where she could find the truth.

20

Opal

OPAL STOOD IN THE FRONT bay window, half-hidden behind a curtain, watching Marina and her brood walk out of sight. She counted to a hundred, making sure that they weren't going to come back for a forgotten binkie or whatever mysterious thing children couldn't live without.

Then she bolted the front door and went straight down to the cellar to break rules two and six.

The yelling and pounding started as soon as she opened the hidden panel. Zander had always been such a drama queen. She couldn't make out all the words between the kicks and punches at the door, but she definitely recognized "bitch" and something that sounded like "yummy pears."

That couldn't be right. She paused and listened.

Gummi Bears? *Good work, Marina.*

She unfastened the head-height hatch in the door but stood to one side so that she couldn't be seen. What she did let him see was a bottle containing the one thing that she knew Zander wanted most in the world right now, other than freedom and maybe a shower: a protein shake.

His hand emerged and snatched it.

"Finally," he said through the hatch. She heard him unscrew the top and there was a pause as he drank. "Listen, Marina, I think we got off on the wrong foot earlier. And I can tell that you feel the same way, too. Thank you for the shake, baby. I knew you'd do something so wonderful and nice for me. I had a feeling. Neither one of us meant what we said, did we? This is all a big misunderstanding. I'm crazy about you, you know that. Whatever's made you upset, we can work it out."

"Somehow, I don't think so," said Opal, and sidestepped so her face was visible in the hatchway. She grinned at him. The expression on Zander's face was priceless: like a man reaching to tickle a baby in a crib only to be confronted by a furious king cobra.

"You—what are you—"

"Happy anniversary," she said. Though technically, their anniversary was tomorrow.

To give Zander credit, he recovered quickly. He always had.

"Why are *you* here?" he demanded.

"To gloat, mostly. I've wanted to see you imprisoned for a long time."

"You can't lie to me. We both know that neither one of us wants me to go to jail." He paused. "How do you know about Marina?"

"Let's say that I follow her on Instagram."

He groaned. "You told her to push me down the fucking stairs? I should have known that you were behind this."

"I'm not, actually. Marina decided to push you all on her own. Not that I blame her." Opal came a little closer, though not close enough for Zander to reach through the hatch and grab her.

Zander was not looking his best. He had dark circles under his eyes, a bit of dried blood on his forehead. His carefully styled hair was in disarray. Still, though: "You've had some work done on your face," she said.

"You're one to talk."

"Well. It's a requirement of the business. You've been a naughty boy, Zander."

"What are you upset about? Because I've started dating again? I never pegged you as the crazy jealous type. You always said you were *different* from all the other women."

"I know your grift. And while we're on the topic, where's my money?"

"Our money."

"My money."

"You never would've had it without me."

"You give yourself too much credit," Opal said. "Let's face it: you were never any good at this."

"And yet, here you are, asking me where your money is."

"And yet, here *you* are, in a well-furnished hole in the ground. You should be ashamed of yourself, frankly. A love rat? A Tinder swindler? A romance scammer? It's low-hanging fruit. The sort of thing they make Netflix documentaries about."

"All I'm doing is going on some dates."

"Uh-huh. And I'm Minnie Mouse."

"If you're besties with Marina, why don't you ask her how much money I've taken from her? I've treated her to meals, bought her flowers, given her gifts. I've kept her *very* satisfied."

"Oh, please."

"She should feel lucky. Let's face it, she's pushed three kids out of there."

"Stop being a pig."

"Just stating facts." He took a swig of his protein shake and sat down on the bed, crossing one leg over another, doing his best impression of being debonair. God, once she'd fallen for it too. "Anyway, none of what I'm doing is against the law."

"What about your fiancée?"

He looked marginally less debonair. "I don't know what you're talking about."

"The little bunny rabbit. The rich librarian."

Zander uncrossed his legs.

"Listen," he said. "I've got to make a living, just like anyone. But you . . . this is kidnapping. And assault. What are you planning to do? Are you going to kill me? Because you think you're clever, but you're not *that* clever. You will never get away with that on your own."

She waved her hand. "No. You're an utter shit, but none of us want you on our consciences. You'll be out of here in twenty-four hours, max."

"Why not now?"

"Because I'm enjoying seeing you helpless, and also because Marina and Lilah need to work through some emotions. Right now they're scared of you going to the police."

"I won't."

"It's easy for you to say that. Before you knew I was involved, you had no reason not to. But now you know that if you go to the police, I will too."

A silence.

"You wouldn't."

"Oh, I would. Seeing you behind bars would be almost worth it. But I don't think I'll need to. You don't want to destroy yourself any more than I want to destroy myself. So you'll keep quiet about your little basement vacation."

"What do you want? Why are you helping them? I know you, and it's not out of altruism."

"I wanted to ruin your plans. And I wanted you to know that I'm watching you." She came closer, so that all he could see through the hatch was her face. "But I'm warning you: when you get out of here, leave Marina and Lilah alone."

"Forget that I asked. I know *exactly* what you want from them."

"My life, my business. Stay away if you know what's good for you."

Zander laughed. "I don't think you'll get it. They'll turn against you sooner rather than later. Women always do, especially when it comes to men."

21

Marina

THE COLLARS WERE CANVAS OR leather, and they fastened with buckles or plastic clips, and you could probably remove them easily enough. Weren't there collars that had little padlocks on them? That could attach to a chain, also with a padlock maybe, and then attach to a bedpost, or . . .

Did Nana Sylvia keep her third husband captive in the bomb shelter until he died?

Or did she shoot him?

Or both?

The idea wasn't as shocking to Marina as it could have been. Her grandmother had never lived by the rules, and while she'd never imagined that Nana Sylvia's eccentricities would extend to murder . . . it was a long time ago, and maybe Barry deserved it.

This was the wrong way to think. Murder was evil, and never justified.

And yet she herself had just pushed her new boyfriend down the stairs seemingly on a whim.

"What sort of dog do you have?"

Marina jumped and came back to the present. She was in a pet shop, full of cat litter and dog treats and the bubbling of multiple aquariums. A young, friendly-looking person stood beside her, wearing a T-shirt bearing the name of the shop.

"Oh," said Marina. "I don't have a dog."

"Oh, that's okay," said the person. "I thought, since you'd been standing here for so long . . . Anyway, that's cool. Some people are just fans of collars?"

"Um."

"It's fine. I don't judge."

Right. Right. She'd been thinking about restraining the man in her basement, and this shop assistant now thought she was a housewife wanting to try a little tame BDSM. "I'd go to a sex shop for that sort of thing," Marina said.

"Well, these are probably sturdier, and pretty adjustable." The assistant pointed to a black leather collar with silver studs. "I mean if that can stand up to a Rottweiler, it's going to stand up to anything. Were you looking for anything in particular?"

"Actually, I was—I got distracted. I wonder if you can tell me, what is the noisiest pet in your shop?"

The assistant frowned, thinking. "We don't have actual dogs here. I'd contact a breeder, or a rescue center."

"Oh. I'm not ready for a dog. But do you have a parrot, maybe? A talking one?"

The possibility of a talking parrot was what had brought her to this pet shop. Or a cockatoo, or a macaw. Anything, really, that made enough noise to cover up thumps and yells from a basement.

Of course, she'd only need to cover up thumps and yells if she kept Xavier in the basement for much longer. Which she wasn't going to do.

Right?

"Is it specifically a bird you're looking for, or is it more the noise you're interested in?"

"It's the noise. My neighbors are doing a lot of construction work." Not technically a lie.

"I might know just the one."

She followed the assistant across the shop to a wall of cages, all containing small rodents. Little white mice, scratching the glass with little pink feet. Gerbils sleeping in fluffy clumps. A rat digging in a pile of sawdust. Guinea pigs squealed in a pen on the floor. And there was a rattle, a rattle, a rattle, a rattle, a thump. A rattle, a rattle, a rattle, a thump.

"What's that?" asked Marina.

"That," said the assistant, pointing to a cage, "is this hamster right here."

The hamster was tan and white, excessively fluffy, or maybe it was fat. It had a pink nose and shiny black eyes. As Marina watched, it hauled itself into its hamster wheel and ran frantically for several seconds, hard enough to rattle the wheel and the cage with its efforts. Then, abruptly, it stopped, and the momentum of the wheel made the hamster keep going, up to the apex of the spin, where gravity took over and the rodent fell, with a thump, onto the sawdust-cushioned bottom of its cage.

Then got up, shook itself, and started all over again.

"His name is Godzilla," said the assistant. "He's lovely. Very friendly. But daft as a brush. When he's not doing the wheel thing, he's gnawing on something or banging his water bottle. I have personally sold him three times. He keeps coming back."

"Godzilla," repeated Marina. "Is he okay with children?"

"Oh yeah. In fact, the only time you can really stop him from being such a brute is when you cuddle him. He loves that. But otherwise, he's a small fluffy noise nuisance." The assistant looked at the hamster fondly. "I'd have him myself, but I live in a flat with thin walls."

Marina thought of Archie and Lucy Rose's faces lighting up when they found they had a pet. She thought of all the comforting hamster-noise that would be in her kitchen. She couldn't afford a pet . . . but she had an emergency credit card, and this definitely qualified as an emergency.

"I'll take him," she said.

* * *

When she stepped out of the shop, laden with cage, food, bedding, water bottle, food dish, wheel, ball, Godzilla, and additional debt, the first person she saw was Nancy. Nancy, who had been leader of her local new moms' group when their first children were infants. Nancy who was now head of the PTA group. Nancy who had perfect children, a husband who loved her, a side business selling handmade crafts, who had posted that #GirlsNightOut pictures of mojitos, and happened to be walking by with little Jocasta in a Bugaboo at the exact same time that Marina emerged from the shop.

Nancy's eyes widened. "Marina!" she exclaimed. Marina could not tell if it was in surprise, delight, disapproval, or contempt.

Marina was *not* going to answer any questions about her new life today.

"Oh hi," she said. "I've got to go pick up the kids from my mom's. Catch up soon?"

"Definitely!" said Nancy.

Marina was already turning in the opposite direction. "Can't wait!"

Who knew it was easier to lie than to apologize?

* * *

"I'm going for a run," said Opal, meeting Marina at the door and barely glancing at the massive amounts of hamster-related stuff she was carrying. "I'll be back in a few hours. Last time I checked, he was asleep."

How quickly Xavier had become merely "he"—a person who was so powerful in their combined lives that he only needed a single pronoun for identification.

Marina and Jake used to talk about Archie like this when he was a newborn. He's hungry. He needs changing. He slept through the night. They revolved around their baby as if he were a tiny, vulnerable god.

Marina went downstairs and checked. Xavier was lying on his back on the cot, snoring lightly. The skeleton had been dumped onto the floor. The Nutella and Gummi Bear sandwich was also lying on the floor, as if he'd thrown it. Another piece of evidence that grown men were basically toddlers.

Back in the kitchen, she had set up Godzilla's cage and was performing the therapeutic task of forcing boiled potatoes through a ricer to make them completely smooth, when the doorbell went. She could barely hear it above the rattle-rattle-rattle-thump.

The shiny-faced man on her doorstop was Mr. Anderson. He didn't even wait for her to say hello before he yelled, "What's this then about you throwing rubbish into our garden?"

"Pardon?"

"You people never stop complaining. I'll have you know that we have a permit from the council. I used to be a councilor myself so I know my rights, and you can stop being a busybody, Karen!"

"My name's Marina. I introduced myself a few weeks ago and tried to give you chocolate mousse."

"It doesn't matter what your name is, I know your type, whining and whining and thinking you can have everything your way and if you don't, you resort to using my property as some sort of trash can!"

He shoved a plastic Waitrose bag at her. Mystified, Marina looked inside. It contained a variety of biscuit wrappers, mostly Oreos, and three empty and crushed cans of Monster energy drink.

"This isn't mine."

"This isn't mine," mimicked Mr. Anderson in a falsetto. "Fake news, Karen, fake news! If it isn't yours, how did it get into my garden over the fence from your house? Did UFOs drop it from space?"

"What part of your garden?"

"Over by that tree of yours. Which you are going to have to cut back, by the way. It's going to drop leaves on our new conservatory roof. You'll be hearing from the council. And if you don't stop using my garden as a dumpster, you'll be hearing from the police too!"

"I really didn't throw this in your garden," said Marina, telling the truth for maybe the first time today, but he had already fumed off. She watched him stump down her front path and through the gate. So much high blood pressure, over a little trash.

She wondered if he would talk with her differently if he knew she had pushed a man down the stairs and imprisoned him in her basement.

She thought that maybe he would be afraid of her.

That should make her feel terrible, but actually, it made her feel powerful.

She brought the bag of rubbish round the side of the house to the trash cans and separated out the recyclables. Then she investigated the garden. The tree that Mr. Anderson was talking about was a horse chestnut, an elderly giant with obligingly low limbs. Many years ago, Nana Sylvia had paid a man to build a ladder against its trunk and a platform in its branches. She and her brother used to climb it in the summers and use the platform as a clubhouse until their parents caught them and told Marina that girls don't climb trees.

Marina gazed up at its lush foliage and sturdy limbs. It had a trunk like an elephant's leg. From up in its branches, you could see all over the neighborhood and a wide glittering swathe of the Thames. One day, Archie would climb it, and so would Lucy Rose, and so would Ewan, and she would cheer them on.

She wasn't going to trim it. Fuck the Andersons.

Something crunched under her foot. Looking down, she identified it immediately: the partly crushed remains of half an Oreo.

She tested the ladder. It was solid enough, so she climbed up and up, through the branches until she reached the platform and stood up on it. It was empty. Searching, she saw something that might be biscuit crumbs, but she couldn't be certain.

What she did notice, however, was something she'd never cared about when she was up on this platform as a child, when she was much more interested in the river and the other houses around her. From up here, if you stood in the middle of the platform and slightly to the right and faced the house where she now lived, you could see straight into the back windows. Including the kitchen, and her bedroom.

22

Lilah

EVIL ALICE WAS AT THE front desk, so Lilah didn't check out any books and gave her a wide berth as she left the library. Her paycheck for this month had come through into her otherwise-emptied bank account, so she had some income. She intended to call an Uber to get her to Richmond, but she had a lot to think about, so instead she walked westward along the high street.

It felt good to walk: glancing into shop windows, being among people who didn't notice her or know any of her problems. It kept her body busy so her mind could travel. She hadn't walked anywhere since that time at the bookshop when someone had followed her.

Some of the things she had just read had given her a different perspective on that event. Now, she wondered if maybe it had just been paranoia that had made her think she was being followed. Paranoia planted there by Zachary, masquerading as concern and love, but with the intent of trying to control her.

Her left hand felt light without the big engagement ring. Something about having it gone made her mind freer, too. Three days ago, she never would have said that Zachary was controlling. But one of the books she'd devoured in the library had been about coercive control. She'd picked it up off the shelf thinking that it would exonerate Zachary, give her some arguments to convince the other women that he wasn't as bad as Opal said. She'd expected (or rather, desperately hoped for) a checklist in which exactly zero items matched the behavior of the man she'd fallen in love with.

But then she read about love bombing. And she thought about all the gifts, all the flattery, all the ways that Zachary had portrayed himself as being exactly the right person for her, all the ways he said he'd keep her safe, all the ways that he made her feel pretty and smart. All the times that she had thought to herself, with delight and no suspicion: *He's too good to be true.*

That wasn't unusual, though, surely? Novels said that was what love was: something precious and over-the-top, something to make you feel wonderful, something you could hardly believe was happening to you.

He'd said he wanted to protect her, and that was what she wanted. So she'd thought it was love when he rang and texted her dozens of times a day to check on her, so often that sometimes she couldn't concentrate. When he chose all the restaurants they went to, the hotel she was staying at, when he said he would pay for everything so she wouldn't have to worry, when he wouldn't allow her to speak to the police without him, when he kept her from speaking with her father's oldest friends at his funeral, when he steered her away from Jimiyu and her other library colleagues who'd come to support her, when he said she shouldn't go back to work.

That was not protecting her. That was isolating her, and controlling her time, and restricting her finances, and keeping her afraid.

Meanwhile he'd been out with Marina and who knew who else, spending Lilah's money and lying. And she had completely fallen for it: hiding in her luxury hotel, looking behind her, carrying pepper spray, watching everyone with suspicion.

Lilah stopped abruptly in the middle of the sidewalk. She'd gone to those elaborate lengths to avoid a stranger in a hat, someone who was probably minding his own business. She must have looked ridiculous.

She cringed.

And then she thought: Hold on a second. If I'm ashamed about this, if I'm afraid to confront it, he has won.

Lilah flagged down a cab and told the driver to take her to Charing Cross Road.

At Cuthbert & Binding, the same bookseller she'd embarrassed herself in front of was behind the register again. Lilah felt a stab of humiliation, but at the same time, the bookseller saw her, and his face lit up into a crooked smile that was actually rather lovely.

"Hi!" he said to her with a little awkward wave. "You came back!"

"I did," she said, approaching the register. Maybe it was the beautiful soothing sight and scent of books, or maybe it was the bookseller's greeting, or maybe it was her own determination, but her discomfort melted away. Well, most of it. "I have money this time."

"I've got your books waiting for you. I was hoping you'd come back for them. Just a sec, I'll be right back." He hurried off through a door behind the till and Lilah had a chance to look around. Since she'd been here last time, many of the books had been taken off the shelves and heaped onto tables marked with large "SALE" signs. She browsed them, and in the short time before the bookseller returned, she'd picked out an illustrated history of London's sewer system and a novel about circus geeks.

"Here they are," said the bookseller, holding up her original stack, and then: "I think you're going to need a tote bag. These ones are seventy-five percent off." He nodded to a display of green canvas bags with the shop name emblazoned on them.

"You're having a big sale."

"Yeah. Stock liquidation." He began scanning her books through again. "The landlord's raised the rent four times in the past two years. I've got to look for a new job, or maybe finally finish my PhD."

"Oh no! I mean—about the bookshop closing, not about the PhD. This was the first bookshop I ever visited when I was a little girl."

He shook his head. "Profit margins are cut to the bone for independent booksellers. It's hard to compete with supermarkets or online retailers, because they can slash prices. We do okay here, but the owners can't keep up with the overhead. Anyway, I'm glad you came back in time."

"Me too." She put four tote bags on her pile. "Thank you for saving my books for me."

"Absolutely, any time."

Despite the sad news about the bookshop, and despite her heavy burden of books, she felt buoyant as she left the shop. Before hailing a taxi to get her to Marina's house, she went into a nearby Tesco to pick up a few items that she realized, now, were necessary.

*   *   *

She arrived at Marina's house at the same time that Opal ran up from the other direction. She had clearly been jogging because her skin was sheened lightly with perspiration, but she didn't have a hair out of place and her lipstick was perfect. Lilah was pretty sure that if she got close enough to smell Opal, she wouldn't smell of sweat but of some expensive skin lotion. She probably didn't even need to use a filter on her social media pictures.

Marina had clearly been watching for them because she opened the door as soon as they set foot on the doorstep. Without consulting, they all went straight to the kitchen in the back of the house. The room was steamy, various pots and pans were in use, and there was a large mixing bowl on the table. There was also a terrible rattling noise.

"What's that?" asked Opal.

Marina, who was wearing a white apron, picked up the bowl and started mixing vigorously, so hard that the muscles stood out on her forearms. "Aligot," she replied, a little out of breath. "It's a specialty of the Auvergne region—a mixture of mashed potatoes and Tomme fraîche, but that's impossible to find here, so I've used mozzarella. I haven't made it in years because my ex-husband said it was too fancy and he always wanted plain old shepherd's pie. You have to rice the potatoes until they're completely smooth, and then beat them until the mixture becomes stretchy." She lifted up the spoon, to show them a long rubbery string of white. It looked disgusting but smelled delicious. "It's absolutely full of carbs and saturated fats. It tastes gorgeous. Z will hate it."

"Fancy thing to call cheesy potatoes," said Opal. "I meant that terrible rattling noise."

"Oh. That's Godzilla. You don't even notice him after a while."

Lilah doubted that.

"That hamster has a death wish," said Opal.

"I sort of like the company. He requires very little of me aside from a few seeds." She moved to the chopping board and used a very large knife to attack some vegetables. "I think someone might be watching my house."

"Did Zachary tell you that?" asked Lilah. "To make you paranoid?"

"No. He's been asleep. I found evidence that someone was in one of the trees in the back of the house. There's a tree house there. It could have been some neighborhood kids."

Opal immediately pulled down the window shades and went out the back door.

"She's not very tactful, is she?" Marina sighed. "How's your day been? Do you want a cup of tea?"

"I've got a better idea." Lilah put one of her tote bags on the table and pulled out one of the bottles of tequila she'd bought at Tesco. "Are you child-free tonight?"

Marina gravitated to the tequila like a moth to a flame. "Yes, they're with my parents. I haven't had a shot of tequila since I was at college. I've got limes in the fridge."

"And salt," said Lilah.

"And Nana Sylvia has a collection of shot glasses somewhere."

When Opal came back in, the other two were busy arranging glasses and slicing limes. "There's no sign of anyone in the tree, but let's keep the blinds closed in case. Are we having a party?"

"We have had a traumatic couple of days," said Lilah. "I thought we should get drunk."

Opal looked Lilah up and down. Lilah steeled herself for Opal to say something mean. Finally, she said, "Good idea, Bunny."

"Don't call me Bunny, please," said Lilah, bravely.

"Okay." Opal pulled out a chair and cracked open one of the bottles.

It had been that easy?

"I've been doing a lot of thinking today," said Lilah. "And the thing is that we're stuck in this situation together but we don't know anything about each other, which is why we're fighting. We have to stop fighting with each other and find some common ground. Other than Zachary."

"At least we can get shitfaced, I'm sure that's something we all agree on," said Opal. She poured a hefty slosh of tequila into each glass. "I don't usually drink because it gives me hot flushes. But fuck it."

"What if Xavier wakes up though?" asked Marina, pausing with a lime wedge halfway to her mouth. "I don't want to get drunk and fall down the stairs or something."

"He won't. I drugged him." Opal licked the back of her hand and shook salt on it.

"You what?"

"I put a couple sleeping pills in a protein shake."

Lilah put down her glass. "But that's against the rules that we agreed on."

"I know. But seriously, Marina has enough to worry about without being at Zander's beck and call and making him fancy French mashed potatoes. I thought I'd give her a break. And also, the more he's awake, the angrier he's going to get. It's better if he has a nice nap. Cheers."

Lilah and Marina exchanged a look, and then downed their tequila shots, too.

"So, that's the plan?" Opal reached for the bottle again. "Drink and bond, somehow? You're going to have to explain this to me. I don't hang out with women that much these days. Or people in general, actually."

"I bought the tequila because I thought we could play Truth."

"I thought it was Truth or Dare," said Marina.

"I don't like dares that much. But I think truth is really important."

"Huh." Opal poured them each another shot, and they all sat around the table. "What are we supposed to tell the truth about, specifically?"

"Well. We can start by saying one nice true thing about each other. But it has to be true."

Opal grimaced. "I'm not good at nice."

"Good idea," said Marina. "Okay, I'll start. Lilah, you have a really beautiful speaking voice. You could be on the radio. And Opal, you are very good at ordering people around."

"Is that a compliment?"

"I meant it as one. I'm not even good at ordering my own children around."

"This feels so fake," said Opal. "Randomly giving other people compliments without wanting something off them."

"The more you practice being kind to people, the easier it gets," said Lilah. "That's what my dad used to say, and he had to practice a lot because he was a mailman. Marina, I think you are stunning. You are the kind of person I always wanted to look like. You just seem so comfortable in your body, which is something I've never been able to be."

"Really?" Marina sat up a little straighter. "I didn't think I came across that way."

"You do. I wish you would give me some fashion tips. Like how do you know how to wear a scarf like that?" She gestured at the green and pink patterned silk scarf that was holding up Marina's hair.

"Oh, it just takes practice. You would look great in this one. Here, try." Marina pulled off the scarf and put it around Lilah's neck, tying it in a loose knot. "It really brings out the color of your eyes."

"Thanks," said Lilah. She took a deep breath and turned to Opal. "It is quite hard for me to say something nice about you because you have been mean to me. But I do actually appreciate that you have taken the trouble to tell Marina and me the truth about Zachary. You didn't have to do that, and maybe we never would have found out until it was too late. So thank you."

"Is it my turn now?" Opal pursed her lips. "I need to do another shot first."

They fortified themselves with salt, tequila, and lime. Opal put her glass down with a bang.

"Okay. Here goes. Marina. I think you are probably a great mother. You seem to always think of your kids first. And you feel so guilty about pushing your boyfriend down the stairs that you bought them a fucking hamster. And Lilah . . ." She took a deep breath, as if this were difficult for her. "I am really quite envious of you."

"Envious?"

"Yes. Because you talk about love so easily. And you seem to actually feel it, even after being betrayed. And when you talk about your dad, you—it's as if he hung the moon for you. I've never felt like that about anyone. But you have, and that makes you very, very lucky. I would give anything to feel something so real and genuine, just once."

Lilah blinked. "Wow. I wasn't expecting . . . wow."

"Yeah," said Marina. "I sort of feel that my compliments were inadequate now."

"Ah, well, apparently practice helps." Opal reached for the bottle, and Marina brought the bowl of aligot to the table along with another of salad with a mustardy, garlicky dressing. She served them all a hefty pile of both. Lilah took a bite of the potato and had to sit for a moment in reverent silence. She had never imagined that mere cheesy potatoes could taste like this.

"This," said Opal after a while, "is really fucking good."

"I know," said Marina.

Lilah took another forkful and in the middle of chewing it, she laughed, choked, swallowed, and laughed again. "I just realized: if this were a book, we've just passed the Bechdel test."

"The what?"

"It's a system for measuring representations of women in the media," Opal told her. "A story passes the Bechdel test if it's got two or more women, who are named in the story, and who talk to each other about something other than a man."

"This is the first time we've actually talked about each other," said Lilah. "We've been talking about Zachary."

"Well," said Opal, loading her fork with salad, "there's a lot to be said about that bastard."

"We have to talk about men," said Marina. "They're everywhere. It's a man's world. They make all the laws and commit all the crimes. *Most* of the crimes," she amended. "If we don't talk about them, we can't work out how to live with them."

"But we need to talk about ourselves too," said Opal. "Otherwise, how do we know how to live with ourselves?"

It was the moment. Lilah put down her fork. Her throat was tight, but that was never going to change unless she did something about it. She picked up the tequila bottle, poured herself a shot and drank it down in one.

"I think I need to tell you a story about a man," she said. "His name was Darren Pine."

23

SEVEN YEARS BEFORE

"HE'S OVER THERE." BEV NUDGED Lilah's arm and pointed across the student union to where Darren Pine sat, next to a group but not part of it. Other people had been talking to him, a whole crowd after his performance, but they had all melted away and Darren was alone. The flashing lights lit up his face and hair in colored patches.

"Talk to him," said Gabby.

"I wouldn't know what to say." Lilah hung back, clutching her bottle of cider, but Bev pushed her forward.

"What are you going to do, stare at him from afar for three years? Go on, be brave."

So Lilah crossed the room, walking in front of the stage where students were clearing up after the open mic night, in preparation for the DJ set that would follow. It felt like miles, but it was only a few feet, and then she was standing right in front of Darren Pine: poet, singer, tragic hero, and the most beautiful man in her class. She'd never been so close to him before.

He shook his fringe out of his soulful eyes and looked up at her. Lilah's heart hammered and the bottle of cider was slippery in her hand. She glanced back at Gabby and Bev, who gave her a thumbs up.

"Hi," she said. "I loved your song."

"Thanks."

"We're in the same Introduction to Creative Writing class."

"Oh."

He didn't seem inclined to say anything else, but he was still looking at her, so she stammered, "I loved the lyrics. Were they about . . . I heard that your girlfriend . . ."

. . . *Is dead. I heard that your girlfriend died before you came to university.* She couldn't say that, could she? Even though he'd already announced it in their writing seminar?

"They were about Aurora, yeah. Everything I write is about Aurora. So I remember her forever, because if I remember her, she will never die."

"That's beautiful."

"Thanks."

"I . . ." Her throat was dry. "I actually can relate. My mom died when I was three. She got pneumonia. I don't really remember her, but my dad and I talk a lot about her so that we both remember."

Darren kept looking at her and she couldn't tell if it was with sympathy, or if it was contempt that she had offered up the death of a parent as an equivalent to the rawness and beauty of his pain. It had been sixteen years ago, after all, and she had only been a child; whereas he had lost the love of his life only months before.

He didn't speak and she swallowed hard and opened her mouth to say *anyway, goodbye,* when he beat her to it by asking, "Do you want to get out of here?"

As they walked across the campus in the dark, the thumping noise of the union fading behind them, Darren lit a cigarette and told her about the meaning of his lyrics and Lilah listened hard. Everyone knew that Darren Pine was going to be famous. He had that glow about him, that center of stillness when he entered a room. Lilah wasn't surprised that he'd never noticed her before; she could barely believe that he had noticed her now. He was a tall shadow holding a brilliant point of light.

They got to his dorm, and then to his room, and she sat on his bed as he talked and rolled another cigarette, and then he was pushing her down onto the mattress.

"Oh," she said. "No, not this."

"You said you could relate," he said, and he rolled on top of her and did not stop. He put his hand around her neck and he whispered, "You said you understood pain."

And then he put his other hand over her mouth.

He was a poet who wrote about love and how sacred it was, how it should never be forgotten, and Lilah lay underneath him, holding her breath, and she could only think about how she wanted this to be finished so that she could forget.

Afterwards, he stood up, buckled his belt, and went to the window to smoke his cigarette. He didn't look at her.

The walk back to the student union was freezing and seemed to take twice as long. Inside the music thumped and the colored lights swam. Lilah saw her abandoned cider bottle on the table where Darren had been sitting. She saw Gabby and Bev dancing near the stage; they'd been joined by her other roommate, Elena. They spotted her at once.

"What happened?" Bev, all grin, squealed over the music. So Lilah told them, and they stopped dancing.

She had met Bev and Gabby and Elena on the first day of freshman week and they had eaten together, studied together, watched television together, read, and confided secrets. She thought she knew them well.

Then Bev's face twisted.

And Elena said, "You're lying to make yourself sound more interesting."

And Gabby said, "Why would *Darren Pine* need to do something like that?"

24

THERE WAS A LONG SILENCE after Lilah's story. Even Godzilla paused.

Lilah accepted the new drink that Opal poured silently for her, but she didn't take a sip.

"I don't know why Darren Pine would do something like that," she said. "I still don't know."

"Did you tell anybody else?" Opal asked.

"No. Not my dad, not anyone. No one was going to believe me. I only had one small bruise, and it was on the side of my neck, it could have been caused by anything. But I couldn't leave my bedroom. I didn't feel like myself anymore. So I . . . disappeared. I tried to stay small. I went home at Christmas and told my dad I wanted to live at home and study in London instead."

"Jesus," said Opal. "Should we track him down?"

"No. This was a long time ago, so. And worse things have happened since. This is the first time I've said his name in eight years, though. Darren Pine. But what my friends did, somehow, felt even worse. Sometimes I think . . . if someone, one person, said they believed me, then I could forget about it, you know? Then I could stop feeling his hands on my neck."

"I believe you," said Marina.

"So do I," said Opal. "It's not an unusual story, either. That's the hell of it. That such a horror story is so normal for so many women."

"Right," Marina said. "In the first restaurant I worked at, none of the female staff were allowed to be alone with the sommelier. He never got fired. And the restaurant was owned by a woman."

"Oh, honey," said Opal. "The stories I could tell."

"You really believe me?" Lilah looked between them.

"We really do."

Marina reached over and squeezed Lilah's hand. To her surprise, Lilah squeezed back.

"Why did you tell us?" Marina asked.

"I'm tired of being frightened."

"I'll drink to that," said Opal. It was probably not a good idea, but Opal slopped tequila into their glasses, and more into Lilah's, which was pretty full already. They all drank solemnly.

The hamster started running again. Rattle-rattle-rattle-thump.

"I am going to be so hungover tomorrow," said Marina.

"So," said Lilah, taking a deep breath and adjusting the scarf around her neck, "what are we going to do about Zachary?"

"We need to let him go," said Marina. "I can't teach my kids about being good people when I've got a man held captive in my basement. Also, I miss them, and I want them to come home."

"I told him we'd let him go tomorrow morning," said Opal.

They stared at her.

"You talked with him?"

"Yeah. It was not a pleasure."

"But you made the rule."

"Made it, and broke it. Sorry, not sorry. Someone had to strike a deal with him. I promise you, though: I have googled *nothing*."

"When we let him free, won't he go to the police?" asked Lilah. "He'll want to punish us."

"He won't. He's not going to say a word. He's going to get the hell out of town."

"How do you know?"

"I just do. I understand how he works."

"Does anyone need more carbs?" Marina spooned more aligot onto the plates.

"Zander is really going to hate this," said Opal. "Save *lots* for him."

"I don't want to be someone who hates men, though," said Lilah. "There are lots of good men out there."

"I have yet to see it," Opal said, chewing. "But I don't like people generally."

"My dad was a good man. Jimiyu, he's the head librarian—he's a very kind man."

"I hope I'm going to raise my sons to be good men," said Marina.

"So we're going to let Zachary go?" said Lilah. "Definitely, tomorrow?" There was a thump from downstairs. Marina winced.

"Definitely," said Opal.

25

Lilah

LILAH SAT ON THE EDGE of the guest room bed, waiting for the first rays of sunshine to peek through the window. This room was a small one in the back of Marina's house, probably a former servant's bedroom, nestled under the eaves. In the end, they'd drunk most of the bottle of tequila and Marina had insisted that they both stay over. Lilah had lain awake, listening to the sounds of the old house around her, the sound of pigeons shuffling on the roof, the distant rattle of Godzilla in the kitchen below.

She felt clear-headed—much more clear-headed than she should feel.

They believed her. These two women who she'd just met. They believed her. They had even offered to track Darren down. No questions, no doubts, no gaslighting—it had been instant, one hundred percent support.

She could stop being scared.

She could do what she needed to do.

It was light enough now that Lilah could get up, retrieve her bum bag and Marina's silk scarf from where they lay beside the bed, put them on, and slip barefoot and quiet out of the room. The other bedroom doors were open; she peeked inside. Marina lay in the center of a king-sized bed in the primary bedroom, wearing only bra, underwear, and socks. She was snoring softly. The next three rooms clearly belonged to the children: one neat, one chaotic, one with a cot and a rocking chair. In the guest room at the front of the house, Opal was also fast asleep, still in her workout gear, with the pillow beside her slightly reddened with lipstick marks.

They'd said they had stories like hers, that had happened to them or to other people that they knew. Somehow, she'd always thought that other women, those who were attractive or popular or confident, moved through life more easily than she did.

But maybe they didn't. Maybe every woman had a hidden shadow self that was full of shame and fear. Not because they deserved it, but because it had been imposed upon them.

Was that why Bev and Gabby and Elena hadn't believed her? They saw their shame embodied in her shame, and it was easier for them to deny it?

She went down the grand staircase, trailing her fingers along the glossy banister, watching them move through the shards of colored light cast through the stained-glass window over the front door. In the kitchen, the detritus of their night still littered the table: plates, glasses, wilted salad, an emptied box of chocolate truffles. There was a strong scent of tequila. The hamster was running around its wheel, as usual. She found a small carrot in the fridge and poked it through the bars of its cage. Godzilla stopped, sniffed, scampered to it, stood on his back legs, and started gnawing away, stowing chunks of carrot in his cheeks.

With the sound of the hamster wheel stopped, Lilah could hear a distinct thumping and muttering through the baby monitor. Zachary was awake.

She unbolted the door to the cellar and carefully made her way down. She was not one for breaking rules, but did the rules even count anymore, now that Opal had broken several?

The thumping got louder the closer she got to the secret door behind it. She'd never operated the catch before, so it took a little fumbling before she got it (this was disappointing; she would have thought that fiction would have prepared her better for discovering hidden passageways and alternate universes). As soon as the shelf slid to one side, Zachary started yelling as well as pounding.

"Opal!" he yelled. "Marina! Hey! What fucking time is it! This toilet stinks!"

This was the first time she'd heard him speaking since his phone call two evenings ago, when he'd rung to tell her he was working late. Of course she now knew this had been an excuse to come here and see Marina instead.

The fury in his voice made her cringe. It drove home that the literature-loving, attentive, considerate man she'd believed she was engaged to was actually a fragile shell disguising the real Zachary, an illusion that could be shattered at any moment. It was only luck and timing, and probably his design, that had stopped him from revealing his true self to her.

"Zachary?" she said softly. She didn't have to fake the tremble in her voice. "Are you okay?"

"Lilah! Oh, thank God! I need to talk to you, sweetheart! Please open the door!"

She opened her bum bag and closed her hand around what was inside. "I have to stay quiet," she said. "I don't want the others to hear me."

"Are you going to let me out, darling? I knew you wouldn't listen to the poisonous things that those other women told you about me. You're so faithful and true. I can explain everything. Just give me a chance, please."

"I want to talk first. Can you come right up to the door? I'll open the hatch."

"Anything, my love."

"Are you there? Come right up close."

"I'm here. Oh, I can't wait to see your sweet face."

"I can't wait to see yours." Her words were truer than he knew. She put her hand on the hatch, ready to open it. With the other, she held up one of the two phones she had found in his jacket on the night Marina had pushed him down the stairs and slipped into her bum bag when no one was watching.

She'd taken them initially because she didn't trust Marina or Opal. Normally she would never look at someone else's phone. It was like snooping through their underwear drawer. But it was the only thing she could think of to do at the time that might give her evidence that Zachary was guilty or innocent of what the other two accused him of.

Now, she didn't need that evidence. She believed Marina and Opal. But she was still curious.

She slid the hatch open. Zachary's face filled it, close enough for her to see the stubble that had grown on his usually clean-shaven cheeks and chin.

"Darling," he said.

His phone recognized his face and unlocked.

"I think someone's moving around upstairs," said Lilah. "I'll be back soon."

She shut and bolted the hatch again, slid the secret door shut, and ran back upstairs to the kitchen, where she perched on a chair and began scrolling through Zachary's phone, keeping one ear open for any signs of anyone stirring other than Godzilla.

She'd been surprised to find not one but two phones in his jacket pocket, both switched off. One was his normal phone, a black Galaxy. She recognized it but in truth, she'd only rarely seen it. Zachary used to say he hated nothing more than people who were on their phones all the time. He would always turn off his phone when they were together, though he texted her often when they were apart. Now, she could see both of those actions as part of his pattern of control and deception.

The second phone was an iPhone. Both were the latest models—Zachary wouldn't have anything less, even for a burner phone, which is what she suspected this second one was. Both worked on facial recognition, but she knew she'd only have enough time to open one of them before he saw what she was doing, so she'd chosen the burner. She braced herself to find soppy messages to Marina, or maybe yet another woman. Online dating apps with multiple profiles. Or God forbid: sexting.

What she found instead was forty-six missed calls from someone called S.

There were no voicemails or messages from this person. There were only two text messages on the phone, both of them from the network provider confirming a pay-as-you-go contract. When she looked back at the call log, the only completed calls registered were to and from this same number, identified only with S. They went back about six months. At first they were infrequent, about one a week, only lasting a few minutes each. Then there were a few longer conversations in May, and a spate of frequent short phone calls in June.

With a chill, she saw that the days with the most recently answered calls were June 12 and 13. The day her dad was murdered, and the day after.

"These are the worst days of my life and you're spending them talking with another woman?" muttered Lilah, stabbing at the phone with her finger. She remembered that Zachary had excused himself several times the day after her father's death, to fetch her drinks and food that she didn't ask for or want. Each time he'd come back with his sympathetic face and his supportive arms and assured her that he loved her, that they would get through this together.

She felt sick.

The forty-six missed calls were all since this Thursday night. Little did S know that her perfect boyfriend was in the company of three other women.

She should tell the others. Whoever this S was, she deserved to know that she was being conned and that her boyfriend was potentially violent. But it was a tricky thing to do via phone. Maybe they should set up another meeting. Maybe the three of them should do more digging, look for more victims. After they set Zachary free, they could set up a support group or something. They couldn't go to the police, obviously, but there were other ways of stopping someone from victimizing others. Look at the MeToo movement. When women started speaking openly about the men who abused them, the men weren't able to get away with it anymore.

She thought about what S might be like. She was most likely on her own. Zachary seemed to pick vulnerable women. Whoever she was, she was probably frantic with worry. Zachary had disappeared without a trace for days. S must have arranged to meet up with him on one of those days, and then he didn't turn up, without so much as a phone call to explain why. If it were Lilah, she'd be going nuts. She'd picture him dead in a ditch, unconscious in a hospital. (She would, before this, never have pictured him trapped in an underground bunker.) This S might have called all the hospitals to check. She might have called the police to report him missing. The sleepless nights, the overwhelming anxiety. Forty-six calls!

It was wrong to impersonate someone else but not when it was for a good cause, right? Lilah quickly keyed in a text message:

```
I'm okay. Don't worry. I'll be in touch soon.
```

She considered signing with a Z but maybe he was using a different name with S, one that started with P or something (P for Penis Head). So she added a small lower case *x*, like Zachary sometimes did in his messages to her, and sent it.

Almost immediately, the phone rang in her hand with a call from S.

She shouldn't answer it. She shouldn't answer it. She *should not* answer it.

She answered it and held it up to her ear without saying anything.

"I appreciate the sentiment, but cute text messages with kisses are not what I'm looking for."

To her surprise, the voice on the other end was not female. Instead, it was a deep male voice, rough in the throat, with a strong south London accent.

"You said I'd have my money last week," he continued. "I remember it well. *I'll definitely get it to you, I swear on my life, mate.*"

The man did a remarkably good impression of Zachary's voice: smooth, charming, confident. Then he went back to his rasp.

"I know you have obligations, but don't we all. I, for example, have a bloody school bill to pay. You agreed, twenty-five grand before the job was done, fifty grand after. I've done my part, I took all the risks while you sat pretty. Now I want my money."

Lilah couldn't breathe. What? Why did Zachary owe—

"Lost for words? That's not like you. Listen, you understand, business is business. If I don't get my fifty grand by five o'clock tonight, it's going up to seventy-five. I've got a reputation, you know? I can't be seen to do business with people who mock me. Where would that get me, eh? My entire reputation is built on respect. I can't exactly advertise, with what I do."

Lilah's heart felt as if it had stopped beating. A loan shark? A drug dealer? What was Zachary mixed up in?

"And mate, it's hard for me to say this, it goes against my nature, but a reminder. I do not do this job for fun. You think I like it? I do not. I don't know what that guy did to you, but to me, he looked like an old man playing with a train set."

A million years passed.

Lilah was a stone.

"And I'm guessing you don't want to end up the same place he did," rumbled S. "It's rude to threaten, and I wouldn't take any pleasure in it, so I'm just saying. A word to the wise. Fifty grand, five o'clock, the place we agreed."

He hung up.

26

THERE WAS ONE THING ABOUT Lilah Nightingale that nobody could deny: when she wanted to research something, she researched it thoroughly.

That was why when she stood in front of the secret door, one hour and seventeen minutes later, she felt no doubt at all. Her heart rate was slightly accelerated, but it wasn't because of what she was about to do, or why she was about to do it, or how.

She felt exactly as she had when she selected the numbers for that final lottery ticket that she'd bought. She always used the same numbers, had for years, a combination of her birthday, her dad's birthday, and her mother's—but that morning at her local newsstand's just down the street from the bungalow in Sidcup, making the same polite inquiries about the owner Jay's family, there was something in the air that was just *right*. A feeling that everything fitted together like a puzzle, that some convergence of the air and land and light was exactly how it had been waiting to be. It was the same feeling she got when she walked into Cuthbert & Bindings bookshop, and when she arranged the book club stacks perfectly at the library.

In short: she was doing not only the right thing, but the only thing that it was possible for her, in a world of infinite possibilities, to do.

"Zachary, honey?" she said through the door. "I'm back. The others aren't with me. Are you awake?"

"Lilah!" She heard his voice from a distance, and then closer. "Darling! Have you come to set me free?"

"Yes, I have," she said. Unlike when she'd spoken with him before, her voice didn't tremble at all. "But before I do, I need to ask you something important."

She opened the hatch. He was standing close to it, though not as close as he had last time, and his face was turned a little to the side. He'd seen the trick she played with the phone last time, and he didn't want her to do it again.

"I'm sorry," she said. "I had to check your phone. I hated to do it, I know it's rude, but I had to. I needed to know if everything that Marina and Opal have told me is true."

"It's not," said Zachary, fervently. "I can explain everything. Those bitches are lying. They've got some sort of vendetta. They've set me up and then stuck me in this place, God knows why. I think they might be after your money. If I could get out, I could sort this."

"Yes, I believe that you have an explanation for everything."

"You and I still have a chance. We can start over, forget all this happened. Start planning our wedding properly! And darling, I'm not a superstitious man . . . I'd be honored if you'd let me come dress shopping with you. What do you think?"

"I don't care much about dresses," said Lilah, almost dreamily. "What I do care about is this. Come a little closer, Zachary. I need to ask you that question."

He came closer. The Peppa Pig Band-Aid had come loose on one side and was hanging free. He wasn't wearing glasses, she noticed. That was another lie.

"Anything," he said. "I'm an open book, darling. Anything you want to know, just ask me."

"Did you pay a man to kill my father?"

He opened his mouth to reply, but Lilah saw the answer in his face before he could speak a word. It was something different than she had seen there before, something darker, uncoated with sugar, something avaricious and cunning, coiling, and hungry for control.

The truth.

With steady hands she raised one of the pair of eighteenth-century antique dueling pistols, cocked and loaded, packed and primed with shot and powder, every working part carefully oiled. She held the pistol with both her hands, arms outstretched, aiming through the hatch.

She tightened her finger on the engraved silver trigger and discharged the pistol directly into the middle of his face.

Lilah had never fired a gun of any kind before, not even a water pistol, and did not expect the enormous noise, or the sparks, or the way the gun kicked her arms backwards and upwards, or the burning sensation of powder on her hands, or the strong scent of sulfur.

But she didn't really notice any of these things, or not much, because her senses were overwhelmed by the sight of Zachary's head exploding in what felt like slow motion. Flesh scattered, blood spattered, an eye seemed to dissolve. Peppa Pig was no more.

A piece of his scalp lifted right off his skull, hair attached, and waved an obscene goodbye.

Lilah had time to see all of this in the never-ending second before Zachary's body collapsed backwards, leaving a red mist in the air where his head had used to be.

She sat on the floor. And waited for her friends . . . because what were friends, after all, but people who would understand when you murdered someone?

27

Opal

IN OPAL'S DREAMS, IT WAS Sunday morning, and she was in one of the village halls where her father held his services. Roof of corrugated iron, walls the color of cigarette smoke, cobwebs drifting like guilty thoughts from the ceiling. Her father was in front of the room on a stage made of milk crates and boards.

"Down on your knees!" he thundered at her.

She did not want to. The floor was hard and strewn with sawdust, and her knees were bare beneath her scratchy skirt, her Sunday best.

"Sinner!" her father roared. "The sky will fall upon you! Repent, or you shall be damned!"

"I didn't mean to," said Opal, kneeling down so the boards dug into her skin. She was a little girl of course, but she was speaking of things that were yet to happen, sins that she had not yet committed but she would, she would.

"Useless," said her father. But he had stopped shouting. His voice rolled over her like honey. This was how he reeled them in: with the forgiveness and the love, the promises of heaven that he snatched away when you were not worthy. And no one was ever worthy. "Whoever sows to please their flesh, from the flesh will reap destruction."

His voice had changed again. She twisted her neck, looked up, and the figure towering above her was Zander. He was grinning, but the glint in his eyes was dangerous as he drew back one booted foot and aimed at her ribs.

"You think you'll win," he said, "but you're going to lo—"

And then the roof fell on them with an almighty bang.

*   *   *

Opal bolted upright in bed, the noise reverberating in her ears. It took a moment before she recognized where she was: the white-painted guest room at Marina's house. Her tongue was stuck to the dry roof of her mouth and her head felt as if it had a spike through it.

Marina appeared in the doorway in her underwear, hair wild. "What was that?" she gasped.

"You heard it too?" Opal glanced upwards, but the ceiling was intact. "Where's Lilah?"

They rushed downstairs. The plates, glasses and cutlery had all been cleared from the kitchen table. In their place sat the box of dueling pistols, open. One pistol was missing.

"Oh shit," said Opal.

The scent of burning and gunpowder were quite clear, even on the stairs going down to the cellar. And another scent: sticky, cloying. Burned flesh.

Lilah was sitting on the floor in front of the shelter, dueling pistol in her hand. She looked shell-shocked.

"What did you do?" cried Marina. "Are you okay? Why are your hands all black? Did the gun explode? How did it explode?"

She knelt by Lilah while Opal looked through the hatch. She hoped that she would find Zander staring back at her, complaining about carbohydrates, but somehow she doubted it.

Instead, it was a scene from a horror film. Prone body lying on the floor. Blood. Skull. Hair.

She didn't want to look too closely. But she couldn't look away, either.

Lilah had shot him in the head.

The articulated skeleton was lying on its back next to Zander, grinning at the ceiling, its white bones covered in his blood. Ironically, it looked more human than he did, because its face was still intact.

"What is it?" Marina said. "What happened?"

"Fuck," said Opal. It was the only thing she could think of. She closed the hatch. She thought she might be sick. She could smell the blood. And scorched hair. And the brains. Were those brains she could smell?

She had seen dead bodies before. She had dealt with them. But this wasn't a body. This . . . was carnage.

She swallowed down bile. She saw Zander's body behind her lids when she blinked.

Marina stood up. "I need to see."

"Maybe steel yourself first," said Opal, shakily.

"I've given birth vaginally three times and had an episiotomy all three times, I've seen plenty of blood."

Still, she took a deep breath before she opened the hatch and looked in. She screamed, staggered back and sat down hard on the floor next to Lilah.

"Oh my god oh my god what did you *do*? *What have we done?*"

28

"I SHOT HIM," SAID LILAH, dreamily.

"Why did you do that?"

"Calm down," said Opal. Strangely, she did not feel panicked, which was directly opposite to how she'd felt the last time she found a dead person. Of course this time, someone else had done the killing.

"We were going to let him go!" cried Marina. She buried her head in her hands and began to cry. "This was all going to be over."

"It's a change of plan." Opal touched the barrel of the dueling pistol with the toe of her shoe. "Did you use this?" Lilah nodded. "Is he dead?"

"If he's not, he's going to need a lot of plastic surgery." Opal crouched down beside the other two women. "Marina, try to pull yourself together."

"I could see his brains," sobbed Marina. "They were . . . they were spattered . . ."

"On the bright side," said Opal, "I guess we have proof now that Zander did have the equipment to think with something other than his dick."

"Did I really kill him?"

"You really did."

"Good," Lilah said, and tried to stand. Opal held her gently down.

"Marina, I think you and Lilah both need a cup of tea with sugar. Three sugars. Could you make them, please?"

As she suspected, Marina instantly got up and went upstairs, still crying but wiping tears from her face. In times of shock, Opal liked strenuous exercise, but preparing food and drink was Marina's happy place. It would calm her down.

Opal sat beside Lilah, who eventually seemed to realize she was still holding the pistol and put it down on the concrete floor.

"I did not expect this," Opal said, mostly to herself.

"He deserved it."

"I thought you didn't care about the money."

"It wasn't about the money. Is he really dead? Are you sure? Can I see?"

"Yes, I'm sure and no, you can't see. Not yet."

Marina came down the stairs with a tray with three mugs. She put it on the floor beside the pistol and sat next to Opal. They each took a mug and blew on it. Opal took a sip. That was more than three sugars, but Marina had stopped being hysterical and Lilah's eyes looked slightly less glassy.

"What are we going to do?" whispered Marina.

"Before we figure that out, we need to know why Lilah killed Zander."

They both stared at Lilah, who was very pale.

"I looked at his phone this morning."

"The phone that we couldn't find?"

"I had it in my bag. I took it from his jacket. But this was a burner phone, not his personal phone. He seems to have only used it for calls to one person named S. Who happens to be the man who Zachary hired to murder my father."

Opal let that sink in. "Wow. That is dark."

"How did you find that out?"

"S called and I answered. I didn't speak, so he thought I was Zachary, and he kept demanding money. Fifty thousand, and then if it weren't paid by five o'clock tonight, the price would rise to seventy-five. This was on top of what he said Zachary already paid him. A deposit, I guess? For a contract killing? And then he implied that if Zachary didn't pay him, that he would murder him. Like he did my father."

"Why would Zander want your father dead?"

"Maybe because he knew that I listened to my father more than anyone else, including him? Maybe because he'd taken out a life insurance policy. That was actually Zachary's idea. I thought it was silly because I had plenty of money already, but Zachary said you could never be too careful and also it wouldn't do any harm."

"Dark," repeated Opal.

"Also," said Lilah, "I just realized. I made a will after I won the lottery, and my father is the main beneficiary. But if I were married to Zachary and my father was dead, then . . ."

"He wouldn't." Marina's eyes were wide.

"If he'd pay at least a hundred thousand dollars to kill a retired mailman, he probably wasn't above bumping off a wife or two," said Opal, grimly.

"I hate him," said Lilah, her knuckles white on her mug handle. "I'm glad I killed him."

"I understand," said Marina.

"I knew you would," said Lilah. "Is that weird?"

"Everything about this is weird," said Opal. "It has been weird since day one."

"Anyway. I did it, I'm responsible, so I'll go to the police and explain everything." She tried to stand up again, but this time Marina stopped her.

"No police," said Opal. "We've agreed on that from the beginning, and nothing has changed."

"But this is murder. I had a good reason, but that doesn't matter. I should go to prison for the rest of my life for this. I don't mind. As long as there are books," she added.

"You wouldn't last five minutes in prison. In any case, nobody is going to prison. We'll deal with this."

"It was my choice, and I'm ready to face the consequences."

"Fuck the consequences."

"We're all responsible," said Marina. "In some way."

"Right. You go to jail for kidnap and murder, and Marina and I go to jail for kidnap and accessory. Marina can have some assault charges thrown in. Oh, and possibly owning a gun without a license."

"Two guns," said Marina. "I really wasn't confident that they worked any more though. How did you load it?"

"I looked it up."

"You didn't use Google, did you?" said Opal with alarm.

"Of course not! I looked it up in the library. In actual books. Which I reshelved, so no one is any the wiser."

"Okay. In any case, if we confess or if we're caught, none of us are going to be seeing Marina's kids again until they're grandparents."

"I'm sorry," said Lilah. "I had to do it. But I should have thought it through, what would be the implication for the two of you. And your children, Marina. Plus, I've made a huge mess of your basement." She sighed. "I should have waited until we'd set him free, and then pushed him off a cliff."

"It doesn't matter," said Marina. "We're in this together. We have been since the beginning, and even more so now."

"Which means," said Opal, "that the three of us have to work together to get the body the hell out of here, and someplace where it won't be found, as soon as we can."

"Before my kids get home. It's Saturday morning, so . . . we've got something less than thirty-six hours. That should be plenty of time, right?"

"This is going to take more than a few baby wipes," said Opal grimly.

"Oh dear," said Lilah. "I'm sorry. I should have used poison."

"If we work together, we can get it done," said Opal. "The main thing is: we have to work quickly, we have to cover our tracks, and no one else can know anything."

It was then that the doorbell rang five times in quick succession.

29

Marina

MARINA LOOKED THROUGH THE PEEPHOLE to see who was at the front door, hoping for a delivery person or a run-of-the-mill scam artist selling dishcloths. For a nightmarish split second, she expected to see a corpse standing there, the remains of its head dripping down its shoulders.

It was her mother.

When Marina reached for the lock, she realized she was holding the spent dueling pistol. She must have taken it from Lilah and unconsciously carried it upstairs for safety. Quickly, she took one of Nana Sylvia's more roomy hats off the hat tree and stuffed the pistol inside, hanging the hat up out of harm's way and little hands' reach.

"Mom!" she said, opening the door. The view through the peephole hadn't been very wide and now she could see that her mother was accompanied by her father, who was holding Ewan. Archie and Lucy Rose stood beside him.

"Mommy!" cried Archie, embracing her leg. Ewan held his arms out to her.

"Mommy wearing underwear!" cried Lucy Rose.

"Why are you answering the door in your underwear?" said her mother.

"I was asleep. Getting a nap in. Before the contractors come." She took Ewan and breathed in the scent of his sweet baby head. "I thought the children were spending the weekend with you?"

Her mother stepped forward, expecting to come in and no doubt have a nose around. Marina, mindful of the open cellar door and the pistol box on the kitchen table, stood in her way.

"I can't come in," her mother said, stymied. "We've got to get on our way."

"On your way where?" Marina smiled down at Archie. "Sweetie, why don't you take Lucy Rose and play in the back garden for a few minutes? Give Nanny and Granddad a kiss first."

"I hate kissing," said Lucy Rose, but she went obediently along with her older brother along the side of the house to the back garden.

"We're going to the steam rally," her father told her, ostentatiously averting his eyes. "In Hungerford. It's been in the calendar for months."

"And you can't take the children?"

"Steam rally's no place for children."

Marina remembered multiple steam rallies from her childhood, with gaggles of children screaming in delight at the tractors.

"We decided to make a weekend of it," said her mother. "We found a sweet little hotel. A little staycation."

"But Mom, you said you could look after the children all weekend, until Sunday evening."

"Oh, well, you know that plans change darling. You really should invest in a nightgown."

Marina gritted her teeth. She had to consciously relax her hold on Ewan so she wouldn't squeeze him too tight.

There were boundaries, and then there were boundaries that you had to set when you had a corpse in your basement. If Lilah could shoot a man, then Marina could stand up to her own mother.

"It's not okay, Mum," she said. "You agreed to do this, and I can't just drop everything so that you can spontaneously go on a staycation. Why can't you have a staycation at home, with your grandchildren? Or rearrange it for a weekend when you *don't* have your grandchildren?"

"Steam rally," said her dad. He deposited the diaper bag on the step and then wandered back down the path, towards the car.

"We have the twins for the next three weekends, and then the soccer season starts, and you know what your father is like. So it's this weekend or nothing. Anyway, you'll cope. Neil and Sally deserve some time to themselves."

That was it.

"Neil deserves some time? What about me? I'm raising these children on my own. Don't I deserve any time?

"It was your own choice to get divorced."

"Why are you always so easy on him and so hard on me?"

"Neil is still dealing with the disappointment of"—her mother sank her voice to a whisper—"his Nana's will."

"Maybe so, but I'm talking about our whole lives. You've always bent over backwards to accommodate Neil, to praise Neil, to make Neil's life easier. Whereas me—you're always poking holes."

"Oh, I expect more from girls. Have you thought about using some cream on those stretch marks?"

She glanced down and moved Ewan over onto her hip, to display her stretch marks to better effect. Then she braced for a fight.

"Don't you think it might have been hard on me, being constantly criticized by you my entire life?"

"I'd never criticize Neil. Boys are so fragile. Anyway, you turned out much better than he did."

Marina blinked. Had she just broken the pattern of a lifetime and stood up to her mother, and in return her mother said something *nice* about her?

"Oh. I um . . . well, thank you, Mom."

Her mother shrugged. "Anyway, my own mother must have loved you more than she loved me since she left everything to you, so you'll be all right."

Having thus ruined the moment, her mother pecked Ewan on the cheek and then turned and went down the path, closing the gate behind her.

Marina craned her neck to see over the hedge to check whether any police cars were converging. There was no sign, so she went inside and straight up to her bedroom, where Ewan entertained her by trying to hide while she got dressed as fast as she could. Fortunately, her phone was still on her bedside table from the night before, so she messaged Lilah and Opal down in the basement:

It was my mum unexpectedly dropping off the kids. Hold on, I'll be back soon.

She tried not to think about how any message she sent could be used as evidence in a future murder enquiry.

In the back garden, Archie was happily building a miniature shelter with small sticks. "Where's your sister?" Marina asked, and he shrugged. "Lucy Rose!" she called, thinking about police, about people hiring murderers, about scattered brains in the cellar, about how she should really set up some security cameras, about how she was a terrible, terrible mother.

Her daughter emerged from a shrubbery, chewing on something. Marina ran across the lawn to her in relief. "There you are! What are you eating?"

Lucy Rose held up a half-eaten Oreo.

"Where did you get that?" She knew the answer before Lucy Rose pointed to the horse chestnut tree.

"Sweetheart, you shouldn't eat things that you find on the ground."

"It's *our* garden," said Lucy Rose, disgruntled, but she handed over the remains of the biscuit. It seemed to be reasonably fresh and still crunchy. Marina went over to the tree and peered upwards, but didn't see anyone. A careful check of the ground underneath revealed nothing more than a few black crumbs, eagerly beset upon by ants.

She took a deep, possibly calming breath. Best-case outcome: Lucy Rose had eaten an ant or two.

Worst-case: there was someone lurking in her tree watching them and dropping poisoned biscuits. Someone who had possibly heard a gunshot.

* * *

Ninety minutes and two bus journeys of carefully watching the perfectly healthy Lucy Rose later, Marina arrived at Jake's new flat, which was apparently also Freya's old flat, in Neasden.

In between rounds of singing "The Wheels on the Bus" and providing her children with snacks, Marina had examined her feelings about the morning's events, and come to a surprising conclusion. She was anxious, yes. She was scared that the police were going to discover what they'd done, yes. She was terrified that her children would be taken from her. She was daunted by the enormous task ahead of her of cleaning up and disposing of a body.

But, to her surprise, now that Xavier was actually dead, her primary emotion wasn't guilt or regret. She didn't feel worse than she'd felt before his death. In fact, she felt better.

As she rang the bell, she decided she would worry about this later, when she had more time.

Freya answered the door, looking both very pregnant and very surprised to see her boyfriend's ex and his three children. "Oh sh-shoot. Is it our weekend?"

"Can I speak with Jake please?"

They waited in the lounge while Freya went to fetch Jake. It took long enough that Marina knew that she'd had to wake him up. He emerged wearing his usual dressing gown open over boxers and a T-shirt. "Hey, kiddos. What are you doing here?"

"I need you to look after the children for the weekend."

Jake yawned and scratched himself through his boxers. "Love to, but I can't. I've got plans this weekend."

The new improved Marina, the badass Marina with a body in her basement, was ready for this.

"You'll have to rearrange your plans. Your children are more important."

"Hey, hang on a minute. I love spending time with the kids, you know that, but—"

"No buts. In our divorce, the agreed custody was every other weekend and half the holidays. You have a lot of missed weekends to catch up on." She passed Ewan to him, in the same way that her father had passed Ewan to her. Ewan grinned and gave his father a slobbery kiss on his unshaven cheek.

"But Freya and I—"

"I know you'll sort it out. You love your children. Plus, I'd hate to have to go to court, wouldn't you?" She handed him the heavy diaper bag and kissed Lucy Rose and Archie. "You can bring them back on Sunday evening, not too late because Archie has school the next day. If Lucy Rose gets a tummy ache, please ring me immediately, okay?

And I think Ewan needs a change, pretty urgently. Have a wonderful time!"

She left her children safely with their father, her heart hammering, but not having apologized once.

Being an accessory to murder wasn't such a bad thing, after all.

30

Opal

WHILE MARINA WAS GONE, OPAL and Lilah found a couple of pairs of yellow latex gloves under the kitchen sink and together, they cleaned the used dueling pistol and wiped it down for prints. Lilah's color had come back and she looked a lot better, but neither of them seemed inclined to speak.

They had a lot to think about. Opal couldn't stop seeing those two bodies lying together on the floor: the skeleton, and Zander. One so dry, and one so . . . wet.

She shook her head and stood up. She needed to be active, to be moving around. "I'm going to gather up all the rags and cleaning equipment I can, are you all right to finish this?"

"Yes, I'm enjoying it," said Lilah absently, polishing the engraved silver grip with a soft cloth. Opal had to admit that she was pretty impressed. Before this morning, she would've expected Lilah to fall to pieces.

There was something else different about her, too, other than Marina's bright scarf around her neck, and watching Lilah's hands in the yellow rubber gloves, she realized what it was. "Where's your engagement ring?"

"I got rid of it yesterday. I didn't feel right wearing it anymore."

"How'd you get rid of it?

"I left it at my father's grave. But I think now that I'll have to go back and get it, if it's still there. I don't want anything that Zachary touched anywhere near my father."

Opal left Lilah in the kitchen and went to rummage around the cupboard. She was not a reflective person, by nature. In fact, she preferred to think as little as possible and focus on action, instead. But something about seeing the man you had married with his head blown off made you reconsider your life choices.

She still had her wedding ring. It was wrapped in tissue, wrapped in a sock, inside the toe of a pair of stilettos that she never wore any more. She had tried to throw it away. She had got as far as standing on the Millennium Bridge with it in her hand, but somehow, she couldn't. So, she'd brought it home and hidden it out of sight and out of mind, where she wouldn't have to think about the ring or what had stopped her from throwing it.

It wasn't as if it was worth anything. Typical of Zander, it looked expensive—a white gold band covered with diamonds—but the diamonds were fake and the gold was plated. If their marriage had lasted longer than a few years, her ring finger would have turned green.

So why had she kept it?

The cupboard was full of hat boxes, rainboots of all different sizes, actual fur coats, and a full-sized dressmaker's mannequin without a head, which was too human for comfort. She pulled them out and left them in a heap behind her. Right in the back, she found a cardboard box containing a mess of tools, with an old-fashioned feather duster poking out of the top. As she was dragging the box out of the cupboard, she thought, *I kept his ring because I couldn't bear to be free of him.*

And right then, she sat down on the parquet floor and burst into tears.

It was a messy cry, the sort of cry she hadn't had in years, maybe never; the kind like a storm that hit from outside, where she wailed and snot came out of her nose and the tears fell and she couldn't do anything but double up in pain and weather it.

She couldn't bear to be free of him. And now she was, and it hurt, and she didn't know why.

"Shhh." Lilah was beside her, an arm around her shoulders. "Shh, it's okay. You're going to be all right. You're strong."

"I'm only strong because of him," Opal sobbed, and that sent her into another paroxysm of sobs that were half a scream, another storm that she could not fight against, only survive.

It passed, eventually. And she realized that she was still sitting on the floor and Lilah was sitting beside her, holding her, stroking her back, making comforting noises.

"It's okay," said Lilah, and Opal pulled away, wiping her face on the sleeve of her sweatshirt. Lilah gave her a cotton handkerchief. "It's all right. You loved him. It's bound to hurt."

"It's not okay," said Opal. She blew her nose.

"You asked me before, so I'm going to ask you now. Did he hit you?"

"Yes," said Opal. Though she had never said this to anyone before. She had tried her best never to think about it.

But now, sitting on the parquet floor next to a heap of fur coats, she told Lilah.

31

FOUR YEARS BEFORE

Opal

THESE STORIES ARE TOO COMMON to be surprising, but here it is: Zander first hit Opal on the same day she discovered she was pregnant.

She had never wanted a baby, and neither did he. Neither had had happy childhoods. Opal had narcissistic parents and Zander grew up in the foster care system. They ran a successful business together that was growing all the time, they did not have time to be parents, and did not know how to be. But the birth control had failed, and she was pregnant, and she was trying to work out how to tell him, and meanwhile they were in the kitchen of her Merseyside apartment arguing over money, and he backhanded her in the face. Quite casually, as if it were the natural order of things.

The shock was not because of the slap. Opal had been hit before. The shock was that up until that moment, she had thought she was the powerful one in their relationship. She had started the business, she had taught him the ropes, the apartment was hers, he was younger than she was.

His hand hitting her face told her that the balance had shifted.

"I'm so sorry," he said immediately. "Darling, I'm so sorry. Are you all right? Let me get you an ice pack. I didn't hurt you, did I? I would never hurt you—I love you. You just make me so angry I can't control myself."

The next morning there were flowers. So many flowers. Roses, lilies, chrysanthemums, orchids. Gerberas and sunflowers, freesias and carnations and tulips. Enough to fill the apartment, and her desk at work, too.

She had always thought: *If you hit me once, it's your fault. If you hit me twice, it's mine.* She had felt contempt for women, like her mother, who voluntarily stayed with abusive men. But when it's actually happening to you, it's more complicated than that.

Their lives were completely intertwined. She couldn't run the business as it was without him. He knew everything about it, and her. She'd never been so vulnerable to anyone before. He knew everything about her life, except that she was expecting his baby. Even though he didn't know, the pregnancy tied her to him.

So she believed him when he said he didn't mean to do it. He wouldn't do it again.

Except the next time, he broke her finger.

And the next time, he kneed her in the stomach. And she started bleeding, and lost the baby that she hadn't told him about yet.

He cried about the baby with her. Neither of them knew they'd wanted it until it was gone. And she couldn't blame him. He hadn't known. She hadn't told him, so it was her fault. They had more secrets between them now. More in common. More reason to stay together.

And he kept buying her flowers. So many flowers. More than enough for a wedding or a funeral, all of them so easily bruised and broken.

32

Lilah

"IT'S ABOUT CONTROL," SAID LILAH. It was scary to see someone like Opal so vulnerable. She took her hand and squeezed it, as Marina had squeezed hers after her own confession. "He didn't hit me, but he didn't need to. He controlled me in other ways."

"When he left, I started working out. I wanted to make myself strong. I wanted to be the most powerful person in the room."

"Is that why you bullied me for acting like a rabbit?"

"No. Maybe. Yes. I don't like weak people. Because . . . they remind me of myself. God, that's fucking pathetic. What an idiot."

"Neither one of us is weak," said Lilah. "You held on to that secret for years. And then when you had the chance to stop him from victimizing other women, you did. A weak person couldn't do that."

"And rabbits don't kill the bad guys."

Lilah looked thoughtful. "Well, I think maybe they do. They put up a good fight, at least, in *Watership Down*. Anyway, he is dead. He can't hurt you anymore."

"I should have flushed his ring down the toilet."

"That's not really good for the plumbing. I'll help you get rid of it, if you want. I'll help you do whatever you want to do."

"Why are you being so nice to me?" Opal asked.

"Because I like you a lot better now."

It was about then that Marina stepped through the front door, lugging several huge bags, and looking quite cheerful. She stopped dead at the sight of them sitting on the floor next to the cupboard.

"Why did you get out all the minks?" she asked, and then immediately: "Oh, good, you found the hacksaw."

33

Marina

IT WAS JUST CLEANING, AFTER all. And she had done plenty of cleaning in her lifetime, even more since becoming a mother: kitchens, bathrooms, toddler potties, back seats of cars. There was one time that Archie had the flu and projectile vomited for twelve hours straight. And Lucy Rose's diapers could get pretty gnarly, too, especially when she went through her beetroot phase.

How hard could it be?

Down in the basement, Marina unpacked the bags of stuff she'd bought: several plastic sheets and tarps, a box of masks, a dozen pairs of rubber gloves, heavy-duty rubbish sacks, bleach, Windex, a lot of paper towels, duct tape, hair nets, sponges, Lysol, Vicks VapoRub (for the smell—she'd seen it on TV), three mops, protective goggles, baby wipes because despite what Opal said they could clean anything, a new dustpan and brush, and two super-size packages of extra-absorbent toddler diapers.

"Why diapers?" asked Lilah, as she helped unpack.

"Along with sanitary towels, they're the most absorbent thing on the planet, and diapers are bigger."

"What did people think while you were buying all this?" Opal asked, taking out three disposable jumpsuits.

"Nobody noticed, are you kidding? Cleaning and decorating supplies and diapers? I couldn't be more of a middle-class cliché if I'd put a large bottle of gin in my basket. Which, come to think of it, I probably should have done."

"So how are we going to do this?" asked Lilah. "Are we going to wrap him up in the plastic sheets and the tarp, and then carry him out of here? Maybe wrap him in a rug? Will we need to hire a car or something?"

"Not keen on that," said Marina. "One, I like all my rugs, and two, it would leave traces in the car, and three, how do we get rid of him?"

"Also, the two of you weren't so great at lifting him when we carried him into the bunker," Opal pointed out. "If we ever kidnap anyone else, we're going to have to put you on a weight training regime beforehand."

"I think we have to cut him into pieces," said Marina. "Take him out in chunks, in a way that isn't obvious."

Opal looked sick. Lilah looked intrigued.

"I thought you were a nurse," Marina said.

"Used to be," said Opal. "And nursing doesn't usually involve cutting off body parts."

"Don't worry," said Marina. "I'll deal with it. I did some butchery as part of my chef training. It will be easiest to sever at the joints."

"You know, Marina," said Opal, "at one point Lilah thought you were a criminal genius, and I'm beginning to wonder if she wasn't right."

"Do we have to carry him out?" asked Lilah. "We could try to bury him here."

"We could toss him over the fence to the Andersons'," said Marina. "I wish. No, my children are going to inherit this house and I don't want them discovering anything unsavory."

Unlike Nana Sylvia, who apparently hadn't been too worried about Marina discovering the skeleton of Husband Number Three. What would have happened if Marina hadn't got divorced and inherited the entire house, and the family had put it on the market? And when the assessment was done, someone noticed that the floor plans didn't match up, and they found Barry's remains, still wearing his bow tie?

It didn't seem like Nana Sylvia to leave things up to chance like that. For such a seemingly carefree woman, she seemed to have planned her life in quite a bit of detail. And possibly gotten away with murder, maybe more than once.

She'd always said she married her first husband for money; her second (Marina's grandfather) for love; and her third for the va-va-voom. Her Grandpa Joe had died of cancer, far too young, and Nana Sylvia had never stopped mourning him—but Nana Sylvia's first husband died when the brakes failed on his Bentley. Nana Sylvia, possibly coincidentally, had worked on the Home Front as a mechanic during the war, a job that would have involved fiddling with brakes.

Standing in the basement with a bottle of Lysol in her hand, Marina for the first time considered that Nana Sylvia might have left her cheating husband Barry behind as a message for Marina, particularly: a message that women didn't have to put up with being disregarded, mistreated, run around on.

Marina had discovered that Jake was cheating on her because of an anonymous email that appeared in her inbox one morning, between the PTA Christmas fair email discussion and a marketing message from Aldi. At the time, she'd assumed it was Freya who sent the email, because she wanted Jake all to herself. But now, she wondered if Nana Sylvia might not have been trying to hasten Marina's divorce. Specifically, so Marina could inherit the house, and find Barry.

A tap on her shoulder. "Marina? Marina, you've been in a daydream. I was just asking you if you had some sort of garden appliance that would help us cut Zachary up. Or a kitchen appliance, maybe. Something more efficient than a hacksaw."

"I really don't think that a Nutribullet is going to be able to handle a human foot," said Opal.

"There's a meat grinder somewhere," said Marina. "But it's not an industrial one. It's only meant for making mince at home. It would take us an age to do a whole man. And we'd have to cut him into smaller pieces first anyway."

"A chainsaw?" suggested Lilah.

"This is going to be a fucking mess," said Opal.

They dressed in the coveralls, tucking the legs into rubber rain boots from Nana Sylvia's impressive collection. Protective goggles, masks, hair nets, hoods up, and hands enclosed in bright yellow rubber gloves. When they were finished, they stood in the basement looking like stunt doubles from *Breaking Bad*.

"You said you wanted fashion tips . . ." said Marina to Lilah, who shook her head.

"Let's get on with this." Opal unbolted the door to the secret room, and the three of them stood, looking in.

Okay. This was much a much worse mess than any child could possibly make. But the principle remained the same: you couldn't focus on the whole picture, because it was too overwhelming. You dealt with what was in front of you and took it bit by bit.

And you tried to ignore the smell.

Some of the blood had dried on the floor and walls, but it was still tacky underfoot as they wordlessly draped plastic sheets over the furniture and used duct tape to hang more sheets from the ceiling so that they wouldn't make the mess any worse. Marina moved Barry aside with her booted foot and they spread a tarp and then a plastic sheet on the floor beside Xavier's body.

The cliché was that dead people looked as if they were sleeping, but even though Marina had never seen Xavier asleep, she was pretty sure he hadn't looked like this. He lay flat on his back with his arms spread, feet splayed. The skin on his hands and neck was mottled. Most of his face was gone, so that was also a major difference.

"Do you want to take the . . ." She hesitated to say "head," but Opal nodded and stationed herself at Xavier's shoulders. Lilah and Marina each took a foot and together, they moved him onto the plastic sheet. He actually felt a little lighter than last time they'd lifted him, but maybe that shouldn't be surprising.

"Excuse me," said Opal, and left the room quickly. Marina could hear her retching.

"I'll do this," said Marina.

"You don't have to do it by yourself. I'm the one who killed him."

"But you loved him. And so did Opal, once upon a time. I didn't. I only had sex with him. It's going to be easier for me to see him as a body, rather than a person."

It was difficult to see Lilah's expression under the mask and goggles, but after a moment, she nodded. "I'll wrap up the pieces as you cut them. And Opal and I can clean up the . . . bits."

"Teamwork makes the dream work," called Opal, from the next room. She appeared in the doorway, adjusting her mask. "Sorry about that."

"I don't blame you," said Marina. "Can you please bring me the sewing scissors from the box, and my set of chef's knives, please? They're on the work bench, rolled up in a canvas holder."

Marina laid the items neatly next to Xavier's left leg. Then she took off Xavier's shoes and socks and handed them to Lilah, who put them into a plastic garbage bag. His feet looked more dead than his hands, for some reason; maybe because she could see how the toes had drained of blood as it settled into the heel portion of his foot. She took off his watch. Trying not to touch his flesh, she used Nana Sylvia's sharp dressmaking scissors to cut up each pant leg, so they were easy for Opal and Lilah to pull off. Then his shirt. She had to brace herself a little before she cut off his underwear; it was more intimate. She had never seen Xavier naked except in the context of pleasure. Something similar must have occurred to Lilah, because she turned away, but Opal helped her remove the bisected boxer-briefs and stuffed them in the bag with the rest of his clothes.

"He's just a man," murmured Opal, gazing down at Xavier's naked body.

Actually, now he's meat, thought Marina.

She should feel guilty for thinking this, but she also knew it was the only way she was going to get through this next bit.

She knelt by Xavier's bare leg. Unrolling her knives was a bit of a ritual, a thing she had done in many kitchens, both professional and at home. Nana Sylvia had bought her this set: German stainless steel, perfectly balanced, honed to whisper-sharp edges, arranged each in its pocket according to size and purpose. The handles were textured to give purchase to slippery hands.

After some thought, she selected a medium-sized paring knife, sharp as a scalpel. The flesh on the knee wasn't thick, but there would be ligaments to sever and joints to cut round, so she might need her cleaver and boning knife.

"Can you get my phone and a plastic ziplock bag, please, Lilah?" she said.

"No googling," Opal reminded her.

"I just want some music," said Marina. "Will you open Spotify and select 'Morning playlist'? And then pop the phone in a bag so it doesn't get anything on it?"

While Lilah did this, she considered Xavier's knee. The skin was waxy and lightly haired. There was a moon-shaped scar on the knee-cap. She didn't know the story behind it, but maybe Opal or Lilah did. It was a complex joint, but maybe not so different from cutting the hock from the ham.

Lilah propped the phone up on the plastic-covered cocktail trolley as it began to play "All the Single Ladies."

Marina took a deep breath to steady her hands. She began to cut.

34

AFTER DARK, MARINA WENT OUT with a blanket-wrapped bundle in a spare baby stroller. Sometimes the only way to get a toddler to sleep is to walk them around and around the block. But she walked farther than that; she walked upstream along the Thames to a path under a bridge, where she carefully lifted the contents of the stroller one by one and dumped them into the river. Three pieces of Xavier's legs—one thigh and two calves with feet still attached, weighted with bricks—and the compostable food waste bag containing the solid parts that were left of Xavier's head. They made four discreet splashes and sank beneath the murky water.

It was probably wrong, but she got a certain satisfaction in the idea that the food waste bag would decay, and fish would be eating Xavier's face, maybe nibbling on his skull, removing evidence of the bullet wound, and not a carb in sight.

Then she made her way back to her house with a much lighter burden. Nobody notices a mother pushing a baby, after all.

* * *

Lilah took a bus. The bookshop tote bags could hold an arm each, cut into two, but she worried because they didn't resemble books that much. Still, people carried all sorts of things in tote bags, even quite heavy things, sometimes. She was also a bit anxious about leakage, but they'd packaged up the arms very well, and the tote bags were lined with nappies, with sanitary towels to fill in the gaps.

She went in the opposite direction from Marina. She'd had a vision of going as far as Westminster Bridge and reciting Wordsworth as she sent pieces of Zachary plummeting down to the river. Sweet revenge: earth has not any thing to show more fair. She and Dad had loved that poem. Zachary had probably lied about reading poetry, too.

But in the end she decided the bridge would be way too busy; instead she emptied her tote bags somewhere in the vicinity of Kingston.

* * *

Opal found what looked like an old army backpack in the attic—Marina explained that it probably had belonged to her grandfather, Nana Sylvia's favorite husband, who had been a captain. Fortunately, Zander had been rather short-waisted and so it was roomy enough to hold Zander's torso. She set off on a run. Zander's torso was heavy, but weight-bearing exercise is especially important for menopausal women, to ward off osteoporosis, so it was all good. She reminded herself to do a TikTok about this soon, preferably after she'd got rid of the torso. She ran to Wandsworth Park.

The main problem wasn't carrying the torso; it was getting it out of the damned rucksack. Getting it in had been a three-woman job—one to lift, one to hold the bag open, one to hold the bag upright—and Opal had not fully appreciated that she would be taking it out again herself, in the dark, in a relatively open area. It wasn't the weight so much as the awkwardness. First she tried lifting it out, but the backpack kept getting caught on the wrapping and she couldn't shake it loose without risking tearing it open and spilling blood and who knew what else all over the grass. The torso was the part with the most problematic contents.

Then she put the backpack on the ground, intending to use gravity to help her: the heavier torso would stay put while she painstakingly slid the backpack off it. This was slightly less awkward, but it was slow going. She'd just freed the shoulders when she heard a noise behind her and froze.

She looked over her shoulder. It was too dark to see clearly. Looked like a young man probably from the way he moved. There was an orange spark and she could smell the odor of weed. He was approaching on the path and had probably seen her silhouette against the light reflecting off the water.

She thought fast. There was no way she could get the torso all the way back into the backpack, put it on, and run out of there before he reached her. She had no weapon on her except her bare hands and a spare key to Marina's house. No phone, not that that would do any good anyway. Years of tae kwon do classes and a bad attitude meant that these days Opal rarely felt threatened in dark spaces with strange men, but this was different. She was trying to dispose of a body undetected.

"You okay there, man?"

She decided to style it out. "All right, mate."

He approached. Damn. "What you trying to do there, sister?"

"Need a place to sleep for the night." She hoped that it was too dark for him to see her Lululemon exercise gear, or her latex gloves, or that the plastic-wrapped torso did not resemble a sleeping bag.

"I hear ya, but it's not safe here, sister. Police patrol here regular. They'll move you on."

"Good tip. Thanks."

"There's a church on Putney Bridge Road, five-ten minutes away, they let folk sleep there in the churchyard, no questions." He gestured away from the river.

"Thank you. Okay, I'll try there."

He held his lit spliff to her. "Need something to help you sleep?"

"No thanks, mate, I want to keep a clear head."

He seemed to accept that. "Give you a hand packing that up." He reached for the torso.

"No, no, no, it's good." She put herself between him and the bag. He seemed kind, but she'd kick him in the balls if she had to.

But he drew back to a respectful distance. "You take care now. Listen, you take this." He reached behind his ear and held out something small and white. It was an unlit spliff. "It's only a little one. If you don't want it, you can sell it and buy something to eat."

"Oh. Thank you."

"No worries." He walked off unhurriedly. Opal waited until he was far enough away and then stuffed the torso back into the pack.

She resumed jogging in the opposite direction to where he'd gone and less than ten minutes later passed a policeman. She kept breathing steadily, inwardly thanking the man with the spliff for the warning, and headed for Wandsworth Bridge.

* * *

When Opal got back, Marina was in the kitchen cooking something that smelled out of this world. "What is it?" Opal asked, stripping off her gloves and washing her hands in the sink, scrubbing under her nails, which were perfectly clean.

"It's a mushroom stroganoff with polenta. We need a proper meal. And after everything, I thought we'd prefer vegetarian."

Opal leaned over her shoulder and breathed in the aroma. Her stomach growled loudly. "That smells so much better than my usual post-workout meal."

"Which is?"

"Steamed fish and salad. And a chlorella smoothie for dessert."

Marina grimaced. "The healthy eating is working for you because you look great, but on Saturday nights maybe you should splash out a little and have some butter."

Lilah came in about fifteen minutes later and groaned with how good it smelled. "I've never had such a big appetite in my life," she confessed.

"It's the workout," said Opal.

"I hope it's not a taste for murder." Marina chopped parsley into a fine chiffonade while they watched. She said, "This is a different knife, by the way."

"I was wondering."

"Dinner will be ready in about twenty minutes."

"Can you make it thirty?" asked Opal. "I need another shower."

"Me too," said Lilah. "I can still smell him in my hair when I turn my head too quickly."

"Try a vinegar rinse." Marina got out a bottle of cider vinegar for her. "I'll keep the food warm until you're both ready. Did you both get everything squared away?"

"It was worryingly easy," said Lilah.

"I almost got caught," said Opal.

"What?"

"How?"

"I did get caught," Opal amended. "But I think I found the nicest man in London. Literally a guardian angel. He warned me that the cops were coming, and then he gave me this." She produced the spliff.

Lilah wrinkled her nose. "What's that?"

"Illegal drugs." Opal grinned. "From the smell, they're good ones. We're doing them after dinner."

35

Marina

JUST OVER TWO HOURS LATER, they were sprawled on various sofas and armchairs in the parlor, a bluish haze hanging in the air.

"That *is* good weed." Marina let her hand languidly trail over an embroidered cushion cover. She'd never noticed how intricate it was until now. Were those birds?

"I haven't smoked weed in thirty years," Opal said, taking another hit and passing it to Lilah.

"I've never smoked weed."

"You do surprise me, Lilah."

"Are there any other laws we can break, while we're at it?" Marina asked. "Might as well get all of them done at once." She sat up in excitement. "Wait, could we put sugar in the gas tanks of all the construction vehicles in my neighbors' garden? That would give us some peace and quiet around here, for once."

"I think dumping a body in the river counts as littering." Lilah's words were breathy. "Wow, my voice sounds strange. Sort of—"

"High," supplied Marina.

"Am I? Is this what it feels like?"

"This is definitely what it feels like."

Marina accepted the spliff and took a long drag, holding the smoke in her lungs.

"I think I'm sort of like the Hulk," she said, smoke puffing out with each word.

"You are *so* high," said Opal.

"No. I mean I am, but. The thing is, that I'm angry all the time. But I have to hide it. I can't get angry at my ex, Jake, because of the children. I don't want them to see me badmouthing their father or losing my temper with him. I can't get angry with his new girlfriend Freya, even though she stole my husband, because you're not supposed to betray the sisterhood or whatever. And I can't get angry with my family, even though they've been objectively terrible to me since Nana Sylvia died, because they're my family and they kept a roof over my head when I needed it most. And I can't get angry at Nana Sylvia for dying in such a stupid, pointless way, because it wasn't her fault. I'd like to be angry at the women who I thought were my friends, for abandoning me when I got divorced, but I know they're just living their lives.

"It's been so long since I've been allowed to show that I'm angry, that I'm not sure I know how it feels. I don't know if I've ever been allowed to be angry, for my whole life. My brother used to have massive tantrums when he didn't get his way, but my mother always said to me 'Thank goodness girls aren't like that' while seeming to think that his tantrums were cute and all part of being a boy." She widened her eyes. "Oh God. I hope I don't raise my children like that."

"You're fine," said Opal. "Those children are steeped in feminism."

"You know what I'm really mad about? It's not even Jake cheating on me, because it led to us getting divorced, and that was a good thing. It's that Jake stole my love of cooking from me. Jake doesn't really care about food, or not my kind of food. He doesn't like anything with strong flavors or distinct textures. He could eat shepherd's pie for dinner every single night. Before we were married, he said he was proud of me for having a career, but then once we were married it changed. He didn't like that I stayed out for long nights at work. He said I always smelled awful after a dinner shift. He said that being a chef wasn't a proper job for a woman, and of course my parents had never been crazy about my job either. So when I got pregnant he said it didn't make any sense for me to work. I wanted to go part time, but he said that it wasn't natural for me to want to be away from my baby. He said we couldn't afford full-time childcare, and my job didn't pay enough to be worth it."

"Which meant that *you* weren't worth it," said Lilah, punctuating her words with a stabbing finger of solidarity.

"I think if when I'd first met Jake, he'd said that he didn't like my job and that he'd expect me to give it up when I had babies, and stay at home and cook him shepherd's pie, I wouldn't have gone on a second date with him. But it happened gradually, bit by bit, until I didn't feel as if I had a choice. And then he left me anyway."

"Fucker," said Opal.

Marina was really in the flow now. "And then from the minute you get pregnant, everyone has an opinion on your body, on what you eat, how much you weigh, how you act, how you should dress your baby and feed your baby and talk to your baby . . . even complete strangers on the street will tell you what to do. Even people who have never had children themselves! And they touch you without your permission. That makes me *furious*. God, I wanted to chop their fingers off.

"And then when you meet other parents of children the same age, especially the stay-at-home parents—I'm sure they're not all like this but the ones I met definitely were—they're competitive while pretending they aren't being competitive at all. It's always who's got the best stroller, whose children walked first, whose children are gifted, whose children are best behaved, who had the easiest breastfeeding experience, whose baby sleeps through the night. And everyone's smiling and smiling, showing off their perfect lives. Sometimes I wish I could do what Lucy Rose does, and *bite* somebody."

"You are the Hulk," said Lilah. "Except not so green."

"I'm always angry, and I'm always apologizing. The angrier I am, the more I apologize. I'm not supposed to be angry, but I can't help it, and anyway, what if anger is the only way that I can change anything? Apologies have never helped. I feel like I've done two things in my life that were purely for me, because I wanted to, without taking anyone else into consideration first. One was my career. And the other one was pushing Xavier down the stairs."

"That's why you said it felt good to do it," said Lilah.

"Yes. Or possibly, I'm genetically predetermined to be a serial killer. But mostly, I think it was the anger."

They sat with that for a while. Time seemed to have slowed down. Opal finished off the spliff and dropped it into a Venetian blown-glass ashtray.

"You know what I really want?" said Lilah dreamily.

"A man who's not going to use you, chew you up, and let you down until you have to shoot him in the face?"

"Well, that would be nice but actually I really, really want ice cream."

They let that sink in for a minute.

"I don't think I have any in the freezer," said Marina. "Maybe some Mini Milks."

"I don't want a Mini Milk. I want double chocolate chip."

"Pistachio," said Opal.

"Also, strawberry."

"Cheesecake. Strawberry cheesecake. Plus, regular strawberry."

"Salted caramel."

"And mango sorbet."

"I can't get off this sofa to get to the store."

"Fortunately," said Lilah, "I have a phone with a delivery app." She dug it out of her fanny pack.

"Ooh." Opal rolled over onto her stomach. "Can we also get some whipped cream? The kind that comes in a can?"

"That stuff is a monstrosity," Marina told her. "I love it."

Lilah concentrated hard on her phone screen for several minutes, screwing her eyes up. Then she made a final tap. "Done."

"Oh my God, I love you," said Marina.

"I love you too," said Lilah, sounding surprised.

"You two are *so high*," pronounced Opal.

"I bet children's television would be hilarious right now." Marina began humming the tune to *Wonder Pets*.

"Listen," said Lilah. "Wait, listen, listen."

They listened.

"What are we listening for?"

"I meant listen to me."

"Oh."

"We need good alibis. We didn't think of that."

"We were all home," said Opal. "We don't even know each other."

"But we met in public. And also, we've been coming and going at this house. Someone must have seen us."

"We're working on a charity together," suggested Marina.

"What kind of charity?"

"Books," said Lilah, at the same time that Marina said, "Children."

"Children's books," decided Opal. "About fitness."

Marina thought about it for a moment. "That is a shit alibi."

"Maybe we should think up something when we're not really wasted."

Lilah found this inexplicably funny and started laughing so hard that she hiccupped, and Marina laughed at her, and then Opal laughed at both of them, and it was a stoned second or two before they heard the doorbell ring.

"Ice cream. *Yessss.*" Marina gathered herself, stood up, and made a rather crooked path through the hallway and to the front door. She threw it open, with a "Thank God you're here!"

It was the police.

36

"OH, HELLO OSSI—OFFI—HELLO." Marina did her best to look casual and relaxed. "Is there a problem?"

"Good evening, ma'am, are you the homeowner?"

"Yes." Minimal answers. Best plan. She didn't want to have to kill this guy.

There was only one of them, which was a good sign. They would send more than one to a murder scene. There would be sirens and forensic vans. Maybe firearms.

"We've had a report about a disturbance."

Gunshot? Music? Women coming and going carrying body parts?

"Oh?"

"Have you noticed anyone trespassing on your property?"

She shook her head. Her pupils were probably crazy dilated. She wished for sunglasses. But then it was after midnight. So that might also be suspicious.

Also, did her house stink of weed? She tried to sniff, surreptitiously, but everything smelled like weed to her anyway.

"My daughter did find an Oreo," she offered.

"An Oreo?"

"Yes."

"I see. Well, your neighbors have made a report of someone climbing over the fence between your property and theirs."

"Tonight?"

"That's correct, ma'am. Would you mind if I had a look at the area of the fence and your garden?"

"This is the Andersons, right?"

"Yes, ma'am."

Was there any incriminating evidence in the back garden? They had collected all the blood-soaked rags and towels and gloves and clothes, plus the rug and other textiles from the bomb shelter, to burn. But all of that was in the cellar. She had a sudden and almost irresistible urge to run and check that it was all still there, safe, and hidden, and not disturbed by whoever was climbing over fences.

"Ma'am?"

"Oh. Yes, of course." She came outside and shut the door behind her. "We can go round the side of the house. I've got some girlfriends over."

And there went the "we don't know each other" alibi out the window. Or had they already decided against that one?

The police officer followed her. "So, your garden is accessible from the front?"

"Yes, if you open the front gate and this side gate."

"Are they normally locked?"

"I don't think so?"

"Do you have any security cameras?"

For a moment she was alarmed, thinking, *Oh no, the security cameras would have recorded everything.* Then she remembered she didn't have any.

"No."

In the back, he went straight to the section with the horse chestnut tree. He shone his flashlight all around the grass and the base of the tree.

"Do you see anything?"

He didn't answer her. She checked over her shoulder to make sure that all the curtains and blinds at the back of the house were still closed. Should she mention that she suspected that someone had been watching the house? But that would just make the police more interested, and that was absolutely the last thing she wanted to happen.

"Is that a tree house?" He shone his flashlight upward into the branches. "How long has it been here?"

"Years. Since I was a little girl."

He examined the ladder, and then went over to the fence.

"Your neighbors say that they've had trash thrown over the fence from this garden."

"They thought it was me throwing it because I complained to them at one point. They have quite a lot of construction going on, you see. It's very noisy."

"Did you throw it?"

"No."

"How about your children?"

"I don't send my children out to play with cans of Monster. Also, they're not tall enough yet to reach the bottom rung of the ladder or throw anything over the fence. So, no."

He nodded, but she couldn't tell if he agreed with her or not. "Well. I don't see any signs of a disturbance, but it would be easy enough to drop into their garden from this tree house, and your back garden is accessible from the street. If your children are playing out here especially, I'd recommend you get a lock for that side gate."

What kind of world did they live in, where you had to lock children in their own back garden? She'd *kill* anyone who threatened her children.

The thought sobered her up a little.

"Construction sites are very popular with thieves," the policeman told her, as they walked back round the side of the house. "The price of copper keeps going up. Pipes, electrical wires. It's a good idea to review your home security. This place is pretty antiquated in that respect." He fiddled with the latch on the gate before shutting it behind them. "A lot of people like those video doorbells. Get your husband to do a bit of research."

It is a bad idea to punch a police officer when you are high and have spent the evening disposing of a body.

A curtain twitched on the side of the house. She glanced up to see Lilah peering through the parlor window, eyes wide. Opal's face appeared above hers. Marina shook her head and shrugged elaborately, and they both ducked behind the curtain.

"Thank you, I will definitely do that."

"Plenty of crazies out there, even in a nice neighborhood like this."

"Oh," she said, "don't worry. I will be very careful." She paused on the front path. "By the way, can you give me some advice while you're here?"

"Of course." He puffed a little.

"I do have some garden waste that I'd like to burn. Just a small, controlled bonfire away from fences and trees. Is that legal?"

"As long as the smoke doesn't create a nuisance for the neighbors," he said, with exaggerated patience. "And you're very careful to keep it away from anything that could go up. And you'll need to keep an eye on your children."

"Thank you so much!" She actually batted her eyelashes at him, but it was probably too dark for him to see. Not a bad thing, because she wasn't sure if she'd done it right. "I'll be sure to do it exactly as you say, so I know I'm on the right side of the law."

"You're welcome. Get a lock for that side gate."

"I will, as soon as possible, I promise," she simpered.

Once back inside, she collapsed against the door with mixed relief and triumph.

Why had she never understood that it could be such an advantage to be underestimated?

37

THE NEXT AFTERNOON, AFTER THE careful, no-nuisance, legally
sanctioned bonfire, the three of them sat in garden chairs drinking
very strong coffee and listening to the digging and banging going on
next door.

"I don't believe that their contractors work on Sunday," said Opal.

"I don't believe that they called the police on *you*," said Lilah.

"There was someone in that tree house," said Marina. "I wish I
knew why. And what they know."

"You should get some security cameras."

"I will. Anyway, there's no way anyone could have seen what was
happening in the basement."

"Do you think it was S?" asked Lilah. "The man who Zachary paid
to kill my father?"

"Did he sound like the kind of man who enjoys Oreos?"

"Not especially. But he was expecting to meet Zachary at about the
time that we were packaging pieces of him up in bin liners. He's got
to be furious and looking for him. He could have traced him here."

"I think you should go to the police," said Marina, and held her hand
up to Opal. "Hear me out. It's natural that you'd report your fiancé

missing anyway, especially given what happened to your dad. And I think you should tell them that you overheard him talking with someone he called S, promising to give him money."

"That makes things complicated," said Opal.

"But it makes things safer for Lilah. This man should not be out there. We can't find him. But maybe the police can. They can investigate your bank accounts, maybe trace the money that he stole and where it went? I don't know how it works. But it seems like the only chance of bringing him to justice. And Lilah deserves that."

Opal frowned, but she nodded. "Okay. In that case, we need to hope that no one saw us together."

"No children's health book charity?"

"That was never going to work."

"We've been lucky so far," said Lilah. "Relatively."

They sank into silence. They were all very tired. It felt weird not to have an immediate crisis to deal with. Weird and . . . unfinished.

Lilah finally said what was on all their minds. "What do we do next? After I go to the police?"

"Back to work tomorrow for me." Opal stretched. "There's no rest for the wicked, or for content creators."

"I miss my kids."

"I want to go back to work too," said Lilah. "And I need to move out of that expensive hotel. But that's not what I meant. I meant: what do the three of us do next? Do you want to make plans?"

"We don't have any more reason to be together," said Opal.

"We . . . could keep in touch," said Marina.

"It's safer not to," said Opal. "The fewer links between us, the better. Especially if Lilah's going to the police and if—well, when—Zander's found and identified. It's the Google principle."

"Oh," said Lilah.

"There's luck, and then there's pushing our luck. We should delete our chat and each other's numbers, never meet up again."

"But what if we have to get in touch?"

"Why should we have to? If we get away with it?"

"What about the person who was watching from the tree house?" asked Marina.

"Occam's razor. Odds are that was just what the police said it was: someone looking to steal from the neighbors."

"I suppose . . ." Lilah sighed. "I suppose I hoped we could stay friends."

Opal stood up and yawned. "We've committed a crime. We want to stay out of jail. Friends are a liability."

"Anyway," said Marina, "we all need to get on with our lives. Move forwards. This was traumatic to say the least. We can't get over it if we keep on reminding each other of it."

"Right." Lilah drew a deep breath and fortified herself. "We need to put it in the past."

They took out their phones and, on the count of three, deleted each other.

"Well," said Lilah.

"That's that," agreed Opal. "It's been interesting knowing you all. Remember ladies: calcium and weight-bearing exercise." She winked, and left.

Lilah worried her lip. "I'll . . . well, I suppose I'll get going too."

"Do you want to take some ice cream with you? Or do you want some before you go? There's a lot left."

"No, no, that's okay. Your kids will enjoy it." She got up.

"You don't need to leave right this minute," tried Marina.

"No. You were right. I've had some big changes in the past few months. I need to grieve for my father and work out what my life is like without him. And I need to understand how I feel about

Zachary's betrayal, and see our whole relationship through the view of what he was really doing. All of this, what we've gone through, and getting to know each other, it has got in the way of processing those emotions. So I have to concentrate on that now. And also, I've had a lot of money stolen and I have to deal with that." She nodded decisively and straightened her shoulders. "The sooner the better."

"The sooner the better," echoed Marina.

Lilah held out her hand. Marina shook it.

And then she was gone, and Marina was all alone.

38

Opal

IT WAS LATE AFTERNOON, AND the sun sparkled off the Thames. Opal stood at the stern of the Thames Clipper as it rounded the Isle of Dogs towards Barking. The water churned in the wake of the boat and foamed white on the brownish water.

Who knew what lay at the bottom of this river, other than Zander. There could be a whole army's worth of people yet to be discovered. There could be lost treasure, Roman coins, an infinite number of soda cans, all of them settling into silt, picked over by intrepid fish. All the secrets in the world could be buried here.

She took her wedding ring out of her pocket. It was just as sparkly and cheap as ever. She knew now why she had kept it—and why she had spent so long looking for him after he was gone. It wasn't because he'd run off with all her money; that was long gone. It was because he had power over her. Because however much she hated Zander, despite all the ways he had mistreated her, he was still the only person she had ever loved. She kept the ring because she needed proof that she could love, and hope, and trust. She needed to know that she could be that person who felt and cared. Even if it turned out badly.

She didn't need the ring anymore. She might end up being alone for the rest of her life, but that was fine. At least now she had learned that she could care.

She wound her arm back and, as hard as she could, she threw the ring out over the Thames. The wake was wide enough, and the ring was small enough that she didn't see where it landed. But that didn't matter. It was enough that it was gone, and Zander was gone, and with him, all her secrets that only he had known. She was free.

She punched the air.

Then, because she had at least an hour before she'd be back at Canary Wharf, she took a burner phone out of her other pocket, and googled Darren Pine.

39

Marina

MARINA HAD PUT THE DUELING pistols in the bomb shelter along with Barry's skeleton, locked the door, and pulled the shelf shut in front of it. She used rags to block up the back of the niche with the secret latch and then placed a jar of distinctly unappetizing preserves in the front. To her murder-addled mind the contents of the jar looked like chunks of flesh swimming in magenta blood, but she thought it was probably beetroot.

She was combing the house for the third time, making sure there were no traces of blood or weed anywhere and putting anything remotely breakable out of harm's way, when the doorbell rang. Her heart lifted in the way it only could when she was going to be reunited with her children—but just to be safe, she checked the peephole.

To her surprise, it wasn't Jake standing there with the children. It was Freya.

"Hi," she said, opening the door. Archie flew to her, and surprisingly, so did Lucy Rose. She embraced them both, tight tight tight, and took Ewan from Freya.

"Everything good?" asked Freya awkwardly.

She wasn't going to try to be friendly, was she, this woman who'd stolen her husband?

"Fine," Marina said with a distinct chill. "Where's Jake?"

"He went to the races."

Marina blinked. "What?"

"Yeah, he had plans with his mates, so."

"*You* looked after the children today?"

"And yesterday, mostly. He was a bit under the weather."

"Hungover?"

"We had fun, didn't we?" Freya said brightly to Archie and Lucy Rose. "We played games and went to the park. And today we also played games and went to a different park."

She sounded exhausted.

"Jake got *you* to look after *his* children all weekend," Marina stated.

"Oh, it was no trouble. It's good practice for me." Freya lay her hand on the swell of her stomach and smiled a feeble smile. "They really do have a lot of energy, don't they?"

"Yes. Well. I didn't mean for you to have to do all the looking after. The children need to spend time with their father, which was what I expected to happen."

"I really don't mind," said Freya. But Marina noticed that she wasn't wearing any makeup, and her hair was shoved into a rubber band.

"We did have a lot of fun," said sweet, peacemaker Archie.

"I didn't bite," added Lucy Rose.

"Because you are excellent children," Marina told them. "And I missed you very much and I'm glad you're home. Look in the kitchen, I have a surprise for you."

"What is it?" Both Archie and Lucy Rose zoomed into the house. Freya stood on the step, arms empty. Marina didn't invite her in.

"Okay, well," said Freya. "I should be getting back. Work tomorrow, and I haven't made dinner. Bye Ewan. Bye Lucy Rose! Bye Archie!" she called, but the two older children were already gone, and Ewan was busy playing with Marina's hoop earring.

Something about the way that Freya walked back down the path to the gate, alone, seemed familiar.

* * *

She deleted all her pictures of herself and Xavier, obviously, and in the following two weeks she filled up her Insta grid instead with photos of pies. It was their new after-school-and-nursery activity: baking. Archie liked measuring flour and sugar, Lucy Rose liked tasting everything and doing the decorations, and Ewan liked sticking his hands in dough. What they made was far from perfect, and sometimes it didn't even taste that good, but it was some of the most fun Marina had ever had cooking.

She had everything that she needed right here. A quiet life with her children. Well, as quiet as it got with Godzilla in the house. Her mother even invited them over for Sunday lunch and although she pointed out as many of Marina's faults as ever, Marina was doing her best to reset her mind to try to understand that her mother thought criticism was a compliment.

And then she tried twice as hard to tell Lucy Rose how great she was, to address the gender imbalance.

"I know," said Lucy Rose, and Marina picked her up and covered her with kisses as she squirmed.

Life was back to normal, but a little bit better. Also, she bought herself a really excellent vibrator online.

So why was she finding herself lying on the sofa by herself again in the evenings, drinking a solitary glass of wine and scrolling through Instagram?

She checked out Opal's feed. They'd had to block each other's numbers but that didn't mean that she couldn't see how she was doing on social media. Opal had been pretty quiet. There were some reposts of old material, and only one new reel, with Opal speaking to the camera about optimal nutrition and the importance of getting enough sleep. Marina thought about leaving a comment about ice cream and staying up all night smoking dope, but she knew that would be stupid.

It felt nice to watch Opal, though, and notice the ways that her online persona was different from her real life. The tough exterior was much glossier online, charming, authoritative. Whereas Marina had learned that in real life, it was armor to protect what was vulnerable inside.

It also felt sad to watch Opal. It made her lonelier.

A message pinged into her Instagram and she read it instantly. To her surprise, it was from Nancy—the PTA mom, she of the many #blessed posts, who she'd avoided on the street.

Hi Marina! It was so nice to see you the other day! How are you doing? Your bakes look a-MAY-zing! I wondered if you wanted to get the kids together for a playdate? It's been so long! How about this Saturday morning, if you're not busy? I would love to catch up with you and chat! Nxxx

She hovered her finger over her phone, ready to send a passive-aggressive reply about being far too busy with a-MAY-zing bakes to meet up with an overly competitive parent who'd ghosted her after her divorce, but then she paused.

She was not too busy. Her calendar yawned with empty days. And her kids and Nancy's had always got along.

Hi, she texted. She might be giving Nancy another chance, but she was not going to give her any exclamation points. Saturday morning sounds good. How about the park?

* * *

The older children squabbled over the slides while Marina and Nancy pushed their toddlers on the swings. They'd spent the first twenty minutes making small talk about mutual acquaintances, schools, and the ins and outs of potty training, and they'd fallen silent. Although Nancy was wearing a fluffy pink sweater and that magic foundation that was meant to make you look well-rested and slightly sparkly, she looked tired, dulled, as if little Jocasta had been keeping her up nights. She also looked as if she wanted to say something.

In the past, Marina would have filled up the silence with accommodating chatter. Now, she stayed quiet, and kept one eye on Lucy Rose to make sure no one was being injured. It all looked good so far.

"I saw your Instagram posts about finding a new fella," Nancy said at last. "I think it's great. You've got this glow about you, like you're really happy."

"Oh. That didn't work out, actually."

"So it's not love that's making you look so good?"

"No. I think it's . . ."

And she didn't know the correct way to finish the sentence. Being independent? Reveling in revenge? Mopping up bits of brain tissue? Finding friends?

"I had some help from some really fabulous women."

"Wow. You're really lucky. I wish I had that."

"You've got Naomi and Nina, right? The three of you are tight."

"I do. We are. But. I just feel like . . . I don't know, I feel like I have to impress them all the time. It's tiring."

Hearing this out loud from Nancy, the queen of performative parenting, was something like a bombshell. Marina stopped pushing Ewan, who immediately clamored for more.

"I don't think you have to impress them," said Marina. "Everyone parents differently, and that should be okay."

"You've heard how they talk about the other mothers at the school gates."

"You talk about the other mothers too."

"That's how I know."

"Did you talk about me when I left the neighborhood?" ventured Marina, pushing again. "That night you all went out for drinks without me?"

"We did."

"Relieved that there wouldn't be a divorcée around to steal your husbands?"

Nancy laughed self-consciously.

"After one cocktail, yes, someone did say that. But after the third we started talking about how we envied you."

Marina knew better than to stop pushing, but she stared at Nancy. "*Envied* me?"

"Yeah. You went through the worst thing. You lost your husband and your house. And everyone knew. And you kept on going. I don't know if I would be able to do that. I don't know if I . . . if I will."

Nancy started crying.

It took some juggling of toddlers and a lot of bribery with snacks before Marina heard the whole story, though some of it was spelled out so as not to be comprehensible to little ears. Jago had been having an affair for the past five years, starting almost on the day that their eldest child was born. Nancy had found out when Jago's other woman had turned up at their door and accused her of giving Jago, and therefore the other woman, gonorrhea. This was, additionally, how Nancy found out that Jago had been paying for sex workers.

"Are you okay?" Marina asked, alarmed.

"Yes. Thank God. Since Jocasta, I've made him wear c-o-n-d-o-m-s. Not that there's been much of that anyway. At least that is a small mercy. I'm allergic to antibiotics."

"What are you going to do?"

"I don't know. I literally do not know. It's better for the kids if we stay together. And we'd have to sell the house and move to somewhere terrible in a suburb. Everyone will talk, I mean *everyone*. He's the one who did something wrong, but I'm the one who looks like an idiot. Like how terrible a wife must I be if he had to do all that? He swears he'll never do it again. But how can I ever trust him?" She turned a tearstained, haunted face to Marina. "You've been through this."

"I have. And it's hard. Really hard. I'm so sorry, Nancy. I feel for you. I hope you can find the strength to discover what it is that you want to do."

"You were the only person I could think to talk to. And you look amazing, you look so happy. You've got it all together. Please, Marina, tell me: what should I do?"

Marina, was, to say the least, flabbergasted.

But, she realized, it was true. She did have it all together—or as much as anyone ever did. Not just from an outside perspective, but from her own perspective. She had a wonderful home and three healthy, happy children; she didn't have Jake around to belittle her; she was working on her relationship with her mother; she'd learned to take it slow with any new man in the future; and she knew, finally, how to stand up for herself, and if that didn't work, she knew how to joint an entire man.

"You could always kill him," Marina suggested. And at least that made Nancy laugh.

40

Lilah

"SO YOU THINK YOUR FATHER was killed by a mysterious contract killer, hired by your fiancé," said Detective Branston.

"That's right. His name was S."

"His name was Ess? Or was it an initial?"

"I think it was an initial."

"But you're not certain? And you don't know what it could be an initial for?"

"No."

"And you happened to overhear your fiancé talking about it, because he had this conversation within your earshot."

"Yes."

"Did he mention any details of the murder in this conversation?"

"No. He just talked about owing the man fifty thousand pounds."

"Could that have been a gambling debt, or a loan?"

"Zachary didn't gamble."

"But he did hire assassins."

"I think so, yes."

"Did you hear this Ess's voice?"

"No," lied Lilah. She wasn't a good liar, but she thought maybe she'd get away with it if she stuck to single syllables.

"So we're looking for a mysterious person named Ess, or something beginning with *S*, no other identifying characteristics, who you have deduced may be a hitman."

"Exactly. Also, I think I was followed by a man in a blue baseball cap."

"When was this?"

"About six weeks after my father was killed."

"And this was before, or after your fiancé disappeared?"

"Before."

Branston sighed and sat back in his chair. He'd offered to come to her house in Chislehurst for this interview, but Lilah didn't dare to go back there, in case S turned up. She was staying in a Premier Inn in Sidcup.

"Your fiancé and your money have both disappeared. This is serious enough, and we've got evidence to go on there, so I'll be passing that on to my colleagues to follow up. It's unlikely that you'll get any of your cash back, sadly. The banks are likely to say you gave him access to it out of your own free will, unless you can prove otherwise."

"Oh, I did," said Lilah. "I completely trusted him."

"Right. Well, maybe we can trace him."

"I hope so," Lilah lied again. "I don't care about the money. I'm just worried about Zachary. Whatever he's done, I don't want him to be hurt."

Branston sighed again. He clearly thought she was delusional, but to give him credit, the parts of her story that he found unconvincing were the parts that she was actually lying about.

"I've worked quite a few homicide cases," he told her. "Contract killings don't tend to look like your father's death. He had no gang connections and no criminal activity. If the purpose was to collect insurance money, it would have been made to look like an accident, not a murder. However, I can see that you are very worried, and that's important. I'll investigate this lead, Miss Nightingale. We'll make an appointment for you to come in and look at some photographs, to see if you can identify the man who you think was following you. And I'll pass on your report to the fraud team who will get in contact with you in due course."

Outside the police station, Lilah paused to look up and down the street, but she didn't see anyone who looked like the man in the blue baseball cap, and no one seemed to be paying any attention to her.

When she'd left Marina's house two days ago, she'd been convinced that she was never going to be frightened of anything ever again. The act of firing a pistol in a murderer's face tended to make you think that you could defend yourself, of course. But more than that, she'd felt as if Marina and Opal had her back. And that gave her courage.

But she didn't have those friends anymore. And the longer she didn't, the more she thought about that there was another killer out there, who wanted the money he was owed for murdering her father in cold blood, and who might think that Lilah was his best chance of getting it. The police clearly weren't going to help. So she had to be cautious, that's all. She wasn't a rabbit; she was something more clever, resourceful, and brave, like . . .

She wished she could talk to Marina and Opal and ask them what kind of animal was clever, resourceful, and brave.

She paused to check her reflection in a window. It had taken her ages this morning to tie her hair up in Marina's silk scarf, and though she hadn't got it exactly right, she thought she'd done a pretty good job. As she was tucking a few errant tendrils back into place, her phone buzzed in her fanny pack.

It was a text from an unknown number.

If it was from S, at least she'd have some evidence to show Detective Branston. She opened it.

```
D PINE IS SERVING A 40-YEAR DRUG TRAFFICKING
SENTENCE IN A BANGKOK PRISON. THOUGHT YOU'D
WANT TO KNOW. DELETE THIS MESSAGE.
```

She smiled. And then she deleted the message.

41

Opal

THEY'D SCHEDULED THE SHOOT MONTHS ago, which meant it had already been paid for. Otherwise, she would have canceled it. Opal arrived ten minutes early, arms laden with boxes.

Faiza met her at the studio door, phone in hand and cross expression on her face. "Where have you been? I've been messaging you, like, five times an hour for days."

"I've been sorting out some things. Getting a little headspace."

"I literally could not find anyone who would agree to do your makeup. So I've got Taylor again, but I promised you would be nice to her. So be nice."

"Taylor? Is that the one with the face tattoos?"

"Taylor is the one with no face tattoos."

"That narrows it down."

"I also had to agree to pay her double." Faiza stepped back, cringing a little, waiting for the onslaught.

"Fair enough."

". . . Fair enough? That's it?"

She handed Faiza the largest of the boxes, a white one with a large pink bow. "This is for you."

Faiza eyed it suspiciously. "What is it? A bomb?"

"Ha ha. Don't open it until we're finished here, all right?"

"Have you heard from GlowUpp?"

"We'll talk about it when we're finished. I don't want to waste Taylor's morning." She swanned into the studio, calling, "Who wants a smoothie and a carrot muffin?"

She brought the box of food and drink over to the corner of the studio, where a person was doing her best to shrink into the background. Opal recognized her.

"Hi, Taylor." Taylor flinched. "Listen, I know I was a cow the last time we met, and I'm sorry. I know you are very good at your job. I'm going to let you get on with it." Opal proffered the smoothie. "Try this, it's full of antioxidants and it will give you energy. You can barely even taste the kale."

Faiza approached her. "What happened to you?"

"Pardon?"

"What happened to you? What's wrong? Why are you acting this way?"

"Let's just say I've learned to appreciate the virtue of working collaboratively." Opal sat in the chair in front of the mirror. "Shall we get started? Remember, last time you had this great idea about extra powder. I think it's going to be magical."

* * *

Taylor took the muffins with her when she left, almost in a daze. Opal had never in her life acted this nice, not without expecting something in return. It wasn't so bad.

"What was that all about?" Faiza asked her.

"I thought you wanted me to be more pleasant to work with," Opal said, wiping the last of the GlowUpp off her face. One bright spot: she wasn't going to have to wear this crap anymore.

"Yes, but this is weird. It's like you've been taken over by aliens. Have you?"

"Open the box."

It was full of roses. The scent burst out into the studio.

"It's a plant," Opal told her. "Bouquets die too easy."

"Why," said Faiza, "are you giving me flowers."

She asked it in much the same manner as you would ask why a dog had pissed on your curtains.

"Because you have been an excellent employee and I have been a terrible employer. You have done everything I've asked you, and more, for very little pay, and you have never failed to call me out on my bullshit even though I never listened. What's more, I like you. So, I owe you an apology, and this is it. Look at what else is in the box."

"Are there thorns?"

"Maybe. Good point. I didn't think of that. Be careful."

Faiza reached in gingerly and took out a long white envelope. As Opal watched, she opened it to reveal quite a large stack of cash.

"I know this doesn't make up for making your life hell," said Opal. "But it's your fair share of the GlowUpp sponsor money. You worked hard to help me land that deal. You deserve it."

Faiza was speechless. Opal threw the cotton pad in the trash and stood up.

"And Faiza? If you were a man, you would have asked for this money months and months ago. Don't be afraid to be a bitch. Sometimes it's the only way to get what you want."

* * *

She'd spoken with GlowUpp the afternoon before. They were terminating their sponsorship; they said they wanted to "concentrate on an up-and-coming consumer base and build brand loyalty from that end."

Thus it ever had been: middle-aged women abandoned for younger models. It was no surprise. At least she could stop looking like a melted candle.

She had a few irons in the fire, but nothing for nearly the same money as GlowUpp had been. And recent events had blown her back-up plan for getting funds. She'd hold on to Faiza for as long as she could, but odds were, she was going to have to let her go soon. That was okay; Faiza was tough and as soon as she recognized her own value, she'd be able to land any job she wanted.

And Opal . . . Opal would be back to using selfie sticks, recording her own videos, building content the old-fashioned way. Or maybe she'd get a job as a personal trainer. Or maybe she'd try something else.

She was a survivor. She would be all right.

She had to be.

It was raining as she emerged from the train station closest to her apartment, but only a light misting, the kind of rain that feels cool against your face, the kind you pray for when you're having hot flushes. She caught herself humming under her breath, and smiled when she recognized the song. "All the Single Ladies"—a song that should be associated in her head with the scent of blood and the sound of slicing cartilage, but wasn't. It made her feel like dancing, right here in the street in the misty rain.

The girls would laugh at me if they saw that, she thought, and sobered.

That was the only real problem. Not the lost sponsorship, or the money she didn't have, or the career that was so precarious that one phone call could ruin it. She was used to all that. She was used to being alone, too.

The problem was that for those few days with Marina and Lilah, for the first time in a long time, she'd had friends. And though she knew that friends were a liability—and she was *fine* with being alone—she didn't like feeling lonely.

She turned the corner and power-walked towards her building. She'd keep going, keep moving. Whatever didn't kill her made her stronger. She would stay strong.

She was so absorbed in her thoughts that she didn't hear the man calling her name the first time.

But the second time, he got her complete attention.

"Opal, can I talk to you for a minute?"

He looked scruffy. He was holding out his phone towards her. He had a rat-like, eager look. Not a policeman, but . . .

"What do you want?"

"I'd like to have a few words with you about Weight&See."

He said it as all one word, like it had been printed on the boxes and promotional material, all those years ago.

Opal turned around. She ran.

42

Lilah

LILAH KNEW THAT GOING BACK to work would help her feel better, safer and less lonely. So she'd been dismayed when she rang Jimiyu and he said he'd already arranged all the work schedules for the month ahead and not included her. Fortunately—well, it was not fortunate, actually, it was a travesty—budget cuts meant that they were understaffed anyway, so Jimiyu was glad when Lilah asked if she could come in and volunteer some extra hours. She'd done Rhyme Time that morning and now she was doing a much-needed tidy of the Military History section, where the Early Modern books had been hopelessly muddled with World War I. It was a remote corner of the library with little foot traffic, which meant that it had been neglected for quite some time. Also, the fluorescent strip lighting here needed maintenance; it cast a frustratingly dim light and flickered constantly, which might have something to do with why all the books had been jumbled.

Even though she had to squint to see the titles and call numbers, it was soothing to remove books that were in the wrong spot, put the ones that needed repairs to one side on the book cart, and then place the ones that were in good shape back in the correct spot, neat and at home where they could be found, lined up with the edge of the shelf just so. She slid out a chunky volume and caught a glimpse of someone on the other side of the shelf, moving quickly out of sight.

Lilah froze, book held in mid-air.

She was in a public place. Of course there were other people around. But something about the way the person had scurried to the side, something about how quiet they had been, so quiet that Lilah never would have known there was anyone there at all . . .

Gripping the handle of the cart, she wheeled it between the shelves and around to the next aisle, into Asian History. It was an old cart and it squeaked, so anyone would be able to tell exactly where Lilah had gone. And there she waited, between Japan and India, listening.

Footsteps. Rubber-soled, cautious. She heard them approaching, on the other side of this shelf, now, where she had been a few minutes ago. The person stood there, but they didn't remove any books from the shelf. Either they were reading the spines, or they were there for another reason. She tried to peer through the shelves, in the space left by the top of the books, but all she could see was a shadow, so she moved a little to the right, stood on tiptoe, craned her neck to see.

A brown eye stared back at her.

Startled, Lilah stumbled backwards, banging her hip against the cart, which squeaked and thudded against the shelf.

Whoever it was, they knew that she knew they were there now.

She rubbed her hip and tried to breathe deeply to calm down. Realistically, a thug who killed people for money wouldn't be lurking in a library, would he?

Would he?

The overhead strip lighting flickered off for a moment, a long moment of paranoia and terror when Lilah expected to be hit on the head and bundled into a burlap sack, and then it came back on. She was still alone in the aisle, and her heart was beating so hard now that she wouldn't be able to hear any footsteps.

This was ridiculous. She was acting . . . like a scared little rabbit.

Reaching into her fanny pack, she abandoned her cart and strode to the end of the aisle. As she rounded the shelf, she pulled out her canister of pepper spray. If it was S, she would face him down. Like she'd faced Zachary down. Like she'd dealt with the death of her father. She'd spray him in the face, and she'd scream and call for help. She would not go down without a fight.

She had nothing to lose.

The lighting went off so all she could see was a shadow, standing right there where she'd been rearranging the books. She aimed at where the shadow's eyes would be and then the light came back on again and the shadow emitted a little squeal.

It wasn't a man. It was Evil Alice.

"What are you doing?" Lilah started out shouting it but then she remembered they were in a library, so she finished the question in a strangled half-whisper.

"I . . . I wanted to talk with you," whispered Evil Alice. "What's that?" She pointed at the pepper spray.

"Oh. Nothing." Lilah put it back in her bag, though she didn't zip it up. "Why are you lurking in the 940s and peering through shelves? Why didn't you just talk to me in the break room?"

She expected something cutting, so she braced herself, but Evil Alice just said, "I thought you might want to talk privately."

"Why?"

"Because . . . well, this is awkward. And I know you and I haven't been the best of friends, so I hope you . . . Anyway. I saw what you were looking up, the other day when you were here."

Lilah stared at Evil Alice whilst she tried to work this out. Was she talking about her research about how to load and shoot eighteenth-century flintlock pistols? Because why would she care that Lilah had been looking that up? Unless she knew something about how Zachary had died, and then.....

Oh God she wasn't going to have to shoot someone else, was she?

"The books on coercive control," Evil Alice clarified. "And narcissistic abuse."

"Oh. You mean . . . those books."

"I don't mean to pry, honestly. I know that none of us know what really goes on in other people's lives. But I couldn't bear to think . . ." She took a deep breath, as if she were fortifying herself. "You were trying to stay unnoticed. Hiding the titles, sitting back there by yourself. And I wanted to say, just in case you needed to hear it, that . . . well, I know what it's like."

"You . . . do?"

"Because I've been through it myself. Before my divorce, and before I moved here. And. Well, it changed me. It made me, you know, very unhappy. He isolated me from everyone, my family, friends, everyone, and I . . . well. I know how work can be the only place you can go to feel sane."

Alice put her hand in her pocket and pulled out a card. "I've written down some resources. And I don't want to assume that you were looking things up for yourself. Maybe it's for a friend, and you can pass this on to her."

Lilah took the card. She didn't know what to say.

"Thank you."

"You're welcome. I don't like to think of anyone going through what I did. But I also know . . . how hard it is to leave. And once you do leave, you think it's over, but it's not. It takes a long time to unlearn everything."

Someone sneezed in another part of the library and Alice glanced over her shoulder. In that moment Lilah saw how frightened Alice was, and how brave.

"Thank you," said Lilah again, and because that seemed totally inadequate, she hugged Alice. The other woman stiffened at the touch, but then relaxed. She didn't quite hug Lilah back, but she did pat her on the shoulder.

"Well," said Alice. "I will get back to the information desk. Just . . . call those numbers, if you need to."

"I will."

Lilah tucked the card into her bag next to the unused pepper spray. She had a lot to think about as she went about the rest of her day. Especially about how Alice had said that you never knew what was going in inside someone else's life. And how other people had secrets that might not be as big as killing someone, secrets that might not even be their own fault, but they were still secrets full of shame and fear, secrets that could eat away at you forever, making you unhappy, or maybe even a little evil, unless you trusted someone enough to share them with.

She had even more to think about the next day when she saw the newspaper article.

43

Marina

IN PARENTING CIRCLES, THEY CALLED this "the morning from hell." Right after her mother had called to cancel, Archie had taken a tumble off the sofa and landed on his face. He was fine, but he'd given himself a bloody nose and that had frightened him so badly that he was still crying twenty minutes after Marina had stopped the bleeding. Then it turned out that Lucy Rose had been yelling "poopy!" at the top of her lungs for about an hour not, as Marina had assumed, because she had decided that she liked the sound of that better than her real name, but because while Marina had been busy with Archie, Ewan had such a horrific poo in his diaper that it had flowed over the top and at the sides of each leg and he had been leaving a snail trail of watery child-feces across most of the first-floor hallway carpet. Ewan had no problem with this whatsoever; in fact, he was remarkably cheerful, if unbelievably smelly. By the time Marina had given him a bath and scrubbed the poo off the carpet and the blood off the sofa and was wondering how she was going to find the stomach to make anyone lunch, and why baby poo was so much worse than actual corpse desecration, Lucy Rose was tugging at her skirt, looking frantic.

"What is it, Luce?" Marina asked, trying her best to sound as if she had infinite patience.

"I lost Godzilla!"

"You lost him? How?"

Sure enough, the cage was empty. No wonder it had been quieter than usual.

"Did you take him out, Lucy Rose?"

"I put him in his ball and then he disappeared!"

Not for the first time, Marina regretted buying the hamster one of those plastic balls that he could run in and propel himself around the entire ground floor of the house. She'd thought maybe the extra exercise would wear him out and keep him a little quieter, since she had no need for him to drown out any noises from the basement anymore. But Godzilla was indefatigable.

"I just have to make a phone call, Lucy Rose, and then I'll look for him."

"Look for him now!"

"Where's Godzilla, Mommy?" asked Archie, wandering in with a carrot.

"Zilla!" yelled Ewan.

It was then that the doorbell rang.

Marina was surprised to see Opal standing on her doorstep. She was wearing workout gear and breathing slightly hard.

"Come in!" cried Marina, delighted. "Oh, it's so good to see you!"

"I know this is unexpected," said Opal, "and I know it's not what we said, but do you think it would be okay for me to stay with you for a few days?"

"Of course! You're very welcome. I've missed you. You can stay in the same room as before. I just changed the sheets."

She noticed that Opal didn't have any bags with her, but before she could ask about that, Lucy Rose was pulling at her skirt again.

"Godzilla's in heaven with Nana Sylvia," Lucy Rose said.

"Oh, sweetheart, I'm sure he isn't."

"What's up with the hamster from hell?" Opal eyed Lucy Rose. "I mean . . . hamster from heck."

"He's rolled off in his ball. He's probably under a chair. Oh my goodness, it's so great to see you. I haven't spoken to an adult in real life for three days."

Lucy Rose abandoned her mother and tugged at Opal's hand instead. "Come help look."

". . . Okay."

With Opal's help, they found the hamster under the piano in under five minutes.

"That hamster looks fatter than he did before," said Opal, extracting the ball and holding it up to the delight of the children. Lucy Rose and Archie bore him off, Ewan toddling behind them. Opal straightened up and brushed her knees.

"You're all dressed up," she said, looking Marina up and down.

"I was meant to be going out for an hour or so. But my mom rang to say she's got a cold and can't babysit."

"I'll do it."

"Really? I thought you hated kids."

"I do, but I can stand anything for a few hours."

Marina beamed. "You are literally a godsend, do you know that? I shouldn't be long. There's plenty of food in the fridge for their lunch, and we made cookies so the tin is full, and if you're lucky at least one of them might go down for a nap. From the looks of what he did before, Ewan shouldn't need changing until I'm back."

"You're not going on a date, are you? If you are, make sure you get a full and verifiable history out of him before you get too involved."

Marina winked. "I'll tell you all about it when I get back."

* * *

On her way to the bubble tea shop, she wondered why Opal hadn't had any luggage with her. She'd turned up looking as if she were mid-run. Was she in trouble of some sort? She'd been the one who was so vehement about the three of them not staying in touch.

Regardless, it felt good to know that she'd be there when Marina got home. It made her feel less lonely, less like everything depending just on her. It made her feel a little braver about what she was about to do.

She paused in the doorway of the bubble tea shop, looking for Freya. Everyone else here seemed to be a teenager, sucking up bubbles through wide straws while expertly scrolling their phones. She spotted Freya sitting at a pastel-colored table by herself. Her hair was in bunches, and she was wearing a pair of dungarees that made her look almost as young as the teens slurping tea, except for her pregnant belly. How old was she, anyway? In her twenties? A good fifteen years younger than Jake. Younger than Marina had been when she had Archie.

She did not seem to be all that that pleased to be here, and when she spotted Marina, she frowned.

Marina ordered a brown sugar milk tea and went over. "Hi. Ooh, you've got a purple one. What's that?"

"Taro without the tea."

"Is it good? I want to try everything on the menu, it all looks delicious. Do you want to try some of mine?"

"I'm not drinking caffeine, because of the baby."

"Oh, fair enough, good for you. I was never able to give up tea when I was expecting mine."

"Why did you ring me?" Freya asked. "I thought you hated me. I tried being friendly the other day when I dropped the kids and you totally shut me down."

Marina put down her cup. She had rehearsed this, late at night when the children were asleep.

"I don't hate you. I don't know you. I've been angry at you, because Jake left me for you."

"But that's not my fault! Jake—"

"I know. Jake was the one who broke up the marriage, not you."

"I was going to say, Jake told me everything. You were separated anyway, so I don't know why you'd be angry."

Marina's eyes widened. "He told you that?"

"Yes, before we even got together. He said you slept in separate rooms, and you didn't even talk. He said that your family had a weird thing about divorce, so he was letting you decide how to tell everyone. He said you were relieved when he told you he and I had fallen in love."

Oh Jake, you weasel.

"We weren't separated. And we didn't sleep in separate rooms. Our sex life was terrible, and I'll admit I wasn't enjoying being married to him, but I had no idea he was having an affair until I found out you were pregnant."

"Oh."

This wasn't the response Marina had expected. She remembered how Lilah had reacted when she'd heard the truth about Zachary. She'd expected, if not a slap, then at least a little bit of arguing and denial.

"You're . . . not surprised about this?" she asked gently.

"I don't know. Maybe. I really . . . the whole thing about your family hating divorce seemed a little far-fetched."

Marina decided to let that go without explanation.

"Jake and I weren't close anymore," Marina said. "That part is true. We weren't happy. So no, I don't hate you, and I'm not angry with you anymore, either. I don't know if I ever really was, or if I just thought that I should be. It's such a cliché, the spurned wife hating the younger mistress, women in rivalry with each other over a man. It's hard to resist these expectations sometimes."

Freya sighed. She pointed at Marina's bubble tea. "Can I try that? It's my favorite. You can try my taro."

Marina pushed it over.

"I didn't mean to get pregnant," Freya said, and took a sip. "Oh, you're right, this is really good. I've had to give up everything I like, and some websites say you shouldn't have caffeine and some say it doesn't matter and it's impossible to find out which one is the truth."

"Welcome to motherhood," said Marina. "Everything you decide is wrong." She tried the taro, and decided she liked hers better, even though it wasn't as colorful.

"Anyway, I never planned to have a baby so early. I love my career, and none of my friends are having babies yet. It's all a lot, you know. I was hoping that, like, if our kids were going to be half-siblings, that you and I could maybe get along at least."

"It is a lot," she agreed. "And I'd like to get along with you, if only because it's better for the children, and also it's spitting in the face of misogynistic stereotypes."

"Hear hear," said Freya, going back to her taro without much enthusiasm. She chewed on a tapioca bubble.

"But also," said Marina, "I need to tell you something that you need to know, before it's too late for you to make a choice. When I married Jake, I also loved my career. I loved who I was when I was at work. I loved myself, too, and I thought that I could keep loving myself while I loved him. But I couldn't. There is something about Jake that made it impossible. Maybe it's him, maybe it's just men in general,

maybe it's not men on their own but actually the patriarchy, whatever
that means. And I'm not blaming him, I'm blaming myself. But the
truth is that within my marriage, when I was in it, I found myself
getting smaller, day by day."

Freya was watching her with wide eyes.

"I got smaller and smaller with every baby I had. Not my ass and
my boobs, those got bigger. I mean myself, who I am. *I* got smaller.
And that's not right, because having children should make you bigger, happier. It should make you love yourself more, because you've
done this amazing thing. *You're* doing this amazing thing right now.
And yet, looking at you . . . I'm not sure you feel that way."

Freya blinked. There were suddenly tears in her eyes.

"You don't know how I feel," Freya said.

"You're right, I don't," said Marina. "My marriage failed, so I am
not the best person to listen to. But I do know, because I've seen it,
that Jake is taking you for granted already. He is already putting his
own needs before yours. I'm guessing that he is already talking about
you giving up your career, which is one of the things that makes you,
you. I'm guessing this, because he told me that you remind him of
me when I was your age, and that he loves your independence and
your spark. But those were the very things that he said he loved about
me, and that he then did his best to destroy."

"What are you trying to say?" Even though a tear had rolled down
her cheek, Freya still sounded defiant. Marina thought this was a good
thing.

"I'm trying to say that you should do exactly what you want."

"I will. You are literally a stranger. I don't need to do what you tell
me to do."

"Good. Your choices might be a lot better than mine. And anyway,
I can't regret my choices, because they led me to having three great
kids who I love more than anything in the world. And I don't think

JULIE MAE COHEN

that Jake is a bad man. I don't think he's much worse than a lot of other men out there. I think he is just a man, who behaves the way he does because he thinks that he is entitled to behave that way. I don't think you're going to change him, but if you want to try, then go ahead. But go ahead with your eyes open. Mostly I want to say that when a man shows you who he is, you should believe him. It will save you a lot of cleanup later."

260

44

Opal

"OPAL?"

"What."

"Why are little worms trying to eat Godzilla?"

For God's sake, Marina had only been gone twenty minutes. Holding Ewan awkwardly in her arms, she followed Archie to the hamster's cage, where Lucy Rose was also peering in.

"Ah," she said. "Those are not worms."

"What are they?" asked Lucy Rose.

"They are baby hamsters. It looks like Godzilla is a mommy."

The children were so delighted that they failed to make noise. Opal helped them count nine babies, all of them pink, squirmy, blind, hairless, and ugly as hell. As they watched, two more emerged. The miracle of birth. It was disgusting.

"How did he make babies?" asked Lucy Rose, in awe.

"That's something you're going to have to ask your mother about."

Opal did not have a burner phone with her, but she figured it was safe enough to google "what to do with baby hamsters." Together, she and the children added bits of soft bedding to the cage and topped up the food and water, being careful not to disturb the litter.

"I wanna make a nest like Godzilla," said Lucy Rose, when they were done, so Opal figured, why not? They built an enormous fort out of the cushions in all the sofas and chairs and from their beds, and draped blankets over the top. It was big enough for all of them to fit inside comfortably. Opal raided the cupboards for everything she could find that was edible and brought it into the nest with them. Archie produced a stack of Dr. Seuss books and Ewan crawled onto her lap and she read them book after book, including *Green Eggs and Ham* three times.

Ewan fell asleep on her first, without even finding out whether Sam-I-Am got that guy to try green eggs and ham. Archie and Lucy Rose conked out sometime near the end of *The Cat in the Hat*.

Opal closed the book and leaned her head back on the cushions. She realized that for at least half the afternoon, she had been too busy to remember her problems.

Through the years, she hadn't allowed herself to think about what kind of mother she would have made if she hadn't lost that baby. Or what kind of mother she'd be if she somehow decided to trust another man enough to love him and make a family with him. She'd walled off those possibilities in her mind and in her life. With the kind of parents she'd had, she was better off not reproducing anyway.

She sniffed Ewan's head. Everyone always went on about how great babies' heads smelled and she always thought it was hype. It was not hype. It was the scent of youth and innocence and hope. If you could bottle this scent and sell it, you would be a billionaire.

It was too late for her to have children of her own, so there was no point in thinking about it now. But given the evidence of this morning, she thought maybe she could be a decent aunt, if she had a chance. She would enjoy it, too.

Too bad she wasn't ever going to get a chance. It was only a matter of days, if not hours, before it was all going to end.

It had been stupid to come here, right to the place where she had the most to lose. But maybe it had been smart, too—because this was the only place where she still had anything that she could lose.

*   *   *

"You know what?" Marina asked the next day, when they were planting bulbs in the beds along the side of the fence in the back garden. Well—the grown-ups were planting bulbs, and the children were having a competition to see who could find the most worms. Delicious scents wafted from the kitchen; Marina had some French chicken dish bubbling on the stove for their Sunday lunch.

Opal had never planted bulbs before. She'd never planted anything. But the damp earth felt good on her hands, and it was an interesting feeling to put these little dead gnarls into the ground with faith that one day, they would emerge as flowers. Not the kind that you got in bouquets, that were already dead, but the kind that were alive and growing.

She wouldn't be around to see them, of course. She wouldn't even be around long enough for Godzilla's babies to open their eyes. But it was sort of nice to think that she'd be leaving at least something behind.

Marina had not asked her any questions. She'd given her a bedroom, a spare toothbrush, one of the good towels, the Wi-Fi password, and an iPad that had to be cleaned of sticky fingerprints before it was fit for use. She didn't seem to be bothered that the very presence of Opal in her house was a risky link to a crime that they'd both committed, or the fact that Opal was obviously running away from someone or something.

263

"Don't you want to know why I'm here?" Opal had asked last night, after the kids had gone to bed and they were curled up on separate sofas in the front room.

Marina had shrugged. "You'll tell me when you want to. Meanwhile I'm enjoying the company. I've been pretty lonely."

"Me too," said Opal, and, miraculously, that had seemed to have been enough.

Now, digging in wormy dirt, enjoying the scent of their future lunch, she knew exactly what Marina was about to say.

"I wish Lilah were here," Opal said for her.

"Bingo."

"Well, maybe one day we'll have another terrible man to take down, and we can get the A-team back together."

At that moment there was a half-timid knock on the garden gate, and it swung open. "Hello? Marina?"

Marina jumped up, squealing in joy. "Lilah! We were just talking about you!"

Opal got up more slowly, while the other two women embraced each other at the gate. "Hello," she said, and Lilah looked startled to see her. Something in her face told Opal exactly why that was.

It was over.

"Thank you for your text," said Lilah, carefully.

"You're welcome," said Opal. "Have you seen the news?" Opal asked. "Is that why you're here?"

"I . . . saw an article when I was tidying the newspapers at the library. And I don't know where you live, so I thought I'd talk it over with Marina."

"An article?" Marina said, and added in a whisper, "Did they find him?"

"No," said Opal. "This one is about me. Am I right, Lilah?"

Lilah glanced over to where the children were playing. "It's all right," said Marina. "They can't hear us over the construction from next door."

"I stole the newspaper, but it was the end of the day so I don't think anyone will mind." She took a folded copy of the *Metro* from her bookshop tote bag and opened it up so that they both could see the front page. There was a full-color photograph of Opal, grabbed from one of her Instagram posts, and another photograph, this one of a young woman, who Opal, with a lurch of her stomach, recognized right away.

The last time she had seen that young woman, she had been dead. The headline was:

FIT OR FRAUD?

WELLNESS INFLUENCER LINKED TO UNEXPLAINED DEATH

45

THREE YEARS BEFORE

Opal

BACK THEN, HER NAME WASN'T Opal. It was Pearl, and she was the CEO and founder of Weight&See, a wellness and weight-loss business that sold dietary supplements and lifestyle coaching in the north of England.

From the outside, her life looked perfect. She had a good-looking husband who was the charming face of the organization, while she ran things behind the scenes. They had started as a small concern, marketing their supplements at wellness fairs, with Pearl handling logistics and Zander as the salesman, but they grew quickly and soon franchised out. People paid to be trained in how to sell Weight&See, and then those people paid the head office a percentage to be paid to train other people to sell Weight&See, and so on and so forth, all in a pyramid. They had branded T-shirts, mugs, scales, and vans, and an Associates' Retreat once a year in a hotel outside of Manchester where Zander gave inspirational seminars to the mostly female associates by day and killed it on the dance floor by night.

Pearl liked the money. Zander loved the grift. Pearl thought sometimes that he was born to be a cult leader.

They had two secrets (aside from the whole pyramid scheme thing). One was that their marriage was far from what it seemed. The other was that Weight&See's premium supplement, SeeMe, while perfectly safe and legal, was also entirely ineffective. The capsules were filled with protein powder, caffeine, corn flour, and enough spirulina to make them taste sufficiently gross to seem healthy. It cost about fifty pence to manufacture a hundred capsules.

Still. People lost weight, maybe because of the exercise and lifestyle coaching, maybe because they believed they would. They told their friends, and *they* told *their* friends, and soon the people who got in on the ground floor were making good money on the back of the poor mugs who were buying algae-laced whey powder at £75 a bottle, and other poor mugs who were paying thousands for the exclusive opportunity to sell algae and whey at £75 a bottle, and Pearl and Zander were making profit out of everything.

It was a scam, but it required more work than Pearl had ever known in a lifetime of hustle. Pearl was so busy that she had to hire an assistant—not anyone who would know what the business was really about, of course, but someone to answer the phone, reply to emails, manage her calendar, work reception, chase invoices, update the website, and handle the social media.

This was how she met Cora Neale.

Cora was short, red-haired, scrappy, pierced, and tattooed. She had grown up in foster care in Barnsley and, at twenty-three, had been working in warehouses for years. She wore Doc Martens, overalls, and sleeveless T-shirts and Pearl liked her from the moment they met. "I don't believe in this dieting shit," she told Pearl at her job interview. "I just want a decent job where I don't have to wear protective clothing."

Pearl hired her on the spot. This was the beginning of the end, though she didn't know it.

Zander did not like Cora. He thought she was too blunt, too Northern, too working-class. "Not aspirational enough" was how he phrased it. "She won't attract customers." By now, Pearl was deferring to him in almost everything, but she held on to Cora. "You never come into the office anyway," she argued. Zander shrugged and said, "Suit yourself. Maybe the marks will relate to her."

It felt like some kind of victory.

That was how pathetic she'd become: she was grateful to be able to hire her own staff. She trained Cora herself, teaching her computer skills and customer care. She thought about how Zander had been when she'd met him—aimless, a drifter, living hand to mouth without many skills except native charm. Cora was like that, but without the streak of dishonesty. She was funny, but not mean. A fighter, not a parasite. She had no family and few friends. Pearl found herself staying late in the office, avoiding going home, getting to know Cora, showing her the ropes. If Pearl was working—at her own damn business—how could Zander complain?

In the first week of December, Pearl got the Christmas decorations down from the office loft and put them on Cora's desk.

"What am I supposed to do with these?" said Cora, turning a bauble round in her hand as if it were some sort of fish.

"Decorate."

"How?"

Pearl shrugged. "However you like."

When she came out at lunchtime, the office was transformed. Pearl stared.

"Is it bad?"

"It looks like a fairy's been vomiting tinsel," Pearl said.

"I've not exactly had a lot of cause to put up Christmas ornaments. I've lived alone in various ratholes since I was sixteen."

"What do you do for Christmas?"

"Get drunk in front of the TV."

"Come to our house," said Pearl, surprising herself. She had never invited anyone before. She did not think that Zander would like it. She thought it might be dangerous to rebel, and she might end up paying later. But she liked Cora.

Strangely, when she told him Cora was coming, Zander didn't object. In fact, he practically laid out the red carpet. They didn't usually follow tradition, but this year he decided to go all-out. He bought a tree. He got in all of Cora's favorite drinks, consulted her about the menu (she was vegan and had various food allergies, and of course he didn't believe in roast potatoes). On Christmas Day, he was charm itself. Apparently he had changed his mind about Cora, or maybe he was just trying to make Pearl happy, or maybe he couldn't bear for anyone not to be impressed by him; but whatever it was, after a few glasses of champagne, Pearl stopped waiting for the other shoe to drop and enjoyed the day. She'd never had a nicer Christmas.

"Cora, I'll admit it," Zander said, leaning back in his chair after the meal, "I wasn't sure about you at first, but you're sound. If you wore something other than overalls, you'd even be pretty."

"He's being an ass," Pearl said. "Don't pay attention to him."

"It's true," said Zander. "I am an ass and you should not pay attention to me. But seriously, you have a knockout smile and a gorgeous face. All you'd have to do is knock off the carbs, lose a few pounds, and buy a pair of jeans."

Pearl shot him a look. Zander winked at Cora, and Cora laughed. "Stop winding up your wife."

"It's too easy," said Zander.

Best not to disturb the peace. She got up to open another bottle and by the time she poured it into their glasses, Zander and Cora were discussing Barnsley's chances in the FA Cup.

They all drank too much that night and Cora stayed in the spare bedroom. Pearl woke the next morning with a hangover and indigestion, but she had to admit it: everything had turned out better than she'd hoped. Maybe Zander was mellowing out. Maybe they'd been going through a bad patch, and they had turned the corner. Since the miscarriage, he'd been more careful with her, gentler.

This could be a new beginning.

Zander was still sleeping. She showered and brought a mug of coffee and a glass of water to the spare room. When she knocked Cora didn't answer, so she quietly opened the door, intending to put the drinks on the bedside table so she'd find them when she woke up.

Cora was lying fully dressed on top of the covers on the bed. Both her hands were clasped to her throat. Her eyes were open, her mouth was agape, and her skin was blue.

Pearl dropped the coffee and the water. "Zander!" she yelled and jumped onto the bed and started doing CPR.

She was doing frantic compressions when Zander appeared in the doorway, disheveled and alarmed. "What the fuck! What's wrong with her?"

"She's not breathing. Call an ambulance."

Zander came up to the bed. "What happened?"

"Fucked if I know, call an ambulance now!" Pearl blew into Cora's mouth, resumed compressions. Nothing was happening. Cora's lips were cold.

"Did she have a heart attack? Young girl like that?"

"Call 911!"

"I think she's dead, Pearl."

"No. No, she's not."

Pearl kept working. Zander peered down at Cora.

"We can't call an ambulance," he said. "It's too late. And also, what does it look like, finding a dead girl in our flat?"

"I don't care what it *looks like*," said Pearl, but she stopped the compressions because Zander was right about that part. It was too late. Cora had been dead for hours, while they'd been fast asleep in the room next door. "Did you hear anything? Did she call for help?"

Zander shook his head. "Looks like an overdose. Did you hire a junkie?"

"She is not a junkie." Numb, breathing hard, Pearl got off the bed and for the first time, she saw the bottle of SeeMe on the nightstand, next to a half-drunk glass of water. She snatched it up. "Where did she get this?"

"I gave her some. She wanted to try."

"You gave her SeeMe?"

"Yeah, she said she wanted to lose a bit of weight. She *asked* for it."

"She is fucking allergic to corn, Zander!"

Her shout echoed in the silence. The two of them stared at each other.

"We have to get rid of her," said Zander, at last.

"What?"

"She took SeeMe and died. We can't have that."

"No. No, we call an ambulance." Pearl started for the door to find her phone.

"No," said Zander, and he came right up to Pearl, and he grabbed her chin and made her look into his face. "You listen. This was an accident. But we cannot have any deaths connected to us and to Weight&See. You know why."

"No," she said.

But he was stronger than her.

46

OPAL

"WE BROUGHT HER BACK TO her apartment, and I tucked her into her bed. I sat with her for a little while. I'll never forget how she looked."

The three of them were sitting on the patio as Opal finished her story.

"It was my fault," Opal said. "That poor girl."

"It wasn't your fault," said Lilah. "Zander gave her the pills."

"I hired her. I brought her to my home. I liked her."

"What happened?" asked Marina in a soft voice.

"They discovered her two days later. By that time, Zander was gone. And all of my money with him. Of course I couldn't go to the police."

"It was a pyramid scheme?" asked Lilah. "Your business?"

"Yes," Opal said. "I'm a con woman. I've been one all my life, ever since I was a kid. That's how I knew Zander's game: I'm the one who taught it to him. And I am responsible for that girl's death. I didn't mean for it to happen, but it was ultimately my fault. I covered it up. After Zander disappeared with all the money, I destroyed the records,

I shut up the business, I changed my name, and I moved to London and got into fitness in a big way."

"But . . . the fitness stuff isn't a con, is it?" asked Marina.

"No. I went straight after Cora died. All the health and exercise advice I give online now are things I do myself, based on actual science, and they are meant to make you feel good and live longer, not make you skinny." She shook her head. "I couldn't live a lie anymore. I owed Cora that much."

"You've been lying to us, though," said Lilah. "By omission, at least."

"Yes. I gave Zander that sleeping pill so that he wouldn't tell you who I was. I'd also reached a deal with him. If we let him go, he couldn't go to the police to inform on you, because if he did, I'd tell them about Weight&See and Cora."

"But that would get you in trouble, too," said Lilah. Opal shrugged.

"Is that why you turned up here yesterday?" Marina pointed at the newspaper that was lying on the table between them. "You knew this was going to break?"

"There was a reporter outside my flat. I was pretty sure the police were next. I needed somewhere safe, and I didn't have cash for a hotel because I'd given it to my assistant. That's another story."

"What's going to happen?"

"I don't know. There might be a warrant out for my arrest, but I'm thinking not yet. It takes some time to put together a case, whether that's for fraud or manslaughter. Anyway. Thanks to your Wi-Fi and the only credit card I haven't maxed out yet, I have a cheap flight to Dubrovnik late tonight. I'll work it out from there."

"Tonight?" said Lilah in dismay.

"But you just got here," said Marina.

"And I have no desire to lead the cops to your door."

"I don't want you to go. The kids are just getting to know you."

Opal steeled herself. "There's something else I need to tell you. And then you'll be glad to get rid of me."

"Shoot," said Lilah, and then wrinkled her nose. "I mean . . . go ahead."

"I went into this whole thing for revenge, like I said. I couldn't bear the thought of Zander cheating and stealing from another woman. But also . . . I needed money. And I have gone straight up till now. But the idea of two gullible rich women . . . to a reformed grifter, that's like a suitcase of free heroin."

"You were going to try to con *us*?"

Opal nodded. "At first I was. Then, after Marina pushed Zander down the stairs, my thoughts were turning more to blackmail. I reckoned I could have the two of you paying me for years, to keep it quiet that you were kidnappers."

"That probably would have worked," said Lilah. "On me, anyway."

"When did you decide not to?" asked Marina.

"Honestly? It was when I spoke with Zander, and he accused me of planning to do it. Then it became a matter of pride. I might need money, but I'm damned if I'm going to conform to what a man expects me to do."

"Patriarchy," said Marina. "Didn't mean to interrupt you. I've been listening to podcasts."

"That's okay, you're right. But the main reason, more important than my own pride, was that I like both of you. And I don't like anyone. I haven't liked a single person since Cora."

Lilah let out a huge and audible breath. "I'm *so glad* you said that. I find it hard to make friends, and then when you said that the three of us shouldn't be in touch anymore, I felt terrible. I've been really sad."

"Me too," said Marina. "It's been lonely."

"Anyway. Now you know everything. You know that I pretended to be your friend so that I could fleece you for all you were worth. I can't be trusted, and I've got the press and probably the police on my tail. So." Opal stood up. "Now that you know the kind of person that I really am, I'll let you get on with the rest of your lives."

She turned to walk away.

And then, something extraordinary happened.

Marina grabbed one of Opal's hands. Lilah grabbed the other. And both held tight, not letting her leave.

"Why are you going?" Lilah asked. "We only just got back together."

"Because I'm a liar and a crook."

"Yeah," said Marina, "but the three of us did . . . you-know-what. That's much worse."

"I was going to make your lives miserable and take whatever money of yours I could get. I was literally doing the same thing that Zander did, without the benefit of sex."

"I keep on telling you, I don't really care about money," said Lilah. "If you need some, I'd be happy to give you some. Cash, no questions asked."

"You don't have any left."

Lilah snorted. "Do you think the lottery gave me sixty-seven million pounds all at once? They spread it out. I'll get another payment in April, for the new tax year."

"I don't have much cash, but you can lay low here for as long as you like," said Marina. "My kids like you."

Opal stared at them both.

"But I've just told you that I'm a terrible person, and that I've always been a terrible person, and I'm about to have my life ripped, quite rightly and very publicly, to shreds. Why would you be so nice to me? Are you both idiots?"

"We're not idiots," said Lilah. "We're your friends."

Then, quite unexpectedly and for only the second time in her adult life, Opal burst into tears.

She hadn't cried when she miscarried, or when she lost all her money, or when Cora Neale died, or when either of her estranged parents died, or any of the other times over the past thirty years when she'd been angry or sad or desperate. She was too strong for that. She had only cried when Zander was dead.

But crying because she was happy: that was a completely different thing.

They hugged her. Archie came over from his dirt pile and patted her on the arm. "S'okay," he told her. "Do you want to see the baby hamsters?"

"No thanks," Opal said, and hiccupped. "I'm fine. I'm sorry . . . I was afraid you two would never want to see me again."

"Stop apologizing," said Marina.

"Stop being a scared little bunny rabbit," said Lilah.

"Well," said a strange male voice. "This is a touching scene. Mind if I join?"

47

Marina

THERE WAS A MAN SHE'D never seen before in the garden with them. He had picked up Lucy Rose and held her around her waist, under his arm like a bundle of sticks. She wriggled to be set free.

"Put down my daughter," Marina said.

"Sure, in a minute," said the man. "We need to talk first."

"You're the person who followed me," said Lilah.

"Good to see you again," said the man, and smiled. He was big, broad, with a thick neck and a barrel chest. He was wearing jeans, a gray sweatshirt, and a blue baseball cap. Aside from the fact that he was holding her daughter against her will, he looked like someone's dad. "Sorry to burst in on you like this, I know it's rude."

Marina didn't take her gaze away from him and her daughter. He was blocking the gate to the front garden. "Opal," she said. "Please get Archie and Ewan now, please."

"Relax, ladies. Everything's going to be fine."

"I wanna get down!" yelled Lucy Rose, squirming and trying to hit him with her little fists.

"Calm down, Princess. I need some information first. Can we go inside the house, please?"

Marina dared to glance behind her. Opal had Archie by the hand and had snatched up Ewan, too. They were safe, for now. But Lucy Rose wasn't.

"If we go inside, will you let my daughter go?"

"There's nothing I'd like better."

"I'm the one you want to talk to," said Lilah. "I'll go with you. Leave the others alone."

"Sadly, I can't do that. I need to keep my eyes on all of you. I think you're more dangerous than you look, you know?"

Lucy Rose let out a squeal that squeezed Marina's heart nearly in two. She could pick up this patio chair and swing for him . . . but she'd hurt her daughter. She could scream for help from the neighbors, or tell Opal to make a run for it with the other two children . . . but would he hurt Lucy Rose if they didn't do what he said?

"Let's go inside," she said, shakily. "Lucy Rose, it's going to be fine. Mommy won't let the man hurt you."

"That's right," said the man, as they all backed slowly towards the French doors to the kitchen. "I've got grandkids. I wouldn't want to hurt anyone."

"Mommy," whimpered Archie. Ewan was crying.

Marina did not know how she was moving, because her brain had no spare capacity for walking; it was focused on her children, where they were, who had them, how frightened they must be.

"Stay with Opal," she told Archie. "Stay right close beside her, okay? I won't let anything bad happen."

She wished she believed what she was saying.

In the kitchen, he closed the French doors and locked them with the key that she kept in the door.

"Smells good in here," he said. "No ideas about grabbing knives, or running off, okay? I'm going to hold on to princess here until we have our business all sorted out."

Marina's gaze darted around the room. The knives were behind him in a block on the counter. Opal brought Archie and Ewan to the corner of the room, not far from the cellar door. Could they get downstairs and barricade themselves into the shelter if Marina distracted this man?

What was he armed with? She couldn't see any weapons, but that didn't mean he wasn't carrying a knife or a gun.

"You killed my father, didn't you." It was a statement from Lilah, not a question.

"I'm looking for your boyfriend," he said. "Where is he?"

"I don't know. I haven't seen Zachary in over a week. I reported him missing to the police."

"Convenient that he ran off, when he owes me a lot of money."

"He owes me more than money. So if you find him, tell him to get in touch."

Somewhere, beneath all the fear, Marina heard how badass Lilah sounded and cheered her on.

"Now, I don't like to call you a liar," said the man, "but I have an inkling that you know exactly where he is."

"What kind of man are you, threatening women and children?" said Lilah calmly. "You attacked my father from behind, when he was alone and unarmed. You're a coward. Just like Zachary. You deserve each other."

"Let's try to keep focused on the issue at hand. The fact is, I have three grandchildren in private schools. I'm just trying to give them the best start in life, you know? So I need my money."

"I'll give it to you," said Lilah. "Put down the little girl, and we'll go to the bank together."

"It's Sunday."

"I'll write you a check."

"A check? What is this, 1986? No, here is what you are going to do. You are going to call your boyfriend and tell him to get here with one hundred thousand pounds, in cash."

"Or what?"

S reached into his back pocket with the hand that wasn't holding Lucy Rose and pulled out a switchblade knife.

Marina screamed, and then quickly covered her mouth with her hand.

"Don't worry, I wouldn't scar her permanently," said the man. "But I'd rather not hurt her at all."

"I hate you," yelled Lucy Rose, kicking fruitlessly. "You're a bad man!"

"I can't call Zachary," said Lilah, "because I don't know where he is."

"I hate to call a lady a liar."

"I can get the money for you, though. I'll give you a hundred and fifty thousand, cash. Your reward for striking down a helpless retired postman while he was playing with his model trains. I'll meet you wherever you want, whenever you want. Just leave my friends alone."

Marina was frozen to the spot, and Opal was shielding the other two children with her body, but Lilah was standing straight and tall and defiant. She took a step closer to S.

"I've got the money in my account right now. All I have to it draw it out. Look, I'll show you." She reached for her fanny pack.

"Hold on a second. Slowly, now. What are you getting out of your bag?"

Lilah paused. "My phone to show you my banking app."

"I don't want your money. Your dad would be rolling over in his grave if you paid me. Have some respect. Why don't you call your boyfriend?"

Marina's entire being was focused on that knife, not three inches from her beautiful, precious child's face. Her eyes. Her throat. He said he didn't want to hurt her, but he was a killer, and she couldn't believe him.

"I can't call him!"

"I'm not going to hurt him, either, as long as he pays me." The man rolled his eyes to the ceiling. "This is the worst part of being self-employed."

"I told you, I don't know where he is!"

"Do you really want to make me hurt this kid?"

"I can't—"

"He's dead," said Opal. Flat, factual, in her tone that brooked no bullshit. "Zachary's dead, and he can't give you the money that you think he owed you. But Lilah can give it to you, like she says. Listen to reason, and put the child down."

"Please," said Marina. "Please let my daughter go."

S glanced from one of them to the other, obviously trying to work out this latest turn of events. Half a smile appeared on his face.

"Ah," he said. "I get it. *That's* what you were all dropping in the river."

"You've been watching us," Opal said.

"Have you been in the treehouse?" Marina gasped. "That was you, with the Oreos?"

"I can't get enough of those things," said S.

"Stop it!" yelled Archie from behind Opal. "Let my sister go!"

"You're a bad man!" yelled Lucy Rose, struggling. "You're a bad bad bad bad bad man!"

"Princess, it'll be all right."

"Let her go," pleaded Marina. "Just put her down, we'll get you your money."

"I can get it for you first thing tomorrow, if you leave us alone. Look, I'll show you."

"You're a bad bad BAD man and I hate you!"

"Calm, now. Just calm down."

S put his hand, the hand with the knife in it, over Lucy Rose's mouth. The blade was so close to her eye, so close to her skin, so close to cutting and blinding her precious, precious child—

Then he screamed. He dropped the knife, which clattered on the tiles. Lucy Rose wriggled from his grip, landed on all fours on the kitchen floor, and scurried across the room to her brothers and Opal.

"She *bit* me!"

In a flash, Lilah reached into her bum bag, grabbed her can of pepper spray, and sprayed it full into S's face.

He staggered backwards, roaring and clawing at his eyes. One of his hands was dripping with blood.

"Get the children out of here, Opal, now!"

"I bited the bad man!" crowed Lucy Rose, as Opal hustled them all out of the kitchen.

S collided with the kitchen island, sending a bowl of fruit crashing to the floor. He sank to his knees and wiped frantically at his face, smearing blood.

Marina dragged in a breath, the first full one since he had arrived. Her children were safe. But they had been threatened by this person, this killer, this bad man. And she was never, ever going to let it happen again.

She stepped past courageous Lilah and writhing S to the stovetop and grabbed the wooden handle of her Le Creuset cast-iron sauté pan, bubbling with chicken chasseur. Without a thought for her hands, her kitchen, her Sunday lunch, her own soul, she brought the hot, heavy pan down on the bad man's head.

Once. Then twice. Three times.

The man collapsed. His mouth open, his eyes staring ahead at nothing. His blood pooling with wine sauce and button mushrooms.

48

Opal

OPAL GOT THE KIDS THROUGH the house to the front door, but Archie refused to walk through it.

"Not without Mommy," he said. "Mommy's with that bad man in the kitchen."

"She wants you to be safe," Opal said. "And she will be safe, too, but she wants you to come with Aunt Opal."

Archie shook his head and planted his feet.

"You're very brave," Opal told him, crouching down to his level. "And listen, I am not going to let anything happen to your mom. She is one of the only two friends I have, and I will protect her with my life. But she loves you more than anyone else in the entire world, and you need to do this for her. You just need to walk out the door."

Archie held her gaze, his mouth set. Opal wondered how she could ever have thought of herself as strong-willed. She was no match for a five-year-old.

"I'll buy you sweets," she tried.

At that moment, Marina came rushing into the front hall. The children cried out and ran to her. Ewan, in Opal's arms, held out his hands.

"My darlings," she said, gathering them to her, taking Ewan from Opal, covering them with kisses. "Everything's okay, we're all okay, we're safe now. The bad man has gone away."

"Is he coming back?" Archie buried his face in her chest.

"No. The police came and took him."

Opal caught Marina's glance above the children. Marina shook her head slightly and then bent to her daughter.

"Are you okay, Lucy Rose? Are you hurt? You are so brave, you are all so brave!"

"I bited him and he tasted bad."

Marina held her close, all three of her children in her arms, cradled tight. Tears were coursing down her face, but she didn't seem to notice them. Opal thought she had never seen anyone look so happy.

She left the family where they were and went back to the kitchen. Lilah was standing over S's prone body. The man's face was splashed with blood and his head wasn't quite the right shape. For a moment, Opal thought that his thumbs had been ripped off and scattered on the floor, but then she realized it was a pair of chicken drumsticks.

"She killed him with our lunch," said Lilah.

Quite deliberately, she leaned forward and spat on S's body.

"That's for Dad."

"Are you okay?" asked Opal, putting her hand on Lilah's shoulder. "You didn't even seem frightened."

"I was very frightened. I just didn't care." She stepped over S and turned off the burner on the cooker. "Are the children all right?"

"Yes." Opal realized something. "Marina trusted me with them. She didn't even have to think about it. Even after everything I told you that I'd done."

"Of course," said Lilah.

"I don't deserve trust like that."

"You do."

They closed the kitchen door behind them and went to find Marina, who was still on the floor with her kids around her.

"Are the police still there?" Archie asked Opal. "Can I see them?"

"They went out the back door," said Opal. "They're taking that guy to jail."

"Did they have guns?"

"I think so."

"Wow."

"Marina, your arms," said Lilah.

Opal took a closer look. The skin on Marina's arms was red and angry where the hot broth had splattered over them. It was already starting to blister and swell.

"Those are second-degree burns," she said. "I'll get you cold compresses. But you need to get to a hospital."

Marina shook her head. "No. I need to take the kids someplace safe. My mum's house, or my brother's."

"I'm not leaving Mummy," said Archie.

Opal made a quick decision. "Right. Lilah, you take Marina and the kids to hospital. You can watch them while she's being treated. And then you can all go together to her mum's."

"But what about . . ."

"I'll clean up the mess in the kitchen."

"No," said Marina. "I made the mess. I'll clean it up."

"We'll *all* clean it up," said Lilah. "But I'll take you to the hospital first, and then we'll take the kids to their gran's, because their Sunday lunch got spilled all over the floor, and they'll need something else to eat."

"And I'll stay here," said Opal, "in case 'the police' need me to answer any extra questions."

"You have a flight to catch."

"I've got loads of time. Don't worry."

"But—"

"The mess will be fine," said Opal sternly.

* * *

But after they'd left, Opal locked all the doors and then went down into the cellar. She found a leftover plastic sheet, and the bucket of rags and cleaning fluids, and a brand-new package of Marigold gloves, and brought them all up to where S's body lay, sauce and blood congealing around him.

Before she got started, she removed S's hoodie, thinking about how, sadly, this was the last man she'd be likely to undress for some time. She cut the hoodie into pieces with kitchen scissors and burnt it, piece by piece in a Dutch oven on top of the cooker, with the fan going full speed. Lucy Rose had been close to it, and Lilah had spat on it, and though she was reasonably sure that neither of them had DNA samples registered with law enforcement, she also wouldn't have put it past Lilah to have sent in a DNA test to a genealogy lab at some point. It seemed like something she would do for fun.

Whatever else happened, she did not want this body being connected with her friends. That meant she'd have to do something about that bite mark, too.

As she worked, she thought about Dubrovnik. Old Town, the mountains, the sea, the wedding-cake buildings, sunshine on palm trees. White boats bobbing on bright blue water. Fresh seafood, Mediterranean diet, people with more money than sense. It was the sort of place where you could reinvent yourself.

If only.

49

Marina

IN THE END, LILAH HAD to feed the children their Sunday lunch at the hospital café while Marina waited to get her arms bandaged, and then they had to take the children all the way to Neil's house in Willesden, which was probably a good thing because by the time they got there, Archie was full of stories about chocolate frosted doughnuts and traveling in a real black cab and he immediately told his cousins about those, not the bad man who had tried to cut his sister's face. With any luck, Marina thought, the doughnuts and the cab would be his lasting memories of the day.

Neil was not particularly pleased to see them at such short notice, until she told him the story of the man who'd broken into her house and grabbed Lucy Rose, but who had been quickly apprehended by the police and taken to jail with no harm done.

"That sort of thing never happens around here," he said. "I bet you wish you'd sold the house now!"

She took the number of his estate agent buddy "just in case." She'd never hear the end of it now, but it cheered Neil up so much that he agreed to keep the children for a sleepover while she went to the police station to give a statement, and that was a small price to pay.

In the cab going back to Richmond, they were stuck in traffic. They asked the driver to turn the radio up and spoke in hushed murmurs in the back seat.

"What are we going to do with him?"

"Same as last time, I suppose."

"I'm going to go bankrupt buying new cooking knives."

"Don't worry about it."

"Opal's getting a flight tonight. So it'll be me and you with the . . . drop-off."

"I'm so sad that she's going. Do you think we can visit her?"

"Eventually."

"I've never been on a girls' holiday before."

"Me neither."

"I wonder if there's one of those resorts with all those activities for kids? Unless you'd prefer to leave them with their dad."

"It's cheaper outside of school holidays, for sure."

"Don't worry about how much."

"Do you think . . . she would have really blackmailed us?"

"She thinks she meant to. She was afraid we wouldn't be her friends anymore when we found out."

"She had a really terrible childhood, didn't she? But it didn't mess her up too much. She's still got a good heart."

"She'll be okay. She'll land on her feet. I hope we can figure out a way to stay in touch."

"You know . . . I thought I would feel terrible if I . . . did that thing. But I don't feel terrible. I feel relieved."

"I know just how you feel. I felt that way too."

"Are we monsters?"

"I think . . . that maybe we are just fed up."

"But . . . we're not going to keep on doing this, are we?"

"Definitely not."

"Right. Definitely."

They listened to Taylor Swift for a moment.

"Do you think my children are going to be all right?"

"I lost my mom when I was really young, and that was traumatic. But I was okay, because I had a parent who loved me more than anything. I think, on balance, they are probably going to be all right."

"They might need therapy. That's going to be expensive."

"Don't worry about it."

"Lilah, I am not going to let you pay for my children's therapy."

"We'll cross that bridge when we come to it. Anyway, it's my fault. He followed me to your house. If I'd gone home, it all would've happened differently."

"Speaking of bridges . . . he saw us at the river. He was watching us the whole time."

"I'm sorry I led him there."

"I'm glad you came to my house. I hate to think of you dealing with that by yourself."

"You know what, though? I think we can deal with anything, as long as we're together."

Marina squeezed Lilah's hand with her uninjured one.

"Does two make us serial . . . ?"

"I'll look it up."

"Not on Google."

"Of course not."

"I don't think I'm going to be able to cook in that Le Creuset again."

"It's a good excuse to get a whole new set."

"You are really a bad influence, do you know that?"

The news came on.

"More details this afternoon about fitness influencer Opal Eliot, better known online as Hot Fit Mess, and her links to fraudulent weight-loss company Weight&See. In addition to cheating customers and associates out of more than three quarter of a million pounds, it has emerged that Eliot, who founded the company, is wanted for questioning regarding the death of Cora Neale, who was her employee. Metropolitan police have issued a statement asking for members of the public who have any tips on her whereabouts to call Crimestoppers."

Marina and Lilah's eyes met.

"Shit," mouthed Marina.

Lilah leaned forward. "Is there any way we can get there faster, please?"

* * *

There was no way to get there faster. It was more than an hour, and long after nightfall, before Lilah paid the driver an exorbitant amount and the two of them rushed into the house. It was dark and quiet.

"Opal!" they called, to no answer. When they went into the kitchen, it was spotless and there was a distinct lack of corpses.

There was, however, a note on the table.

DON'T LOOK FOR ME. BURN THIS. LOVE YOU. O

They searched the house and cellar and garden, but without much hope, and reconvened in the kitchen.

"What did she do." Lilah sank into a chair.

"Exactly what we told her not to do. I hope she caught her plane." Marina scoured the kitchen. It was the cleanest it had ever been. The Le Creuset sat, empty and without even a dent, on the top of the cooker. She sniffed: bleach, lemon cleaner, and the slightest whiff of something burnt.

"How could she do all of this, and then get rid of—that, by herself?" Lilah looked distressed. "It took us all day with Zachary."

"Maybe she carried him whole."

"How?"

"She did say that she was able to bench-press 150 pounds, no problem."

"Yes but . . . I didn't *expect* her to." Lilah got up to pace the kitchen while Marina sat down. "And he weighed more than that, for sure."

"Do you think the police got her?" Marina chewed her lip.

"Oh no."

"The police are looking for her and she tries disposing of a dead body on her own."

"Oh, goodness."

"Unless she just went straight to the airport, with . . ."

"How?"

"There are some large suitcases in the attic. Nana Sylvia never traveled light."

"You can't check a dead body into a plane! Can you?"

"I honestly don't know. I mean, people must. When Nana Sylvia died we flew her back, but I think she was in a coffin."

"You must need a permit of some sort though. Not just . . . stuffed into a suitcase."

"I'll go check."

In the attic, there was a suitcase missing. Marina didn't remember what it looked like, or how big it was, but there was a space without dust on the floor where it used to be.

Back downstairs, Lilah was burning the note from Opal in the sink.

"She doesn't want us to find her, but we have to try."

"We can't call her. We deleted her number."

"Check the news."

The news websites didn't have any new items about Opal, just repeats of what they'd heard in the taxi. Photographs of Opal were now paired with photos of a young woman. The caption said *Cora Neale may have died after taking a food supplement.*

"Everybody dies around us," said Lilah, starting to hyperventilate. Marina put an arm around her.

"That's not true. None of us are dying. And my children aren't dying. We saved Lucy Rose's life today. Opal is a survivor. Breathe."

"But what are we going to do?"

"Let's have a cup of tea."

The cup of tea did not actually help, but it gave Marina something to do for five minutes before they checked all the news websites again.

"She felt terrible about Cora dying," said Lilah. "And it wasn't even really her fault. It was a mistake. Not like you and me, who actually killed someone on purpose. What if they find her? Will she go to prison?"

"No, she'll be okay." Marina thought about it. "Though no one would mess with her in prison. Within like five minutes she'd be leading all the prisoners in exercise classes."

"We could visit her."

"Maybe we'll all end up there together."

"At least we'd be together."

"I love my brother, but I don't want him raising my kids."

"Have you checked Opal's Instagram lately?" Lilah asked.

"She's not going to post while the police are looking for her." But Marina tapped on the app anyway, and found Opal's profile.

"Wait," she said. "Oh my God. Opal posted a video five minutes ago."

"She did?" Lilah scooted over and peered at the screen. "It's dark."

"And I've got it muted. Just a second, I'll go back to the beginning and turn on the sound."

Music blared from the phone. It was "All the Single Ladies."

As they watched, Opal's face appeared in the picture, and she began to speak.

50

VIDEO FROM THE INTERNET ARCHIVE, ORIGINALLY POSTED ON INSTAGRAM BY @HOT_FIT_MESS:

MUSIC FADES INTO BACKGROUND. The scene is dark, an alley some-where, with brick walls and peeling posters. There's a streetlight casting a faint orangish glow. A striking woman with short hair and red lipstick appears in frame and speaks to the camera.

"Hi everyone, it's me, Opal. Today's video is a little bit different from the normal stuff, but hey, it hasn't been a normal day, has it? If you've seen the news, you know that the name I was born with is Pearl Howe, and my married name was Pearl Bolt. That was the name that Cora Neale knew me by, and before I go any further with this video, I want to say something to anyone who knew Cora, something that I haven't been able to say publicly before, but everyone knows who I am now, so screw it.

"I am so sorry that Cora died. I wish she were still alive. There isn't a day that goes by that I don't think of her. Especially recently, when I've learned more about what it's really like to care about people. I wish she'd never taken those tablets. If I could trade my life for hers, I would. She lost her life, and what for? To try to lose weight? Those supplements were supposed to be harmless, but the idea behind them was pure poison. Pardon my French, but there's something fucked up about a society that tells women that they're only valid and attractive if they're thin. She was beautiful just as she was."

Opal looks into the camera for a beat, and then glances away, at something by her side.

"Anyway. I didn't want Cora to die. But I did want this guy to."

The camera pans down to a large open suitcase on the ground. In it lies the body of a man. His limbs have been curled into a fetal position to fit into the suitcase. His eyes are open, he is not moving, and he looks very dead.

Back to Opal. She speaks with the ease of someone who is used to doing a lot of social media posts.

"This guy is a villain. He's a criminal associate of my ex-husband, who is a man known as Zander Bolt. I found him when I was tracking down Zander, and he's a very bad dude, with a line in extortion, murder, and assault. Fortunately, ladies? You don't have to worry about him anymore, because he's dead. Blunt instrument to the skull. It felt great.

"So yes, this video is my confession! But keep watching, because for those of you who usually watch my fitness videos—and I'm grateful to all of you and sorry that they have to end now—I've got one last exercise demonstration for you. Hold on a sec. I'm doing this on my own here, so I have to prop up the phone on a wall."

The video wobbles, and there's a close-up of Opal's shoulder, but when it steadies, there's a wider view of the alley. More brick walls, more peeling posters. The open suitcase lies on the ground next to an open green dumpster. Opal appears, a full-body-length view now. She waves cheerfully and speaks to the camera again.

"I call this move 'Taking Out the Trash.' Now remember: don't try this unless you've already learned the proper techniques for weight training. Ideally, you should have a spotter, but of course we don't want to implicate anyone else in our crimes so in this case, I'm going it alone."

Opal bends over the suitcase and addresses the camera.

"I'm going to zip up the suitcase before I demo this move, so say goodbye to your friend, everybody. I've turned on location services for this reel, though, so once I've posted it, if you want to find him, you shouldn't have any problems. With any luck, I'll be long gone by then."

She lifts the body's arm, as if to wave, but there's no hand at the end of it, only a bloody stump.

"Whoops. Sorry, wrong arm. Dude seems to have lost his left hand. Not sure where that went. So, that's about a pound off the lift total, but the principle remains the same. I'll tuck that back in and zip up the suitcase. That doesn't really affect the weight, but it makes the whole package tidier, more centered, and easier to lift. Here we go. Remember: lift from the legs, not your back. Get a good hold, you don't want to drop him, because postmortem injuries might mess up the autopsy, and those pathologists have a hard enough job, am I right? Okay, now: brace, lift, and hold."

Opal hoists the suitcase and holds it at waist height, her arm muscles bulging.

"Now remember what I always say: if it hurts, that's your body's way of telling you to back off. Maybe find another way to get rid of your dead man that doesn't require so much lifting. An unfinished building site, or an abandoned quarry. For example. I don't officially endorse any particular method, this is just what works for me. You do you, boo! Right, so finally, you turn—and remember, your legs are your base now—and you just send that bad guy right into the skip with the rest of the rubbish, where he belongs."

She matches her actions to her words as she talks, and tips the suitcase into the dumpster, on top of several bin bags. Then she turns back to the camera with a smile, wiping her hands on her leggings.

"So there you have it: Whole Man Disposal Services, an internet meme come to life. I hope you've enjoyed today's demo and it's inspired you to make healthy changes in your lifestyle. If you want to learn more, or you're curious about what ever happened to my lying, cheating husband, Zander Bolt, you can find one I've prepared earlier by checking out the location link in my bio. Have a great day, ladies, and don't forget: stay strong!"

Reel ends.

The comment attached to the reel reads:

OH AND BY THE WAY, @GLOWUPP _ MAKEUP SUCKS.

Post deleted by Metropolitan Police, after it was viewed 50k times and liked by 20.5k accounts.

51

Opal

THE VIDEO COULDN'T SHOW HOW the alley stank of rotten fish and urine. Opal thought that was fitting for the final resting place of someone who pulled knives on children and murdered elderly retired postmen. Aside from that, S didn't seem like such a bad person, and it was a shame that his grandkids wouldn't get to go to private school, but c'est la vie. She'd gone to public school, and she'd done all right for herself.

Well. Compared to Zander and S. Sure, she was broke, and she was a fugitive from the law, but least she was still alive. And she had friends.

She scheduled the Instagram post for an hour in the future, tossed her phone into the dumpster next to the body, pulled up her hood, and put on a face mask. She knew she wasn't going to be able to get on that plane to Croatia, or indeed anywhere that she needed to show a passport, but that didn't mean that she wanted to make herself easy to find. She figured: Euston, Liverpool, Belfast, lay low and make some phone calls. It was an extremely long shot.

But what happened to her wasn't important. The important thing was to loudly divert suspicion away from Lilah and Marina.

She hadn't been glib when she said she would swap her life for Cora's. But that wasn't possible, so she was swapping her life for Marina and Lilah's.

The narrative here was easy. Opal was a crook. Opal caused an innocent woman to die. Opal killed her husband. Opal killed another man because hell, why not? She was going to prison anyway.

As long as she was the chief suspect in a crime, no one was going to look at a mother of three and a mild-mannered librarian. Never, ever in her entire life had a single person given her automatic trust and acceptance like Marina and Lilah did. She owed everything to them.

She wiped off her hands with a baby wipe (Marina was right; they cleaned anything). Then she threw the wipe and the packet into the dumpster and took off running.

It was a nice, easy nine miles to Euston, but she had to avoid busy areas and anyplace likely to be covered extensively by CCTV, and also she'd given herself a lumbar strain hoisting S into the dumpster so she couldn't take it at her usual pace. By the time she reached Kensington she was limping, and the pain had radiated down her left leg to a level that was difficult to ignore. She stopped to stretch it out against the side of a deli, but she'd barely started when she saw the reflection of blue lights in the window.

She didn't even turn around. She took off sprinting down the road, dodged down a side street, vaulted an iron fence into a private square, pelted across it to the other side, sneakers wet in the grass, and jumped that fence too back into the street.

Did she hear running footsteps behind her, the clump of the police? She couldn't tell above the sound of her own breath in the mask, the searing pain in her back. It seemed too soon for the reel to have posted to Instagram, but maybe they were after her already because of the newspaper story. She glanced behind her and saw two dark figures running, a distance away but not nearly far enough.

Good luck, fuckers, she thought, running harder than she'd ever done. *You're about to be beaten by a middle-aged woman with sciatica.*

Down another side street, going north now instead of west, trying to put them off her tail, and then cutting across towards Marylebone. Crossing Baker Street, she ran straight into a tour group led by a man dressed as a Victorian. "Pardon me!" she yelled, dodging between anoraks and umbrellas. She stumbled on a curb, stomped her other foot into a puddle, splashing water up the guide's pants and her own leg. Right ankle twisted now. She skipped forward as best as she could on her left leg, the sore one, until she dared put down her right foot. Sore, but okay.

As she rounded the corner, she looked behind her and saw nothing but bemused tourists. No blue lights, no one in uniform. It seemed too good to be true, that she'd lost them.

But she couldn't run properly now. Her left leg was heavy, and her spine was on fire. Even at peak fitness she would be in trouble, and she'd been neglecting her workouts in favor of trying to sort out her life. Plus, she had already cleaned the kitchen, hoisted a large man halfway across Richmond, and blown up her entire life. Adrenaline and cortisol could only do so much for a girl.

With relief she saw Gower Street. Slowing to a walk, she pulled her hood a bit further over her face and checked her watch as she approached Euston. The reel would have posted half an hour ago. But she couldn't see any police around the station, just the normal travelers, walking slowly with suitcases, quickly with backpacks, wheeling bicycles, checking their phones. She joined them entering Euston.

Train to Liverpool was departing in seven minutes. Luck was on her side. Ticket. Barrier. Weaving as quickly as she could between luggage and dawdlers. The last carriage on the train was the least crowded one in theory, but when she entered it, nearly every seat was full. Acutely aware of her appearance, mud-spattered and sweaty, limping and sodden, masked and hooded, no doubt smelling of bleach and fish, she found an aisle seat next to a young woman wearing a head-scarf and whispered an apology. Then she slumped back in the seat, closed her eyes, massaged her hamstring, and waited for the train to move, taking her north, somewhere that she might have a chance.

She wondered what Lilah and Marina thought when they'd come home to a clean, corpse-free house. Maybe they'd seen her video by now. She'd give a lot to see the expressions on their faces when they realized what she'd done.

Opal was chuckling softly to herself when something shifted. Conversation in the carriage stopped, and then started up again in a murmur. Casually, she leaned to the side and peered down the aisle.

There were two police officers at the front of the carriage. They were looking at each of the passengers, heading in her direction. At least one of them seemed puffed, like he'd been running more than he was accustomed.

There was an exit behind her. Quick quick, she could dodge off the train, onto another, hide in a toilet. She was fast, she was lithe, she was unstoppable.

She slipped out of her seat and saw another two police officers advancing from the back of the carriage.

She wasn't unstoppable after all. But she could stay strong, and save her friends.

Opal pulled off her mask. She stood tall and put a big, undefeated smile on her face. "Hello, lads. Are you looking for me?"

52

Marina

THEY DIDN'T SLEEP THAT NIGHT. Between checking the news, refreshing Opal's Instagram account, and obsessively looking at social media, they racked up an impressive dossier of evidence for anyone looking to implicate them, but they did not care. They had to know, and anyway, everyone seemed to be doing the same thing as they were. The comments on Opal's reel kept appearing, registering shock and dismay, and perhaps surprisingly, plenty of admiration and glee, and not surprisingly at all, creepy male commentary on her body.

As they refreshed and clicked, they tried to come to terms with what was going on.

"We need to tell the police," said Lilah. "She can't go down for this all by herself. It's not fair. She didn't even kill anybody; that was us."

"She decided to do this." Marina was still stunned.

"But why?" asked Lilah. "We could have hidden S together. We could have got away with it, all three of us. We would've figured it out."

"Maybe she didn't think so."

"Maybe she'll get away. She could still get away, right?"

They kept swiping.

About ten o'clock, someone posted a link on Instagram to a video on Twitter. When Lilah opened it, she paled and beckoned Marina over and played it again.

Taken over the headrests on a train carriage: Opal in the aisle, her arms behind her as four officers led her off the train, two in front and two behind. She was smiling. When she passed the person who was filming, she winked at the camera. The user's caption: *Guys they caught @Hot_Fit_Mess on my train, when I am arrested for murder I want to look this good!*

"They got her."

"Oh my God."

They played it three more times. Lilah stood.

"Where are you going?"

"The police."

Marina grabbed her arm and pulled her back down to her chair at the kitchen table. "Lilah, Opal wanted to do this. This is what she wanted to happen."

"But why?"

"Because she loves us. She said so in her note."

"That's no reason!"

"For Opal, it is."

"We have to save her!"

"We can't save her. But we can let her save us."

Lilah stared, and began quietly crying. Marina kissed the top of her head, tenderly, like a mother; then she went down to the cellar and came back with a bottle of 2011 Château Pétrus. She uncorked it, decanted it, and lovingly poured three glasses. One for her, one for Lilah, and one for Opal.

Right there, she made herself a promise: she would always pour one for Opal.

"Drink this," she said, pushing a glass over to Lilah. "We've got a long road ahead of us, if we're going to do this."

"Do what?" Lilah sniffed and wrapped her hands around the stem of the glass.

"It's going to take a lot of planning. Especially without being able to use Google. It might take years. But with your research skills, and what we've learned already . . ."

"Research what?"

"First, a toast." Marina chimed her glass on the side of Lilah's. "To friendship."

"To friendship."

They drank.

"Wow," said Lilah. "This is . . . crazy good."

"It should be. It's the second most expensive bottle in the cellar."

"Why the second?"

Marina took a contemplative sip of wine, and rolled it in her mouth, savoring the bouquet, before she answered. "I'm saving the most valuable bottle for when we break Opal out of prison."

Epilogue (1)

TWO WEEKS LATER

Lilah

SHE'D DONE IT.

The last train, the last piece of track, the last tiny human being, all of it to precise scale: she'd wrapped every single one of them carefully in paper and put them in labeled boxes. The back room of the Chislehurst house was full of them now, stacked nearly to her waist.

Marina and the two older children had helped her pack up the books in her library, the photograph albums, the board games, personal things that she wanted to take with her. With Marina's support, she'd also been able to select a few bits of Dad's clothing that she could keep as a memento. His woolly cardigan, which she could wear on cold days; his old Post Office sweater with the worn-through elbows. They were both way too big for her, but she felt safe and happy when she put them on. She didn't need clothes to remember her dad, but she liked them anyway.

Most of the furniture would be sold with the house. She'd never been particularly attached to it. In the garden, she and Marina had already chosen a few of her father's favorite roses and a small Japanese maple to transplant to Marina's in Richmond, for now at least, until Lilah had a garden of her own.

But Lilah wanted to do this last bit, this hardest bit, by herself.

This was the room where S had killed her father, hired by the man she thought she'd loved. It was where Dad had taken his last, painful breath. Before she set foot in it, she wasn't sure that she could even bear to be in it.

But when she gathered her courage and went into the room, she remembered that this was also where Dad had spent hours and hours creating his own little perfect world. It was the place where he was happiest. A whole miniature England, with cheerful trains and chocolate box shops; people with painted smiles and trees that were always the green of late spring.

It was Dad's world. Everything made sense here. It all had its own order, its own logic, and every single part of it was infused with her father's attention and care.

As she packed up the train set she found little sparks of joy, too—jokes that he'd created, little scenes to amuse himself. There was a tiny dog, chasing a tinier cat, chasing a barely visible mouse. A trainspotter stood on a platform, complete with anorak and notebook. The barber shop had a sign saying BARBER STREISAND and the chip shop was called FISHCOTEQUE.

Best of all there was a mailman wearing a sweater with worn-through elbows and hauling a bulging sack of packages. There was a young woman wearing a fanny pack and carrying a stack of books. She slipped those two figures into her bag, wrapped up in a tissue to keep them safe and together.

In the end, Dad's life was much more powerful than Dad's death. It took her hours to disassemble the tracks and the trains, but she loved every minute. She handled these small intricate things that her father had before her. She could almost hear his voice explaining to her, gently, what everything was.

It was sad, yes. Sometimes she cried, alone in that room where her father had lived and died. And she had to take breaks; she couldn't do it all in one day. But it was also one of the nicest goodbyes that she could imagine.

And now the last carriage had been wrapped up and packed, and the courier would be here in an hour to take it all to a charity she'd found that matched train sets with children fighting cancer.

Then the estate agent would be in to take photographs of the empty house to put it on the market. Lilah had moved out of the Premier Inn. She'd found a nice two-bedroom flat with lots of bookcases in Twickenham, not ten minutes' walk from Marina's house. She was renting it for now. She liked being close to Marina, close enough to pop in to share meals and go for walks together, to play with her children, take them to the park, and be called "Auntie Lilah." And the building allowed cats.

She gazed around the room and felt at peace. She was still grieving her dad, she knew that; just as she was still recovering from being manipulated and betrayed. But this was a good step forward into a new life.

* * *

The bell over the door at Cuthbert & Binding was just as cheerful as it ever had been, but the shelves were sparsely populated, and the wonderful bookshop smell was slightly diluted with the scent of cleaning fluid. There were still SALE signs everywhere.

"Welcome," said the man at the till, and then he looked up and a smile lit up his face. "Oh hi! It's you."

"It is me," said Lilah. "And it's you."

"My name's Mychal, by the way."

"I'm Lilah."

"I see you've got your Cuthbert & Binding tote bag."

"Yes, it's very useful for carrying things." She remembered that this had included both of Zachary's arms, and blushed a little. She said quickly, "I'm celebrating something, and I need to buy a lot of books."

"That is the best kind of celebration," said Mychal. "Can I help you find anything?"

They went upstairs to the children's section together, Lilah explaining the ages and personalities of Archie, Lucy Rose, and Ewan and the bookseller saying he knew just the thing. When he'd helped her choose a stack of picture and story books, and then they'd gone to the cookery section and found a book on Vietnamese food for Marina, who'd expressed an interest in pho, and then gone to the fantasy and science fiction section, where Mychal introduced her to a trilogy by a new author, and she introduced him to a book of short stories by one of her old favorites, and they'd had a long conversation about which Discworld novel was the best and why, Lilah peered around at the shelves and said, "Well, you've got a lot of gaps here now."

"Yeah. I hate to see all the stock being sold off. It's been hard not to buy most of it myself. But . . . space."

"Are the owners sad about closing it?"

"Yes, but also they've been wanting to retire to France. So it's bittersweet for them."

"What do you think this shop will be used for?"

He shrugged sadly. "London souvenirs? Key chains? Bobblehead King Charles?"

"That's such a shame."

"I know."

They walked back to the till together. She'd chosen so many books that he had to help her carry them. And she'd meant to stop by the self-help section, to see if there were any books she could give to

Formerly Evil Alice, as a sort of thank-you, but she had started to get an idea that was taking up most of her head space. An idea that would be a celebration of her father's life, and her friendship with Marina and her children and with Opal, too.

Mychal glanced at her several times while he rang up her books, but she didn't really notice. She was thinking too hard. She automatically handed over her debit card when he was finished, and he packed up the books for her in her tote bag and a few more.

"Well," he said, when he was finished. "Those should last you a little while."

"Yes," she said, but she didn't pick up the bags or move away. She gnawed on her lip, and she looked at Mychal, and she thought about how he had a nice smile, and he knew a lot about books, and seemed to like them a whole lot, and how it would be lovely to talk with him every day.

"I think—" she said, at the same time that he said, "Would you—"
They both stopped.

"Sorry," Lilah said. "You go first."

"No, please, you go first."

"I was going to say, that I think I might like to buy this bookshop."

His eyes widened. "Oh wow," he said. "Wow, really? And keep it a bookshop?"

"Yes. What do you think?"

"I think that's a great idea. But . . ."

"But what? Is the business not for sale?"

"It's definitely for sale. I was just thinking . . . that if you were going to be my boss, then I probably shouldn't ask you what I was going to ask you."

"What were you going to ask me?"

"If you'd like to go for pizza with me sometime."

"Oh," said Lilah. "I see. Actually, I think that is also a really great idea."

Epilogue (2)

Marina

THE YELLOW CRIME SCENE TAPE and the white forensic tents had been up next door for nearly two weeks. Apparently the Andersons were staying in their second home in Cornwall.

Marina brought a tray of coffee to some of the reporters hanging around on the pavement outside.

"Have they found anything yet?" she asked casually, passing round a plate of her children's homemade biscuits.

"Don't think so," said the BBC woman.

"I think that bitch was lying," said the man from the *Mail*. "I don't think she buried her husband there at all. He's probably alive and well and living it up in the Maldives."

"Underneath the patio is a classic, though," said a dark-haired man with a scruffy dog and a microphone. Marina thought maybe he was a podcaster. "It was good enough for Fred and Rosemary West . . ."

"Why do they think that there's a body there at all?" asked Marina, innocently. "I'm not clear on that part. What did this woman have to do with the Andersons?"

"It was the coordinates she gave on her confession video." The podcaster sipped coffee. "And she mentioned disposing of a body in a building site. They've been doing a lot of construction here, haven't they?"

"They sure have," said Marina, with feeling.

"No knowing what these posh idiots have buried in their back gardens," said the man from the *Mirror*. "No offense, love."

"They've finished with the garden and the patio, though," added the woman from the BBC. "They're taking down the extension now."

"Oh, and that's the *real* shocker," said the man from the *Sun*. The others crowded round. "Turns out the owners never had planning permission for any of the work they did. So once this lot comes down, it's not going back up. Whether they find a body or not."

"What a shame," said Marina.

"If they do find a body, it's not going to be great for property prices," said the man from the *Telegraph*.

Marina told them she had something in the oven to attend to, so please leave the mugs inside her front gate, she'd collect them later.

I love you, she said silently to Opal.

* * *

Just over an hour later, she held a warm casserole dish in both hands and rang the bell for Jake's flat with her elbow. Actually, it was still Freya's flat, but Jake was staying in it until he could find a place of his own. Freya was staying with her parents in Chelmsford.

Jake opened the door: unshaven, pale, his hair greasy, dark circles under his eyes, wearing baggy gray sweatpants and a T-shirt with food stains on the shoulder.

"Thank God you're here," he said, and behind him, the children shouted "Mummy!" and Archie and Lucy Rose crowded the door to hug her legs.

"Careful darlings, Mummy has a hot dish," she said. "Let me take this through to the kitchen and then we can have a cuddle."

The kitchen looked as if a bomb had hit it. Dirty dishes and spilled food littered the table; the counters were covered with opened packets; the dishwasher was full and open and more dishes were piled up in the sink. A bottle of milk lay on its side. There were small handprints on all the cupboards and the front of the refrigerator. Marina hoped they were that color because they were chocolate.

She put the casserole dish on the top of the stove and scooped up Archie and Lucy Rose. "Did you have a fun weekend?"

"Yeah!" said Archie, sweet and loyal as he was.

"I eat the yellow Play-Doh," said Lucy Rose.

"It's probably the best-tasting flavor. Where's Ewan?"

"I only just got him down for a nap," said Jake. He leaned against the counter, looking like he could do with a nap, too.

"Did *you* have a fun weekend?" Marina couldn't stop herself from asking. "You know, I think this is the first weekend ever that you've had the kids all to yourself since they were born."

"I don't think I'm going to be able to make it into work tomorrow. Maybe I'm coming down with something."

She turned to Archie and picked a Cheerio out of his hair. "Have you packed your stuff, sweetheart? Or do you need me to help?"

"I do it." Lucy Rose marched out of the room, Archie following.

"Have you heard from Freya?" asked Marina. She should not savor Jake's pained expression. She really shouldn't.

"I don't understand it," exploded Jake. "One day everything was great, and then suddenly she's all like 'I need to look at my options' and 'I think a co-parenting situation would be better than a romantic partnership.' I don't know what happened to her. Maybe she's been watching those feminist videos."

"You can't trust YouTube these days," agreed Marina. "Anyway, I hate to think of you here all on your own eating nothing but ready meals, so I knocked together something for you. It's your favorite."

Jake peeled the foil off the top and inhaled. "Shepherd's pie. Thank God. I thought you were going to say it was some of that foreign gunk that you like so much."

"Would I do that to you?" She smiled. "Now, this is all for you, so don't share it. I made it specially."

He found a spoon and dipped in. "Not bad."

"Glad you like it. I've got a few more in my freezer with your name on them, when you've eaten that one."

In the freezer, where she'd kept the piece of Xavier's left thigh, wrapping it in foil and sneaking it into the drawer next to bags of frozen peas and corn, when she was supposed to be packing it away in her pushchair with the rest of the body parts, to be dumped into the Thames.

Thawed, filleted and ground, it turned out to be beautifully lean—so much so that she'd had to add a little fatty lamb mince so the meat part of the pie wasn't too dry.

Apparently that no-carb diet had worked wonders for Xavier.

Jake said, "I don't know how you managed to put on so much weight when you were at home with the kids. I barely had a minute to sit down and eat anything all weekend." He took another big spoonful of shepherd's pie.

"It must be the female metabolism," said Marina, cheerful and not in the slightest bit angry. She went to the spare bedroom to help her children pack and to wake up Ewan, warm and sleepy and snuggly, so she could take them all home.

Lilah was coming for supper. They would eat vegetarian food and start making plans.

ACKNOWLEDGMENTS

THANK YOU TO TERESA CHRIS, who this year will have been my agent for twenty years—it wouldn't have been the same without you, Teresa.

Thank you to the team at Bonnier UK: Ben Willis, Ruth Logan, Isabella Boyne, Georgia Marshall, Isabel Smith, Holly Milnes, Ellie Pilcher, and Ross Jamieson.

Thank you to the team at Abrams US: Zack Knoll, Andrew Gibeley, Christian Westermann, Ruby Pucillo, Michael Sand, Jamison Stoltz, and Christine Edwards.

Thank you to Darren Faulkner, who bid in the Young Lives vs Cancer auction to have a character named after his daughter, Lucy Rose Faulkner, who is known for her cheeky laugh. Thank you for inspiring me to write a Chekhov's toddler.

Thank you to Ruth Ng, who gave me tips on life as a librarian; to my brother Matt Cohen M.D., who gave me tips on dissection; to Mychal Threets (@mychal3ts), who inspires readers of all ages and who gave permission for me to name a cute bookseller after him; to Janie and Mickey Wilson, Charlie, and the late well-beloved Rory at Chez Castillon; to my mom and dad and teenager and of course my dog Meg.

Thank you to the independent booksellers, including Bert's Books, Kemptown Bookshop, the Edinburgh Bookshop, and many, many more, who are a godsend to authors and readers.

Apologies to Elizabeth Gilbert.

Mostly, thank you to my female friends, who are everything to me.